Hell

A Novel of the Desert War

R.R. SMITH

WILLIAM KIMBER. LONDON

First published in 1987 by
William Kimber & Co. Limited
100 Jermyn Street, London, SW1Y 6EE

© R.R. Smith, 1987
ISBN 0-7183-0666-X

This book is copyright. No part of it may be reproduced in any form without permission in writing from the publishers except by a reviewer who wishes to quote brief passages in a review written for inclusion in a newspaper, magazine, radio or television broadcast.

Typeset by PRINTIT-NOW LTD
and printed and bound in Great Britain by
Biddles Limited, Guildford and King's Lynn.

This book is dedicated to a small elite: to the men of the Royal Horse Artillery who, down through the history of this country, have gone to war. To all who have served in peace and in war and who still serve today. To the absent friends of our youth and in particular to the men of the:

        4th Regiment Royal Horse Artillery,
            7th Motor Brigade,
          7th Armoured Division,
              Eighth Army.

The 4th Regiment RHA was one of the original units that formed the 7th Support Group (later known as the 7th Motor Brigade) of the famous Desert Rats, 7th Armoured Division.

The characters in this novel are fictitious and bear no relationship to any person, living or dead.

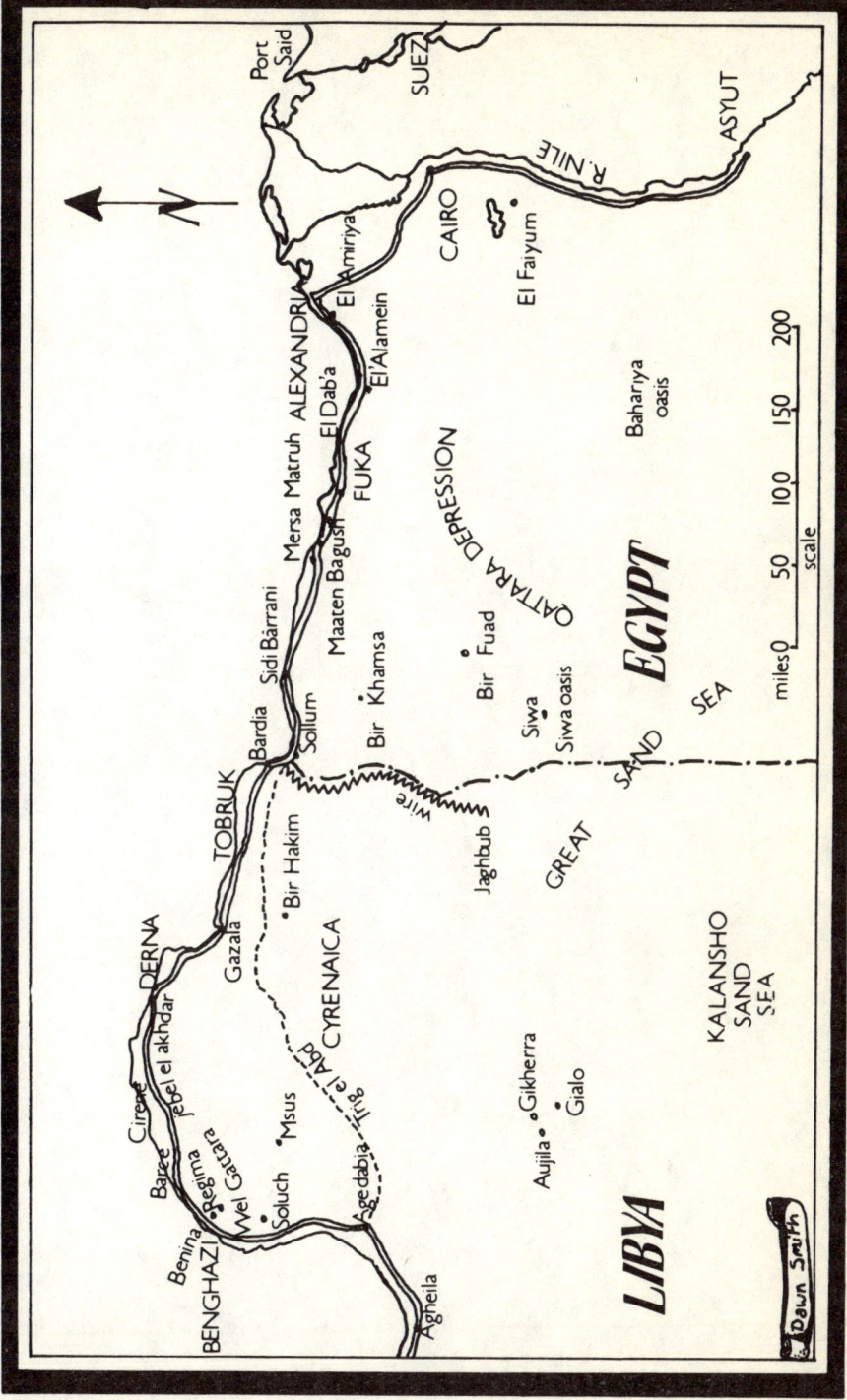

I

The wet desert night was one of black intensity. The lashing stair rods of vertical monsoon-like rain bounced viciously off windscreens, hundreds of units of the Eighth Army and thousands of men were on the move: corps, divisions and brigades. The 7th Motor Brigade, original Desert Rats and, until recently, an integral part of 7th Armoured Division, was now part of 1st Armoured Division. Somewhere in that flood of guns, tanks and vehicles they moved along the divisional axis.

The direction of their advance was simple: head west. Nose to tail in dozens of columns, seeing only the rear of the vehicle ahead, they crawled doggedly on. To the north came the flashes of the RAF's night bombers attacking the coast road. Flares hung lazily above the fleeing Afrika Korps. There was no shortage of targets in that log jam of desperation that stretched as far as the Libyan border.

The last twenty-five pounder gun in the regiment of Royal Horse Artillery was known as 'Kelly's Eye'. The term was affectionate and practical. The gun detachment or guncrew shortened it to Kelly. They were 'A' Sub-section and in the troop of four guns were invariably the right-hand gun, number one gun of the troop when firing.

The rain bounced, drummed and cascaded off the gun-tower roof (practically, the vehicle was called a quad - it was four-wheel drive) in torrents that hit the soaked ground. Once there it chuckled away into gullies and wheel tracks. Steadily the level rose. Earlier the quad had been followed by other vehicles. Now it was the tailend of the regimental column.

Inside the quad conversation was sparse. The only indication that men sat there was the occasional and surreptitious glow of lighted cigarettes. Sergeant 'Geordie' James eased his rump slightly and watched silently the vague patch of white paint on the muzzle cover of the gun ahead.

His vision was a horizontal foot-long, two-inch wide cleaned area of glass, in the oil and sand smeared divided windscreen. Even the rain had failed to shift the oil and sand on the glass. Smoking was forbidden inside vehicles and even more on night moves. This time, however, it was different. Now they were chasing Rommel. Well at least, thought James, that was what they called it. It was more like a funeral march. Still, it was unlikely the Germans had any aircraft up. Even if they did, it was even more unlikely they had any idea of where their own troops were.

He thought back over the past fourteen days and nights of the Alamein battle. For the guns and the gunners it had been sheer graft. He imagined briefly how rich the crew of Kelly would be now, if only they had paid a bonus of a 100 Acker note for every round fired. Could be enough to set them all up in civvie street. That is, if any of them reached that far-off goal.

Pity about this bloody rain though; no one had expected it. Monty, he thought, would be chewing his bloody chin-strap and so would the Colonel for that matter. Struggling up, he raised the roof hatch to peer out into the stygian blackness. It was pissing down. It was now thirty-six hours since it started.

Every now and then a darker shape materialised at the side of the quagmire. Vague figures in the familiar leather jerkins were digging and pushing, and cursing their luck. Fragments of shouted abuse whipped in through the open hatch. These were mingled with the scream and whine of engines being pushed to their limit.

At any other time help would have been readily given, unconscious desert custom, but tonight was different, not counting the weather of course. If Rommel and his forces could be cut off and the remnants annihilated, the push to Tripoli and beyond would be little more than a 'Cook's tour'. So stragglers and breakdowns were on their own and deliberately left to fend for themselves. He closed the hatch and lowered himself on to the pad of rubber that was called a seat. Shaking his head distributed a spray of water into the steamy fuggy atmosphere. Protesting groans informed him that the crew did not appreciate his largesse.

He rested his right knee against the engine cover. It was hard and warm. He hoped the throbbing six-cylinder Morris engine would keep up the good work. A twinge of uneasiness at the thought of the present fuel consumption crossed his mind. Two miles to the gallon in this mud and in permanent four-wheel drive. At this rate and in this weather the navigator, whoever he was, would soon need a boat. Maybe, he thought idly, we could reach the Med, if we had the boats.

One consolation was that at this speed one could get out for a piss and take as much time as you liked. Reaching behind he tapped a knee. Guardedly the lighted cigarette was passed inside the hollowed palm. James bent, held the lit end in the first and second fingers of his right hand with the thumb on his chin. The pitching and lurching of the quad made no difference, lit and unlit cigarettes fused together in rock-like solidity.

It saved a lot of crushed cigarettes and was a relic of his mounted days. James could do it at any pace on a horse or anywhere else. He passed the cigarette back and stretched his right leg along the engine cover. A bolt head caught the side of his right knee and reminded him forcibly of another time, a time when he had been the lead driver of a six-horse gunteam. Then he had come close to getting a steel trace of the harness down his protective leg-iron. That had been painful and left him with a permanent tenderness.

Gingerly he moved his leg away from the steel cover and sat hunched uncomfortably on the thinly covered seat. Tiredness swept over him. Chalky, the quad driver, was a reliable regular soldier, he could trust him not to do anything daft. He closed his eyes for a moment. The time dragged on. Suddenly he was awake with no idea of time but aware that the quad had stopped.

'What's up, Chalky?' he rapped out to the man at the wheel.

'Stuck, Sarge. It's like treacle and the bloody engine's conked - petrol trouble, I think - ' his voice sounded as weary as he felt.

'Fuckin' Hell!'

James spat the expletive out with weary disgust and pent-up anger. All the crew were veteran Desert Rats and tempers, particularly directed at inanimate objects, were normally on a short fuse. He swung his legs around and opened the wide quad door.

'Come on, you lazy shower. All out, *Jildi - Jildi* - Hurry, let's take a *shufti*.'

The cool desert wind swept into the quad making him glad

of the overcoat he was wearing. The thick mud he landed in sucked at his untied boots. Slowly, slopping and swearing, he reached the rear wheel of the quad. He heard the other door crash against the metal body. It was still raining. He bent and felt; the mud was up to the axle.

Swearing, stumbling and squelching he ground his way back to the open door.

'All right. Relax,' he shouted to the bulky figures moving about in the close confines of the vehicle. He pulled himself up into the quad and pulled the door shut. The opposite door closed.

'What's up, Sarge? Are we in deep?' enquired a voice. James gave an unseen grin.

'Deep? Any further down, we'd be diggin' coal. Engine's passed out an' we're up to the hubs. We'll hang on till first light - can't do anythink now. Bulb's gone in the inspection lamp anyway.' James reached under his overcoat and retrieved his issue watch from his blouse pocket. The illuminated dial showed 1-45. He listened for a moment to the whisper of the wind and the drum of the rain. Through the cleared windscreen slit the sky was inky black. Swivelling round in his seat he said:

'Umm. Looks like everyone's gone home to bed. Lackery - you there?'

'Christ, Geordie, can't you let a bloke 'ave a kip?'

The voice came from a bulky figure in the corner by the fuel tank. James made out the faint whites of eyes as the figure leaned forward.

'Better 'ave a guard on,' he said, 'we're pretty far behind I should imagine, an' we don't know how many loose Jerries are floatin' around. Take the next two who's due for guard. Let's see - ' He thought for a moment. 'Bell an' Rayburn - ' raising his voice - 'get your *bundooks* - rifles - ready. You'll only 'ave a couple of hours to do, give or take an hour.'

Over the movement of the two men he caught the whispered curses. James smiled to himself particularly when another voice, recognised as Dodger Green's, say:

'Come on, you lucky people. You said you could do it. Get out there an' protect us - an' don't wake me too early.'

'Bollocks.' The retort in unison created a giggle from the remainder. James said:

'First light - don't forget - .' The door slammed. They heard the soft sucking squelch of boots as the two figures moved away. There was a general movement of bodies as the remainder of the crew took advantage of the extra room.

James let his head drop, his eyes closed and in seconds he was asleep.

Outside the rain was tailing off. It was now more a heavy drizzle with a light wind that was cool and getting colder. The cold was normal in the desert winter months. Even in the summer the nights were cold although the days were roastingly hot, a heat that fortunately, was devoid of humidity. The two men, rifles slung, squelched silently around the gun and quad. They stopped by common consent in front of the gunshield now covered by the travelling gun cover. For a few moments that dragged into minutes they stood there gazing mutely into the surrounding blackness. At last Rayburn cleared his throat. He was of medium height but even under the bulky overcoat one could sense the tremendous chunky solidness of a powerful physique.

'This could be a bit tricky, Ding-a-Dong. Don't like to think that we're on our tod. Anythink' could 'appen an' probably will.'

Bell grunted an affirmative. He was never what could be described as a talkative man. Joining the battery in 1939, he was one of the band of reinforcements that had had the label 'Moon Men' tagged on to them. The first night the bulk of the draft had gone over to the canteen still wearing their pith tropical helmets. This was long after dark with a moon riding high in the sky. Hence the nickname.

By now, in the early days of November 1942 the nickname was no longer one of derision. That draft had proved in many ways, in many actions and by many sacrifices, that they were the equals and in some cases better Horse Artillerymen than their regular army comrades. The regiment, indeed the 7th Motor Brigade, were always aware of the Moon Men because the draft still used the term. But now it was with pride.

Although Rayburn and Bell had soldiered in the same gun crew from the early days of 1940 there had always seemed to be a barrier of service between them. By now the barrier was paper-thin. Bell thought over what Rayburn had said. Not easily scared he had to admit it was not a pleasant feeling to be away from the battery. It was like being away from home.

There had been too many incidents on 'Jock' columns over the past two and a half years. Incidents where trucks isolated from the column for one reason or another, had disappeared without trace. The desert could be a friend. It could also be an implacable enemy. Bell shuddered inwardly at the thought. If the battery was moving, well, it was like a family moving, all together. If you got bounced, well at least there was always someone to bury you and mark the grave.

If, on the other hand, you were on your own you could hit a mine or thermos bomb and nobody would ever find the remains. Muscles was talking again; the reason for his nickname was obvious as was his own and the Bombardier Wood's 'Lackery', meaning wood. Sergeant James was a Geordie, Dodger was dodger because his name was Green. Cockney because he was from the smoke.

His attention came back to what Rayburn was saying. Not again, thought Bell. He was talking about India. These bloody regulars were always talking about India. Always somewhere where one had not been. Talking about the times they had got drunk or the time when the Loosewallahs, the native thieves, had cleaned the bungalow out. Or of the tremendous heat, the earthquakes, the snakes, the Urdu terms for bread, jam, water and so on. Tea was always *chah*, sugar was *cheeni* and milk was *lebben*. Bell had heard it all before, even used a lot of the Urdu terms and phrases himself, but it all got a little wearying.

He realised that as usual, he was being unfair. Letting the slow murmur of Rayburn's voice drift past his ears he felt slightly ashamed of his thoughts and attitude. Bell was a loner, knew he was and since that first day in the army, had chosen to be. His trouble was a basic inability to come down to other people's level. He had always felt a superiority to most other men but disguised it effectively by a cryptic economy of speech. Rarely did he pass an opinion. He confided in no one. Sometimes he felt sorry, wanted to be one of the lads, mates, muckers. Usually the feeling came from a memory of how the regulars had helped him and all the other Moon Men. They had been taught how to survive, for that he was grateful. The feeling passed, he thought of home. That bitch.

If only she had written. She'd be out having a good time maybe with a Yank. Overpaid, over-sexed and over here. He could just picture her laughing face. The teasing way she had, the warmth of her body, smoothness of her lips, the evocative fragrance. Maybe she had picked up with a black man with a big tool. He realised suddenly that the rain had ceased.

Racked by the torment of thoughts that wouldn't go away he moved away from the gunshield. Rayburn watched him go, used as he was, as they all were, to the moody detached quietness of Bell; he didn't expect confidences. He waited, eyes trying to pierce the darkness that enveloped their little world without success. Thirty minutes later the faint glow of the false dawn tinged the blackness to the east. The silence could almost be felt. He moved away from the gunshield and squelched round the side of the quad. He joined Bell in front of the quad.

'I should think that we'll soon pick them up again - if we follow the coast road, Muscles - that is, if we get the bloody quad moving. Where do you think we are?' asked Bell, more for something to say than because he thought Rayburn could answer his questions.

'I 'aven't a clue, Ding. Somewhere south of Fuka, I expect. Geordie 'ull tell us when it gets light. He knows 'is job.'

Bell nodded. James did know his job and so did 'Lackery' Wood, the bombardier. For that matter they all knew their jobs. You learned quick in a fighting regiment. If you didn't, you were dead. When one thought back he realised how lucky that draft of theirs had been. Instead of being posted to a regular regiment they could have been posted to a shower where men like James and Wood were few and far between.

In this regiment men like those two were the rule rather than the exception. James had been wounded twice. Wood just once and at Sidi Rezegh the whole crew had been taken prisoner. That was nearly a year ago. Even now the thought of that confused holocaust that had lasted for three weeks, made his skin crawl and break out in a cold sweat. There had been no hiding places there.

This regiment, this mob, as it was more familiarly known to them all, had been in every campaign since 10th June 1940. It still had the majority of those who had left Cairo two and a half years ago. Outwardly they looked the same, a deeper shade of brown, thinner if anything, built like whippets and moved just as fast, mused Bell. The innocence of pre-action, before the first rounds fired in anger, had vanished. They now wore the cloak of assurance woven by years of experience in action.

'Better wake 'em, Muscles.'

'Aye, suppose so. I've got a mouth like the bottom of a birdcage. Could do wi' a brew. 'Ave to wait 'till it's light. Roll on - '

They moved to opposite sides and each opened a quad door. James was awake instantly.

'What's the time?' he queried.

'After four, Sarge - ' answered Rayburn.

James shook the men behind him. Inside three minutes they were all out of the quad doing the usual dawn exercises. Stretching, scratching, yawning and emptying throats lined with phlegm and rubbing eyelids encrusted with sleep. One of the quad's side lockers was opened and out came the green-painted ammunition charge box. This contained their rations. Two ex-German gas mask containers, cylindrical in shape and ridged held the tea and the sugar.

The sergeant climbed back into the quad, lifted the hatch and studied the landscape with captured German binoculars. They appeared to be in a fold of dead ground. To the south the escarpment rose some miles away and was just visible in the light growing stronger by the minute. To their left front about five hundred yards away was a slight rise. To the north appeared gently rising scrub desert. Behind them, to the east was flat, a sea of mud criss-crossed with hundreds of tracks, wheeled and tracked. The stronger light reflected sheets of water and deep ruts that were miniature canals. In a full circle there was no sign of life, no vehicles.

Clouds hung heavily and looked ready to unload. James climbed down from the quad and got his mapcase out. The rest of the crew had the guncover off and were folding it tightly to rope on to the ammunition trailer. No one called it anything but a limber. Another relic of the mounted days. James squelched away from the quad and with his prismatic compass took a bearing on a mound of stones on the northern horizon. It was a trig point; which one he had no idea. He slipped and slithered back to the quad and looked at the map. With a *tck* of disgust he clipped the canvas cover closed and tossed the case on to his seat.

Chalky White, the quad driver, had the bonnet up and the carburettor stripped. For some reason James felt uneasy, naked. They were vulnerable in their present position, immobile and sitting ducks if a dirty great Mark VI Panzer came over that slight rise to their left front. He looked over Chalky's shoulder.

'How's it goin', Chalky?'

The driver's head remained bent over his task. 'Not bad, Sarge. Half the bloody desert in this filter an' the jet's filthy. Musta' bin dregs in that jerrican, yesterday. I'll be ready in ten minutes.'

James nodded, pleased at the reply. He slopped his way over the invisible track, mud sucking at his boots and found reasonably firm ground thirty yards away. Sizing up the situation, he gave orders to unhook the gun. Out came the shovels and the sand channels. Soon they had a firm base in front of the quad rear wheels into which they laid the steel perforated channels.

The bonnet cover clanged down and Chalky slipped behind the driver's seat. He held up two fingers, crossed. The others stood all wearing expectant expressions. Choke out, black starter button, a reluctant wheeze of six cold pistons that suddenly caught, fired and 1.5.3.6.2.4. smoothly and powerfully burst into life. A ragged cheer went up from the spectators.

'We knew you could do it.' Chalky answered the delighted grins with one of his, but he, like everyone else, knew it was just the first step.

'Release the winch.' Chalky moved the winch lever to free the cable on the rear bracket of the quad. Cockney Wells fastened the shackle round the trailer eye. James waited another five minutes. It was nearly full daylight, full for November anyway. He pointed out the patch of firm ground to Chalky and told him to start when ready.

In first gear and four wheel drive Chalky gently moved forward on to the sand channels, along them and across the rutted flooded quagmire to the firm ground. The winch cable played out behind the quad. Once on firm ground the winch was put in gear and the gun with the limber was reeled in like a fisherman landing a fish. It took another six operations before they were at the base of the slight rise on firm ground.

James walked forward to find that the main track, so far as he could guess, jinked to the right and north. To his front was another rise of ground. This was much steeper. He looked back and could just see the quad. He clambered up the slope to just short of the crest. The quad was invisible and remained so until he was halfway down the slope.

What he thought was the main track was a quagmire and even worse after it jinked right. He noted a possible alternative that followed the base of the rising ground, and felt sure that after the slopes the main escarpment would begin and offer much better going. James was desert wise, could recognise country he had travelled over in the past. This part, and he thought they were south of Fuka, was new to him. The map was not a lot of help either. The one in 500,000 scale showed no contours. Neither did the one in 100,000. Navigation in the desert was by dead reckoning, he thought. If you reckoned you were there and you weren't, you were in the shit. At the moment he only thought he knew where they were.

As he walked back to the quad because he had been thinking about maps he recalled a map he had used. It was covering the Segnali area, over the Wire, in Libya. On it was marked 'Large Bush'. The bush turned out to be five feet high and four feet wide. Its significance lay in the fact that it was the only bush in hundreds of square miles.

Back at the quad Lackery passed him a tannic-stained enamel mug of tea. He grasped it gratefully and took the first deep swallow. Lighting a cigarette and drinking the first brew of the day, 'gunfire' the gunners called it. The world was a different place. Even the sky seemed to lighten and for a change, they were free of the tormenting black ubiquitous flies.

The crew sat for another five minutes enjoying the slow start to another day. James explained where he thought they were and which direction they would go.

'We'll head for Bir Khamsa. Pre-move briefing gave that out as the regiment's leaguer area. It's west and south of Matruh. We'll have to go west for a bit yet. We'll get better going off the tracks - they'll be like glue anyway.'

He looked round at the attentive stubble-flecked faces. Lackery, a close friend, ten years' service, tall and thin with a gaunt, tanned face. Muscles Rayburn, broad-faced, placid but steady, six years' service. Bell, bit of an enigma, good gunner, a Moon Man, moody bugger hadn't got a word for the cat, but intelligent. Dodger Green, another Moon Man, a Londoner, small chirpy, like a bloody sparrow and always looked half-starved. Cockney Wells, a mucker of Dodger's and a Moon Man, he could use himself; quick, humorous and sharp as a whip and, James thought, one of the best gunlayers in their mob. Chalky was the last, the longest serving man with twelve years in. Useful at anything including taking care of himself. He was Liverpool, a scouse and a capable driver mechanic.

He knew them all like the back of his hand, knew them and liked them, for most of the time anyway. He even had a rough affection for them. None of these emotions was betrayed by his craggy features. Suddenly he stiffened and turned to face the rise in front of them. Faintly he could hear the sound of a straining engine. So had the others.

Quickly he rapped out, 'On your feet! Unhook the gun - slightly behind the quad. Get five rounds HE out then run the limber over there, behind the bank. Chalky, start the quad. I want it at this angle - ' he demonstrated.

'Pick up the *pialas*. Put 'em in the box. Leave the doors open. Let the quad door swing. Open the hatch. Scatter a few things about. That's it. We want it to look like a derelict - open all the lockers.'

He moved round to the gun, removed the steel tube of the trail handspike and slotted it swiftly in the steel orifice above the trail spade. Lackery and Bell had unhooked the limber and were pulling frantically away from the gun. James shouted to them to stop.

'Open the doors and leave 'em!' He and the others pulled the gun back on to the steel circular gun platform. James hoisted the trail and moved round in a 180 degree half circle, before dumping the heavy trail. Now they were pointing in the right direction as Cockney slid into the layer's seat and removed the leather eye-piece protector off the telescope, and unclamped the piece.

Bell removed the muzzle cover, Dodger the breech cover. Lackery had brought two rounds of HE 119 over. Rayburn carried the three HE shells as though they weighed no more than a cigarette packet. Dodger fetched a box of six charges. James held up one finger and mouthed AP to Rayburn. Bell opened the breech, wooden brass-bound rammer under his arm.

'Let's 'ave a bit of hush!' James called. They all paused, everyone listening. The straining engine, still muffled by the slope in front was nearer. They all caught another sound, an unmistakable one to them all. The squeal and screech of steel tracks. Glances locked with invisible beams of awareness.

James moved behind Cockney.

'Sight on that point. Depress - a bit more - ' He was looking down the barrel. 'Right, that's it - that's the line. 'He's got to get to that point before he can see us. Load the AP ! Chalky, back up a bit. That's it - whoa - '

The breech clanged shut, the gun loaded with armour-piercing shot and super-charge. James removed his overcoat and draped it carelessly to hang down in the quad door opening.

'Four hundred!' His voice was crisp. At that range it didn't matter what came over the top of that ridge. Cockney acknowledged the order with 'Ready!'

'Chalky, I want you to move the quad forward - when I give the word - on to that firm ground. And fast! Give that engine all the revs she can take. Until then I want you slumped over the wheel - *Dead*. OK?'

Chalky gave a grin and a nod and obligingly slumped over the wheel with one eye cocked on the ridge. The gun was now shielded completely by the side of the quad. James hoped he had his angles right. He reached into the quad and brought out the Bren and the Tommy gun. He tossed the Tommy to Lackery, cocked the Bren and flipped the safety on.

'Right! Everyone less Dodger under cover. Dodger, sprawl out in front. You're dead, too - an' look it, for Chrissake. An' don't fuckin' move when we open up. Wait until we've finished.'

James was now flat, partly behind the quad rear wheel, binoculars in his hands, Bren alongside him. Lackery was kneeling in the number one's position at the side of the trail. Rayburn kneeling with a round of HE on his knee with brass charges and the other shells on the ground behind him. Cockney, relaxed on the circular wooden seat. Bell doing number two, his job to open and close the breech and ram the shell into the barrel.

No one spoke. Lips suddenly felt like dry moth's wings. They waited. The straining engine and track noises grew louder. James kept his binoculars focussed on the ridge. He always marvelled at how sound carried so far and so clearly over the morning air. That engine must have been five or six miles away when he first heard it.

He said to Chalky. 'Switch off. It'll be warm enough now.'

The quad engine died. The note of the other engine was pitched higher. Then suddenly, it was there. It came over the top of the ridge and stopped.

'Come on, you bastards!' James whispered. He saw a figure stand up in the front of what looked like an armoured troop carrier. Through his binoculars James caught the dull gleam of helmeted heads behind the standing figure.

'Keep still,' warned James softly. The breeze flicked idly at the quad's camouflage netting. The quad engine gave a barely audible crack. From somewhere came the slow drip of water. He felt his elbows getting sore, sweat trickled into his eyes. Still the troop carrier stood there, a faint gleam of sunlight catching and reflecting the glint of the German's binoculars.

By now James was certain that the half tracked carrier was the smaller type. It was either three or five tons in weight. They rarely carried more than eight men. Sometimes carried a *Flammenwerfer*, a flame thrower. The seconds that seemed like hours ticked by. He watched the upright figure, willing him to come down, come on - get this torture of waiting over.

James heard the loud whisper from Dodger in front.

'Cor, Sarge, what wouldn't I give for a bleedin' fag? What's the bastards doin' now?'

'Nothin'. Just standin' there. You'll have to wait for your fag. I'll bet there's a section of infantry in that carrier. I don't think he's suspicious yet - well, no more than usual. Anyway, he's not movin' until he's sure. They're Jerries all right. They'll probably 'ave two light machine guns, so don't get careless.'

'Fuckin' good job it ain't a Mark four special,' came a whisper.

'You're tellin' me,' James replied. 'Uh, uh. Here he comes. Chalky, start up. Take it easy now. Wait until I give the word. Aim for the radiator. We'll follow up with a round of HE.'

The troop carrier, tracks squealing, moved slowly down the slope. The quad engine started, James felt the wheel move slightly as Chalky engaged the clutch. He slithered back with the Bren across his forearms. He was now behind the line of the shield and protected from the whiplash of the muzzle blast. He dropped the tripod legs of the Bren and cradled the stock. Safety off, he was ready and he hoped like hell that he hadn't forgotten anything.

The half track held its course. Cockney had his eye glued to the telescopic sight. James sucked in his breath. It was time.

'*Chalky, go*! Fire!'

The quad engine screamed, the vehicle leapt forward, a split second later came the roar of the gun.

'Load!' from James. He watched the tracer of the solid shot hit the front of the carrier which disintegrated under the impact. There was a fireball explosion; at the same time he heard the ripping calico sound of the German machine gun parting the air above him. He was firing in short bursts at two figures that had been hurled from the half track. The round of HE hit the carrier which had slewed broadside on to the twenty-five pounder. Intense flames followed by black oily smoke outlined the skeleton frame of the tracked vehicle. They could all feel the intense heat and now further explosions as the ammunition crackled. There was no sign of life. James put the safety on. He stood up and looked around.

His heart sank as his eyes fell on the bombardier's body sprawled in the loose-limbed posture of the dead. He felt an awful loneliness, a hole in the stomach bereftness. It was gone as suddenly as it had been felt. The trained experienced mind took over. No time. Lackery's chest had collapsed under that short burst of enemy machine gun fire. James closed the surprised eyes and blinked back a welling tear. He turned to the gun.

'Cease fire!'

To the frozen attitudes and the four pairs of pleading eyes, he said, 'Lackery's dead.' His flat neutral tone broke the tableau.

'Bastards.' The word was repeated again and again, it came from the Cockney. 'If - if I'd only fired a bit quicker. The sods - the bloody sods.' He put his head between his hands with his forehead resting against the bracket of the dial sight. His shoulders heaved.

James moved over and put a comforting arm over the shaking shoulders. 'Pack it in, Cockney. It was nobody's fault. You couldn't have fired any quicker without blowing the quad apart. It could 'ave 'appened to any of us. You know that fuckin' shield only stops rain, it could 'ave 'bin you. Now, forget it. It's over.

Nothin' any of us can do about it.' He patted the shoulder and turned away.

He waved to Chalky to reverse the quad back to hook up. Very lights intermingled with the staccato crackle of small arms ammunition. The variegated plumes of colour scattering in all directions from the vertical to the horizontal. James picked up the Tommy and passed it to Cockney.

'Keep an eye on the bonfire - ' and turning to the others, 'Right - get limbered up, then breakfast. We'll bury Lackery right after. We'll take a shufti at the half track when it cools down. Get weaving.' His voice was still flat, neutral and as impersonal as he could make it.

He moved over to Cockney Wells who was standing in front of the gunshield cradling the Tommy and gazing with a hit dog expression, at the burning half track.

James stopped in front of him and turned to face him. 'You all right, Wells?'

Recognition dawned in the hurt eyes. 'Yes, Sarge. Just the shock - Lackery gettin' knocked off. It's different, y'know, when it's - ' His voice trailed off.

James nodded. 'I know - who should know better - different when it's a friend, a mucker. Not the same if it's another gun crew or someone else in the battery. We all 'ave the same chance. Look at what's left behind me - they had a chance too. That was different; they were the enemy - the fuckin' Nazis or maybe they weren't. Maybe they were innocent, finished up out here. Maybe they had no say. But they had a job - we had a job too. This time we won - after a fashion. I knew Lackery for over ten years. He was more than a brother, he was half of me - '

He paused to spit the rising lump from his throat.

'You've seen men killed, plenty of them. Theirs and ours. We feel for them, deeply, but, take it from me, kid, you're glad it's not you. An', in the long run, that's what matters - survival. Get it?'

Cockney nodded the eyes hardening and face muscles tightening. 'Thanks, Sarge - '

James forced a grin. 'Just now - that was good shootin'. Two rounds, two hits. Can't fault that. As Lackery would say, a bit more practice an' you could be good. Mind you,' James said thoughtfully, 'if you'd missed at that range, I'd have had your bollocks for footballs.'

Cockney forced a grin, emotions now fully controlled. James went to see to the limbering up. Cockney had grown up a little more today. They had to use the winch again but soon afterwards the gun and trailer were hitched up behind the quad.

Out came the half petrol cans, quickly filled with sand and soaked with petrol. The two cans, were lit, on went the brew can of the same construction with a matchstick in the water. This swallowed any smoke. The cooking tin, the same size, got a tin of Soya bean sausages and a tin of American bacon. Oleo margarine provided the fat. Within ten minutes everyone was eating, all of them with spoons, the handiest cutlery in the desert.

They ate fast, habit of the life they had led for the past two and a half years. With food inside them, cigarettes in their mouths and drinking the strong desert brew spirits were recovering. Acceptance too. They had seen the last of Lackery as they had known him. He had been posted. No one would say much about Lackery today, maybe not tomorrow or the next day. In a week's time they would remember him in their conversation, feel ready to accept the memory in their hearts. Joke about him and have a certain pride that they had been mates.

The meal over and the utensils cleaned in the sand, the lockers were loaded and out came the two shovels for the grim task that lay ahead. James walked over to the body. Funny, he thought. It's not Lackery, it's just another body. He bent and emptied the pockets of his friend. Identity discs, he would need them, ten Victory V cigarettes, one paybook, the amounts drawn entered neatly by the officer who paid them, a wallet with two hundred piastres and a set of obscene French photographs. James glanced at them. The memories commenced. Ruthlessly he suppressed the thoughts, tore up the photographs and got to his feet. For a moment he thought: who would remember Lackery? And starkly, back came the answer: only us.

He walked over to the quad and took down the bombardier's bedding roll off the roof rack. He unrolled it. From it he took the US blanket. The blanket that of the original three issued was termed unserviceable, two GS general service, one US. It was a burying blanket. In India coffin money was deducted from a man's pay. No one in the frontline troops had just three blankets: by hook but mainly by crook the bedding rolls grew to as many as ten blankets. Constantly on the move the extra blankets provided just that bit more comfort during the cold nights.

James unrolled the blanket by the body. All helped to carry the remains of their bombardier off the track to the north and open desert. They took turns in digging the grave. No one spoke. Gently they lowered what had become another statistic. KIA Western Desert, November 1942.

Each of them dropped a handful of desert into the grave with an inaudible murmur, James stood for a silent moment. He felt curiously inept, inadequate as he struggled to find suitable words that would fit the sad moment. Eventually he commenced the Lord's Prayer. Raggedly the others followed their voices getting stronger as the prayer progressed.

'Amen,' said James. 'Lackery was a good friend of us all. He was a fine soldier. I knew him a long time - we all did. Today he was unlucky. Those Jerry bullets had his name and number on them. We won't forget him. So, Lackery, this is goodbye. We were proud to have served with you - ashes to ashes, dust to dust - rest in peace an' don't take any duff rupees, Sahib.'

He threw the first shovel of moist sand into the trench. James still couldn't think of it as a grave. It was another slit trench, one of thousands they had dug over the past years, from Agheila to Alamein, up and down like bloody yo-yo's. Slit trenches that they had all spent a lot of time in, that had saved countless lives and had always had a double purpose. For the living and for the dead.

II

Silent, they retraced their steps back to the quad. The half track, twisted and grotesque smouldered and sizzled in front of them. A slab of heavy steel yards away from the carrier, probably the cover protecting the engine, bore the white-edged black cross of the Wehrmacht. The front wheel tyres were now providing the densest black smoke, and smell.

James opened one of the quad lockers. He searched around inside for a few seconds before his fingers came into contact with two pieces of petrol boxwood that he now withdrew. Placing one of the flat pieces on the quad floor he started to inscribe, with an indelible pencil, the number, rank and name of the bombardier. Lackery, he thought, Wood on Wood.

Wetting the pencil constantly with his lips he went over the numerals and letters again and again. Finally the inscription was to his satisfaction. Taking a spare bootlace, army issue leather, out of his small pack, he bound the two pieces of wood together. Wood from petrol boxes was scarce now. The wooden boxes used to contain two four gallon tin cans of petrol. Now they came in jerricans, unboxed. The jerricans were a typically efficient German product that had been copied and manufactured in Egypt.

Giving a grunt of satisfaction at the result of his efforts he walked back to the mound of fresh desert. There he stood for a moment before placing the roughly made cross at the head of the lonely grave. He stepped back and saluted, turned smartly away and pushing all thoughts of the bombardier out of his mind, walked back to the gun .

'Come on, let's take a *shufti*!' He picked up the Bren and Cockney fell in beside him holding the Tommy. They squelched along, climbing the slope to the distorted wreck which was giving off mainly smoke, bearing the acrid stench of burning rubber. Mingled with that was a sweet, porkish scent.

Wells' expression was grim. His colour had returned and with it, his confidence. The memory of the bombardier was fading.

The first shock, the realisation had affected Wells more than any other member of the guncrew. In this mob everyone lived in little families for months on end. All of them part of larger families. The smallest, the driver and co-driver of a truck. Then the six men of the guncrew, the 220 or so men of the battery to the largest of all, the family of the regiment. Each family had a head whose word was law; this law was administered down from the matriarch/patriarch, - the Colonel, head of the tightly-knit clan.

To Wells, losing Lackery was like losing an elder brother. Even more in some ways, mostly because, like a good sheepdog, Lackery had watched over them all including Geordie, without ever seeming to be over protective.

The tips and wrinkles that he had passed on to them in his casual manner, came from a seemingly inexhaustible source of information. Information that had, Wells knew, been garnered from the barrack rooms of Woolwich, Newport, Aldershot and Trowbridge. From the North-West Frontier of India to the sands of this limitless desert they were in.

Wells owed his position as gunlayer to him. All the crew had been trained as layers as well as any other gun number. They were gunners. But he was the regular gunlayer of Kelly and his speed and accuracy had been put there by long periods of supervision by the bombardier.

No man breathing, even in the Royal Horse Artillery, reached that standard in five minutes. Lackery had been the spur, the guide and mentor. He had spotted the talent of Cockney. The ambidextrous digital efficency. The retentive memory, sharp ears, quick eyes and instant response. It had all been there but a coach like Lackery had honed the blade of that potential into something else, professionalism.

At Sidi Rezegh Wells had come into his own. He felt a warm glow of pride at the memory. That shambles had not been due to them, not to the crew of Kelly.

He switched his thoughts off as they got to within fifty yards of the wrecked half track. The pungent tang of burning rubber, and something else too, wrinkled his nostrils: roasting flesh. Automatically as they walked he had counted the strides from the gun. Admiringly he glanced over at James. Anyone would think he carried a rangefinder in his head. They reached the wreck. Four hundred yards, nearly to the bloody inch.

The scene was chaotic and forlorn. There were only three bodies all blood-soaked. One with the head missing. Fifteen yards away lay another figure, huddled with the grey overcoat smouldering. Of the two nearest, one was just a torso, nothing else. Wells walked over to the furthest body. James had gone round to the rear of the half track.

The single oblong door swung drunkenly outwards on one twisted hinge. Inside was a roasting charnel house. Must have had a *Flammenwerfer*, thought James. The intense heat that had scarred and melted the interior had not been caused by high explosive.

The light machine gun resting vertically on its bracket was a fused length of barely recognisable metal. Of its recent occupants there was little left that resembled human beings. On the still redly glowing steel floor, fat bubbled and spat giving off a distinctive odour. He turned away in disgust. James had a strong stomach but he felt the rising bile in his throat. He hawked and spat.

Wells stood in front of him. 'Sarge, that one over there, I think he's still alive. Anyway he seems to be breathing.'

They walked over to the huddled figure without the coal scuttle helmet and in a foetal posture. James kneeled and put his finger on the neck artery. He felt a steady pulse, opened an eyelid then looked at the head wound that was seeping bright red blood that had soaked the collar of the uniform.

'Pass us your field dressin', Cockney.'

Wells dug in his pocket, found the sealed field dressing and passed it over. James scratched the flap open. Between them they rolled the man over on to his back. A groan came from the pale lips. The face was that of a young man in his early twenties. Regular features and the skin white with shock. His rumpled black hair matted to the gash, bleeding freely, over his left temple. James placed the field dressing over the wound and with Wells holding the German's head, wound the brown-coloured bandage, attached to the sterile dressing, around the survivor's skull. Gently they laid the unconscious man's body back on the ground.

James and Wells stood up, James to see where the others were, Wells to light a cigarette and sort out his jumbled emotions. In the past hour he had experienced, sorrow, despair, frustration, anger, revenge and, in the last seconds, triumph, fulfilment and now pity. His eyes flicked to the smouldering wreck. He had done that. He was pleased and proud - a bullseye, blown the fuckin' thing to smithereens. Eyes flicked to the headless torso. Hard cheddar, Fritz. You coulda been the bastard who killed Lackery. Then again it coulda been you - as he glanced at the lad on the ground.

Lad. He grinned inwardly. He could be older than me. The flicker of pity he had experienced had gone back into a hard carapace deep within him. He remembered Lackery's favourite expression when wanting a kip. Well, I'm off to practise a short course of death. Wells grinned. All of them at some time said similar things, like 'Roll on, death. Let's have a long sleep.' He felt better, on top of things, controlled - normal.

Bell and Rayburn in company with Chalky had, once it was obvious no threat would come from the carrier, wandered back towards the quad. Dodger just stood there, looking. He was pleased they had knocked the half track out, horrified at the result and thoroughly disgusted that there was no loot. He was also only barely recovered from his shattering experience of having the gun fire over his body. His hair still felt singed and his facial skin stretched. On top of that he was still slightly deaf from the concussion. Sounds were faraway, in another cottonwool world. He heard James shout. The retreating figures of the other three turned and commenced their slipping ungainly way back. Even from where he was standing he could see the disgusted reluctance on their faces. He walked over to James and Cockney.

'Come on,' James said as the four straggled up to him. 'We'll 'ave to tek this one with us. Hump 'im over to the quad - there's nuthin' we can do here. The desert 'ull 'ave to take care of 'em.'

Rayburn and Bell, the tallest of the crew, got the German up on his feet. They each put an arm under the shoulders, Chalky took the legs. James had taken a look at the white piping around the epaulettes. It meant nothing to him. So far as he was concerned any designation was immaterial. They were Germans, that was enough.

It was rare for gunners to be in as close contact with the enemy as they had been today. Excepting Rezegh, and nothing had remotely resembled reality or normality there. He remembered the troop running out of ammunition, the panzers with their machine guns sweeping the gun positions helped by their mates, such as these had been in the half track. For a time, a long time, it had seemed to James, they had given a good imitation of moles.

Back at the quad they placed the prisoner in Lackery's corner seat. He was breathing heavily, so were the men who had carried him. Rayburn took two potato masher grenades out of the prisoner's belt. They had an official name, Rayburn thought, but all the crew called them potato mashers because that was what they looked like. James came up and saw what Rayburn was holding.

'Give 'em to me, Muscles. They might come in handy. You just pull the string and throw 'em.'

Relieved, Muscles handed them over, he was not a violent personality.

'Who d'y think they were, Sarge?' came Dodger's question. James thought for a moment. 'Dunno' really. Could be part of 90th Light - the cream. I'll bet they got a shock when our AP hit 'em.'

'Nothin' to the bloody shock I got when they came over that bleedin' 'ill, Sarge. My chuffin' teeth were rattlin' like castanets. Strewth it was all right for you lot. Me, I wus on me own, in front feelin' like a plucked chicken. Difference wus, the chicken wus as big as a bleedin' elefunt. I'll tell you straight,' his voice sank to a confidential whisper, 'I didn't know whether to 'ave a shit, shave, or a bleedin' 'aircut.'

Though not a true cockney, Dodger was pretty close to it, as was his wit. James grinned as he put the German grenades on the quad floor between the engine cover and his small pack. He wasn't short of comedians in his crew.

'You lyin' git,' Cockney said. 'Everyone knows you wus asleep. He wus fuckin' snorin'. I'nt that right, Chalky?'

Chalky nodded grinning, more at the change in Dodger's expression, which resembled an outraged turkey, than at Cockney's remark. Piling coals on the fire: 'Yeah, come to think of it, I reckon he got bit by a tsetse fly. Can't keep awake. If you ask me, the poor little bastard's 'ad it. He's got sleepin' sickness.' Adding with unction like an out of work priest, 'He'll be dead in six months.'

A wave of laughter went up. Dodger made a rush for Chalky who enveloped him in long arms, patted his head and crooned to him like a baby.

'OK, pack it in,' James said.

The horseplay stopped as he gave out orders. In less than fifteen minutes the gun and quad were free of the track mud, past where it jinked right and standing on much firmer ground. James left them there whilst he walked past the smoking half track to the crest of the ridge. He carried the Bren over his right shoulder as he trudged over the stony scree and up the hill.

He had put his mud-caked overcoat on. The faint gleam of a reluctant sun was doing its utmost to break through the cloud mass. The desert had that fresh newly washed look. Rain came so rarely in these parts; the old timers said only once or twice in six or seven years. When it did the desert shed the cloak of barren mediocrity over large tracts.

Tomorrow there would be flowers. They would last only for a few hours. Some parts would be a carpet of small delicate blooms, the colour soft, varied and magnificent and an impossibility that was a fact. The mantle of colour brought a new meaning and beauty to the normal harsh appearance. The first time James had seen this desert blooming all the quads and trucks had detoured. No one wished to sully or destroy such beauty.

He reached the top of the ridge. From a prone position he cautiously scanned the country beyond. He heaved a sigh of relief as his binoculars traversed the horizon. The ground was less stony, the typical camel thorn humps, which compelled any transport to perform the weaving dance, so typical of desert movement.

Within the scope of his vision scattered knocked-out tanks and trucks of the 'B' Echelon's occupied their final and unexpected terminus. Rough wooden crosses over the scattered and isolated graves with sand heaped to and almost burying the centrepieces. His eye caught a quick movement three hundred yards away. He stared intently then relaxed; it was a gazelle.

The small clusters of vehicles and tanks were the only tangible evidence of the retreat from Gazala and Tobruk in June. He got to his feet and slithered down to the quad. They had been lucky this morning. The half track could have been mounting a 37 or even a 50mm. He thought about the breakout at Alamein. He could only guess. The rain would have bogged down both tanks and trucks. Even on the coast road progress would be limited. Off the tarmac surface it would be mud and strewn with mines. It was possible, even likely that the frontier wire had been reached. Sollum and Capuzzo captured. Then again, they might be stuck around El Daba or Fuka.

He thought about Fuka, just a spot on the map, landing grounds for the RAF. It was also a regimental saying, meant to be sarcastic and humorous. A cynical put down, meant to be a joke, to convince scared and often frightened men that a tense and extremely dangerous situation was not that at all - black sardonic humour - like the man who gets his leg blown off, and his mate says: 'What'yer groanin' at? You've still got yer wedding tackle, ain't ya?' There are a thousand such examples - cruel, merciless, biting, cynical observations, made out of the depths of despair - a cocked snook at the officers, the generals, the politicians and everyone else not in his particular predicament, where the justice was often measured in seconds.

James had the type of craggy features that betrayed little or no expression. To an anxious enquirer his reply might be: 'Rommel has lost all his tanks. But he's just got another five hundred Mark IV specials. Seriously though - an' this is pukkha dink - the real truth: there's fuckin' hell on at Fuka.'

He would leave his enquirer pondering on what significant event was happening or had happened at Fuka. If anything ever happened at Fuka, it would be the first time unless the boys in blue had run out of talcum powder. Until the Afrika Korps occupied the landing grounds it had been a backwater, subject only to air raids.

So far, James could see no reason to alter his decision to head for where he knew the regiment would be, Bir Khamsa. True, there were old minefields scattered all over the place, booby traps, old thermos bombs, poisoned wells and spare Jerries. The same hazards would apply to the trip to the coast road north of here. And James thought, there would be a traffic jam for fifty miles. Anyway he liked the desert, the room and he supposed, the challenge. He was not ignoring the fact that Rommel had turned the tables before. The Afrika Korps did not give up easily.

He thought briefly about Lackery. They had mucked in for six years. One did not forget that. He had even refused promotion to stay with James and the troop. Now he had left it for good. James had noted down the map reference of the grave from the sketchy information derived from the trig point. Eventually, after this lot was over the grave would be found, that is if anyone could find a minute spot on the map. If they did, the War Graves Commission would bury him decently in a recognised Military Cemetery.

They all stood around the quad drinking the tea that had been brewed for his return. He took his steaming mug and lit a cigarette. The reaction of the morning's events still lingered but were fading as each in his own way adjusted and, more practically, thought of what lay ahead.

James finished his tea and threw the dregs away. He went for a quick walk of inspection around the quad and gun. He knew that everything would be spot on but it was his habit. The crew knew it and accepted the ritual. Being together for so long they had developed a smooth fast way of working. Their home was the quad. Five minutes from receiving the shouted order to 'Prepare to Move', they were packed and rolling.

It was the same when they dropped into action. To an observer the sheer speed of the operation was staggering. To the crew it was routine, as it was to any of the twenty-four guncrews that made up the regiment. They were professionals. A split second might save a life, either their own or that of someone, lying in a trench five thousand yards in front of them, who desperately needed fire support.

Throwing the butt of his cigarette away, James said, 'Right, gather round.'

He looked at each in turn. They were a motley collection. Like a tribe of bloody gypsies.

'I don't need to tell you,' he began, 'but I'm goin' to. That punch-up we had this mornin' - could happen again.'

The flat tone made each word drop like a pebble in a limpid pool. Five pairs of eyes focussed on his lips. He went on:

'There's too many things we don't know. F'rinstance, we don't know how many spare Jerries are floating around, or what they're floatin' around in. We don't know how far the advance has gone. It could be any one of half a dozen places, Daba, Fuka,

Matruh, Sidi Barrani, Buq Buq, Sollum, Hellfire, or even El Adem. Take your pick.'

He watched the changing expressions on the faces before him. Bell looked worried, Dodger searching for a quip, Rayburn, open trust. Chalky, nonchalant, Cockney a mixture of confidence, trust, humour and determination.

'That's right. We're bloody ignorant. But we do know it. We also know that the regiment was heading for Bir Khamsa and then on to El Adem.' He paused to light a cigarette and took the first drag. 'If we head for the coast road, we'll be heading for the biggest traffic jam and *snafu** we've ever seen. And on the way, who knows? We could even end up in the bag. So - we're goin' to Khamsa.'

Heads nodded in agreement, only one shook in dismay.

'This has certain advantages. First, we'll be followin' the regiment. We have a target to aim at. Second, away from the coast they won't have 'ad as much rain an' the goin' 'ull be better. Third, we've more room, the risk should be less. Any questions?'

No one spoke for a moment then Bell moved closer. James raised his eyebrows expectantly. Bell cleared his throat and hesitantly said:

'Well, I've been thinking, Sarge. We've no guarantee that the regiment will be at Khamsa, have we?'

James thought for a brief moment before replying, his tanned face wooden, only the eyes betraying slight irritation.

'No, you're right. We've no guarantee they'll be there. But then again, we've no guarantees about anything in this war. We don't even know if we'll be alive in an hour's time, do we?'

The others let slow grins appear. James went on:

'Seriously though, we know the biggest part of the army kept to the coast road, so did Rommel. We could meet up with a lot more up there than we did this mornin'. It's my job to get all of you and Kelly back to the troop, *Jildi*. We're no good here an' no good in the bag. Anyway, there's no place like home. So, mount up! We'll press on and *marleesh* the torpedoes.'

There was a general murmur of amusement that contained a measure of relief. James knew from experience how not

---

**Situation normal all fucked up*

knowing what was going on affected men. It was a factor that he had always thought important. Tell them what you knew, even if half was conjecture and they settled down, accepted. On the other hand James was not the kind of senior NCO who encouraged parliamentary debates regarding decisions he was solely responsible for.

They followed each other into the quad. James picked up his anti-magnetic oil compass from under his seat. This was loot from a crashed Italian tri-motored S79 bomber. He had won it in July 1940. Ideal for accurate travel and unaffected by the metal of any vehicle. His own prismatic compass varied, as all prismatics did by up to thirty degrees from a bearing taken thirty yards away.

'How's the Jerry?' asked James.

'Still spark out, Sarge,' came Cockney's reply.

James glanced at the slumped figure of their prisoner. Even in the gloom of the quad interior the white face stood out, like an hallowe'en mask.

'Keep an eye on him then.' James leaned down to Chalky. 'Let's get around the bottom of this hill. I'll take a bearing there when you stop.'

Chalky nodded and let the clutch in and the quad moved forward. Brew and fire cans rattled as their home on runflat tyres gripped the surface. The quad resembled an enormous beetle. It was piled high, on the sloping rear roof, with the spare wheel and the bedding rolls of the crew. Kitbags, jerricans, water cans, tools, shovels, camouflage net, sand channels: all had their place. The gun limber carried the gun cover, spare shovels, picks, machetes, water and more jerricans of petrol. Every locker on the quad was used to the full capacity. Total length of quad, gun and trailer was over fifty feet.

They crawled around the base of the hill into a wadi which came to an end a hundred yards further on. They now faced the vista James had scanned with his binoculars. Chalky stopped. James directed him to the left. The bearing was two hundred and fifty degrees, just south of west. They moved on, bouncing and jinking their way through the humps of camel thorn, the ground damp but fairly firm. James picked out a tiny V on the horizon and pointed it out to Chalky.

They looked to be crossing a huge bowl that under the lowering sky offered no invitation. James put his mind in neutral, lit a cigarette, leaned on the edge of the hatch and enjoyed the purr of the engine and the solitude. It was a bonus to be free of dust that clogged eyes, mouth, hair and ears. The further they left the wrecked half track behind, the less the weight on his mind. They would never see it again. For that matter they would never see Cairo again. The latter caused him to think, at the moment, that was the last thing he wanted to do.

He was, as he knew they all were, feeling the enervating post-action effects. Most of the crew would be asleep, nature's way of providing a recharging of the nervous system. James closed his eyes, his body automatically swaying to the movement of the quad. Maybe the desperate tiredness could be explained by a doctor. Maybe the only solution was to stop the war. But it always happened, one could sleep on a clothes line afterwards. Come to think of it though, whose reflexes were faster than the fighting man's? Only the big cats, the wild life of the jungle, and look how they sleep, all bloody day.

A hand pulled at his overcoat skirt. He was back to the present in the blink of an eyelid. Aware, his instincts and reflexes razor-edged - just like a wild animal, the thought flashed and went. He bent down. Cockney said:

'It's the Jerry - he's coming to.'

The prisoner occupying the late bombardier's seat had opened his eyes and was gazing muzzily at his travelling companions. James took a quick glance at his watch. Much to his surprise he saw that they had been on the move for over two hours.

'Pull up, Chalky,' he ordered. The quad slowed down and rolled to a halt.

'OK. Wakey wakey!' James shouted. 'All out. Let's brew up and 'ave some *connor* - grub. We'll move off in an hour.'

There was a general exodus through slammed open doors followed by the clanging of opened locker lids. Dodger and Muscles had taken charge in the cookery department. Bell and Cockney had each taken a shovel and were walking away from the quad to dig their personal latrines. Chalky was topping up the tank he was running on. The quad had two tanks, one each side with the filler pipe and cap high up on the side near the rear.

James looked at the German. Comprehension was slowly creeping over the young, still white face. His lips looked cracked and dry.

'You speak English?' The sharp voice of James was enough to penetrate the fog that surrounded the German's brain.

'*Bitte? Ja*, I speak a little *Engleesh*. Who are you?'

The words were enunciated slowly and painfully, the German let his head drop into his hands. James tapped the man's shoulder. The dark-pain filled eyes slowly met his. James tapped his own chest.

'Me *Feldwebel* - Sergeant - compree? You prisoner - prisoner *de guerre*. As your mates say, for you the war is over. *Coloss, ogeia*, over, finished.' The dark head lifted again. The eyes pleaded.

'*Wasser, bitte. Wasser.* Please, you give me to drink, *ja* yes?'

James poked his head out of the quad door.

'Chah up yet? When it is, bring us a couple of *pialas*.' The grunt of acknowledgement came from Rayburn. James turned back to the forlorn figure.

'Be here in a minute - *une momento* - *teek hai*. All right?'

'*Une momento - grazie dankeschön*, Sergeant,' his prize of war replied.

Two minutes later the urchin features of Dodger made their appearance in the open doorway.

''Ere y'are, Sarge. An' one for the honoured guest.' Dodger made sure he sounded the H in that one. James thanked him and took the steaming mugs. He noticed one was Lackery's.

The irony of the situation struck him. This could be the man who killed Lackery. But he didn't feel hatred for the forlorn figure drinking out of the bombardier's mug. Concern, yes, pity, no and certainly not hatred. That was war. It did a lot to you. Widened your vision and provided a deeper insight into people. Under pitiless shelling or bombing and strafing it created hate, a powerful hate that demanded revenge, particularly if you were unable to hit back.

At the moment of Lackery's death James would have shot this man out of hand. Now, hours afterwards he felt a kind of sorrow for him but no more than he would for an injured dog. In action, when they were hitting back it wasn't hate. It was some kind of joy, mocking joy, the same kind of joy that one got in a football match when your team was four down in the first half, and then you scored five goals to win.

James picked up the oblong messtin that Dodger had placed

on the quad floor. It held four slices of bully beef, crisply fried and a packet of issue biscuits. He broke open the packet and handed half to the German then showed him how to pick up the bully with two biscuits, to make a sandwich. He watched as the prisoner bit into the iron hard offering of the British Empire. The German's face was a study as he started to chew slowly.

'Good?' James held up the biscuit sandwich.

'*Ja* - yes - but hard, like rock - you know?' he said, between chews.

'I know,' said James. 'Believe me. I've been chewin' 'em for the last two an' a half years. Good for your teeth.'

'Teeth? How so?' asked his prisoner.

'Eat 'em long enough an' your bloody fillin's drop out with the vibration,' quipped James.

The German's eyes widened, then he comprehended. He laughed, then gave a quick grimace of pain. James thought he would have a king-sized headache. He listened to the fractured English and thought, 'I'll sound the same to him.'

'Ah, you make joke, *ja?*'

'No joke,' said James, 'it's dead serious. Eating biscuits, I mean. We've had plenty of practice.' He regarded the man half-humorously.

'Tell me - you infantry?'

'*Ja* - me paratrooper. Sent to Ninetieth Light. Good division, you know?' James nodded in agreement.

The German went on, 'Alamein - pretty hot, huh? We go south, breakdown, spend much time - not *gut* - then we look for no mud. Then - I doan-no, I am here, in this - this.' He indicated the quad with an expressive gesture, shrugged then smiled carefully.

'Maybe now I spend war in Cairo or Alex?' He seemed happy at the thought.

'Yeah, you could at that. For the time bein' you'all 'ave to come with us. You'll get back to Cairo *baadin*.'

'*Baadin*. 'Ow you mean?' with an alarmed look.

'Later,' James said easily. '*Baadin* is later. It's Arabic for later.'

'So, *baadin* - later - Arabic. *Baadin* - yes, yes, *gut*. OK.'

James took a look out of the quad door and glanced at his watch. They still had twenty minutes of the hour left. He took another swallow of tea, opened a tin of Players cigarettes and passed one to the German. He lit them both, they sat smoking, taking an occasional drink of tea, each occupied with their own thoughts.

Since they had followed the dense mass of vehicles through the 'Supercharge' gap at Alamein and the resultant breakdown, he had followed his instincts. In the past two and a half hours they had covered thirty-five miles. He was now questioning the decisions he had arrived at. He knew it was not always the wisest thing to do. But, as he thought back, he was not infallible and the more he thought about the situation, the more he became convinced that he might be wrong. Wrong about where they were when they had broken down.

He picked up the mapcase and studied the map. He followed the line of the escarpment from the ringed circle he had marked. It dawned on him that they were already on the escarpment, had been since their enforced stop. He swore under his breath and felt chagrin at his mistake. He reassessed their probable position and tentatively marked another circle. Moodily he realised he could still be ten miles out either way. Not feeling very confident and still piqued he laid his protractor base on the marked ring and took a line on Bir Khamsa. Two hundred degrees, well, that would have to do, further south than he had guessed.

No damage had been done and they might even meet up with some of their own troops before then. They had plenty of fuel and water with rations to last them a week. He tried to remember the date but gave up in disgust. No one ever remembered what day it was, that is unless the padre held a church service, That didn't always mean it was Sunday either.

He looked at the German. '*Ezmah*- kay? - what's your name *nom - was ist - ?*' He searched his mind for another term. 'Monicker?' Understanding dawned in the dark eyes.

'*Ja - fustan* - understand - Schwarze - Karl -' It was followed by stream of what James took to be German. He waved his hand weakly to stop the flow.

'*Chubbarow, escott*, shut up. *Husty - husty -* slowly - *vu ist* Karl Schwarze hein?'' he said, slowly and distinctly.

The prisoner carefully kept his head rigid and grinned.

'*Gut* - you know - me Karl. OK?'

James said. 'Right, you're Karl. Me, Sar-gent.'

He took both mugs and the messtin and put them on the floor near the doorway.

'OK, you lot, drop your cocks and grab your socks. Let's get movin'.'

Groans and laughter greeted his shout as they threw dregs of tea on the ground, packed the mugs and messtins away, hung the brew and cooking cans on the outside of the quad at the rear, and closed the locker lids. They crowded into the quad with the rifles and Tommy gun going into the racks. James picked up his Bren and changed the magazine. He beckoned to Wells and Rayburn.

They leaned forward and he whispered.

'Watch the arms. It's still a Jerry we've got. His name is Karl Schwarze. Call him Karl, but watch him. He's not in very good shape - he's got a headache. Keep on your toes.'

They moved off. The sky was still heavy with grey, almost stationary clouds and a chill in the air. The sun, by this time, although not visible, betrayed its presence by the lighter sky overhead. James indicated the line to follow and the quad bore left to follow the new bearing. The ground was drying out, the going was flat and good. It bore no evidence of other vehicles. James took off his overcoat, folded it and put it on the edge of the hatch behind him. Bracing his legs he leaned back on the improvised cushion.

The wind plucked at his jerkin. Just riding in a vehicle let alone standing, as he was, one's bones could get very tired. He narrowed his eyes, an automatic concession to the breeze and uncertain light. Ahead looked like virgin desert that had seen no war.

There were no burnt out wrecks here and few travellers could have known its loneliness. It was strange, mused James, how often one found this sort of emptiness completely unsullied.

Quite recently, before Alamein in early October, the regiment had moved back to a name on the map called Khatatba, halfway between Alex and Cairo. There they had received some new and reconditioned vehicles and equipment. Only a few miles west into the desert they had stumbled across a petrified mass of giant treetrunks horizontal and scattered for miles. They had the ring of iron when hit with a hammer. Further south and west of where they were now, they had come across two hundred foot cliffs bearing a solid glittering cover of mica. Dig a slit trench and find sea shells.

He recalled the first trenches they had dug, at Gerawla in May 1940. They had sea shells by the shovel. It had been a flypast by RAF Blenheim bombers, its purpose to show what two thousand feet altitude looked like to the man on the ground. Over that height, *they* said, small arms fire was useless. *They* had said a lot of things over the past years, thought James, without making a lot of sense. On 10th June, 1940 they were at war with Italy. They were part of what was known as Western Desert Force. In England, Lady Astor had attacked the brown knees and Vee necks, that to her indicated that all their time had been spent sun bathing and swimming in the blue sea.

Maybe now, she was regretting those words. Those same men, in company with the Aussies, New Zealanders and the Indians, many now in lonely desert graves had held the Italians in September of that year. In December as part of Wavell's thirty thousand they had defeated an army many times their size in conditions that in England dog owners would not have tolerated for their pets.

He remembered the names etched indelibly on his mind like a roll of honour. Sidi Barrani, Buq Buq, Halfaya Pass, Capuzzo, Sollum, Sidi Omar, Sherferzen, Maddalena, the two Sofafis, the Rabia track, Charing Cross, Bardia, Tobruk, El Adem, Sidi Rezegh, El Duda, Bomba, Gazala, Cyrene, Mechili, Bir Hacheim, Retma Box, Msus, Sceledeima, Antalat, Segnali, Ghemines, Beda Fomm, Agadabia, Agheila. So many names, there were dozens more, familiar, nostalgic, like Tobruk for instance. He had been cut off there in the first siege for seven weeks before finally reaching Alexandria by the destroyer *Decoy*.

Risalpur, the name meant cavalry station, on the North-West Frontier of India, twenty-eight miles from Peshawar and close to the Waziristan border. Names, operational names. The first one called 'Operation Compass' began the Italian campaign under Wavell. Then in June 1941 came the first against the Afrika Korps, 'Battleaxe'. That was a disaster. 'Crusader', the three-week long battles of Sidi Rezegh, a series of disasters. Alamein was the most recent, the most successful and for the first time, a complete victory.

They were entering a wadi. There was no point in looking at the map, for it wouldn't be shown on the 1 in 500,000 map he had been forced to use. Fortunately it was nearly dry and after two miles they were back on good going. He gave instructions for a slight correction in direction to Chalky. He glanced inside the quad. Karl was asleep, so were Bell and Dodger. The other two grinned at him. He bent further and lit a cigarette before resuming his stance.

A faint gleam of sunshine illuminated the bonnet of the quad. It picked out in sharp relief the unit number of the regiment. 64 on the red and blue divided square. On the near side was the Jerboa, the desert rat. A red square bearing a white circle with the desert rodent facing out from the vehicle. It was said that the white circle was the eye of the desert rat, which never slept. The number 64 in the view of the Italian propaganda machine was the 64th Division that they had wiped out in their advance to Sidi Barrani in September of 1940. They had announced, too, that the trams in the city had recommenced. James smiled at the thought of the four shells of buildings that comprised that dot on the map ever needing a tram service.

He started to hum a tune, as he dropped down into his seat. Still humming, the words eluding him he looked at the others. They were all awake except Karl. He looked like death warmed up. One by one the crew joined in the humming their minds searching for the lyrics. There were plenty of would be lyricists in the regiment. Some were known but the majority were anonymous. Often they would parody one of Kipling's Barrack Room Ballads. This one's tune suddenly registered, 'Foolish but it's fun'. Cockney started it and the others swiftly joined in. The words described a battery commander who was rather eccentric:

> Every morning with the rising sun,
> We hook the limber to the gun,
> To chase the Eyetie and the Hun,
> It's foolish but it's fun.

The six voices grew in strength, as Chalky joined the choir.

> Old happy Jack with his hunting horn,
> Wakes the leaguer every morn,

The silly old bastard should never 'abin born,
It's foolish but it's fun.

The last verse brought in the other Desert Rats in the 7th Motor Brigade. Units they had fought with since June 1940. The initials not the full titles were cleverly brought in.

The KRR's, the KDG's
11th Hussars, the 2 RB's
The poor old bastards - ,
Are on their knees.
It's foolish but it's fun.

Once started the crew took some stopping as they roared out repeats of every verse. They were all forgetting for the moment, the grave behind them and what might lie in front.
James sat swivelled in his seat enjoying the spontaneous sing-song. Once started the crew would go through the whole repertoire. It was all part of coming back to normal. Like pain, one only felt one at a time as with toothache. He didn't need to be psychic in order to know what was coming next. Dodger led off and the rest joined in, Bell as usual, thought James, unable or unwilling, just mouthing the words. Karl should really be in dock, James knew that sort of pallor. He joined in:

South of the Libyan border,
The Eyeties were staging a show,
When over came three British bombers,
And dropped all their bombs in a row.

Singing:

Here's one for old Mussolini,
Here's one for Ciano as well,
Here's one for you olive-skinned bastards,
Who thought that you could conquer us.
The lines were laid out *boat Jildi.
The bearing was six oh degrees,

*Very quickly (Urdu)

A few rounds of gunfire were fired,
The shells they did buzz like bees.

Singing -

They repeated the chorus.

Now this is the end of my story,
The Eyeties are far away,
But if there's a job you want doing,
Just send for the fourth RHA.

Singing -

They were now thoroughly caught up in what was a part of their history, desert lore, memories, their life, indeed all their lives woven together. Their quad, their gun, their regiment. Entertainment was of their own devising and reminiscence, nostalgia played a large, frequently major part of their existence.

James took a look through the slit in the windscreen glass and checked the aircraft compass bearing. Miles and miles of sweet fuckall. The same lowering sky could be Scotland; all they wanted was sheep.

Cockney shouted, 'What about the *Berka* one, Sarge? You know - the brothel one - down in old Cairo, there is a street of shame, Sharia El Berka is its fuckin' name.' James thought for a moment. The song, fairly filthy was sung to the hymn tune 'Abide with me'. He didn't think it was a time for hymn tunes even parodied.

'*Lah Lah* Summat cheerful Saieeda Bint.'

'*Haiwa*. Yes. *Tumam howie* - that's the best' - crowed Dodger.

'All together - 'James joined in the lilting song, another parody.

Saieeda Bint, (Greeting's Girl.)
I love your charming manner,
To be with you would be my only joy.
A dirty little yashmak, two eyes of sapphire blue,
You make me say - to other bints,
Musquoise, mafeesh faloose. (No good, no money.)

Two eyes afire,
that make me *stanaswire*, (Wait a little.)
To dance with you, would be my only joy.
I think I'll call you Nina,
'Cause your eyes say *Taala Heena*, (Come here)
Oh my little gyppo bint,
You're *quoise kateer*. (Very good)

They finished off with a roar of laughter. James stood up and put his head and shoulders through the hatch. He whistled softly to himself. He was concerned about the German and didn't like the look of him. The poor sod was still asleep. Below him the crew had fallen silent relaxed and smoking.

Rayburn was thinking about the next cool beer. Bell was depressed and worried. How long, he wondered. Dodger was thinking of home and Ann Shelton.

The quad purred along and Kelly bounced easily behind.

III

His peripheral vision caught a flash, low down below the cloud to the north-west. His binoculars seemed to come up of their own volition. An aircraft. One look was enough.

'Pull up, Chalky. Bale out. Me 110- *'Raus , Luftwaffe!*' he roared.

He hoped Karl would *malamm* - understand - his sketchy German, if he was awake. The quad stopped. Both doors crashed open and the crew shot out like corks out of a bottle. Rayburn was dragging, half lifting a dazed, half-conscious German behind him with his rifle in the other hand. He was heading for the end of an arm of the imagined X that would bisect the gun and quad. It was the aim of everyone to reach one of those points, as far, and as quickly as possible.

Heart pounding like a steam hammer, breath whistling through his teeth, the Bren weighing a ton, James galloped across the sandy waste. No slit trenches here. Air attack was the last thing he expected. With the advance, heavy rain, with the Luftwaffe restricted to rear airfields and their losses from the RAF the LRDG helped by the SAS, it had seemed remote. How wrong can you be. Just our fuckin' luck.

He reached his goal arriving on his stomach like a baseball player and rolled over, cocked the Bren and looked for the Messerschmitt. He saw the reflection on the perspex cockpit canopy and hoped desperately that the observer had missed them. The hope vanished as quickly as it had come. The plane was low, below five hundred feet. On this flat landscape they would stick out like flies on a tablecloth. James, in common with everyone else in the desert, had never got used to the feeling of naked exposure when under attack from the air.

He got to one knee, the butt of the Bren snuggled in the hollow of his right hip. The Messerschmitt 110 was a twin-engined fighter bomber armed with cannon and machine guns: it also carried bombs. He watched it come in from the north-east in a flat shallow dive, hearing the Vroom-Vroom of the twin engines getting louder and echoing around the empty landscape. James was on the south-east tip of the X. Rayburn and the German on the north-west tip. Wells, with the Tommy and Dodger with his rifle on the north-east. Bell and Chalky, both with rifles on the south-west.

The ME was going to make the first pass from stern to stem. Christ, it was fast, thought James as he caught the winking of muzzle flashes. James led off fifteen degrees and followed the streaking shape now no higher than fifty feet: the tracers of the Bren stitched a pattern along the fuselage. He heard the fast ripple, calico-tearing, baby-shitting sound of the machine guns interspersed with the deeper thud of the cannon. The thud of the Bren stopped as he released the trigger. Rifle shots had come from the four corners and the faster snarl of the Tommy gun. His had been only a short burst, maybe thirty rounds. He knew he had hit and could have sworn the aircraft had staggered.

The ME had pulled up from the dive towards the south-west. It swept in a bank to the north. This bastard's not joking, must have a liver on. Why the fuck don't you go home? James thought sourly. He steeled himself for the next attack and wished vainly that he had a quadrupled set of 20mm ack-ack cannon. Better still, a 40mm Bofors. The ME was going to come in abeam of the quad. He moved round and waited. As in so many situations in the past, time slowed down. It was the eerie feeling of watching a slow motion film. Even though at the back of his subconscious mind he knew the ME was slicing through the air at three hundred miles an hour.

The image of the sleek shape of the Messerschmitt barrelling towards him, the flame-winking spurts of cannon and machine gun fire were burnt on the retinas of his eyes. The timeless moment was devoid of any noise, his ears encased in cotton wool. He was hardly aware, in this dreamlike void, of the vibration of the Bren and the stream of tracer, locked like a magnet on to the hurtling mass of steel and aluminium sweeping towards his quad and gun.

Suddenly the moment ended. The 110 was past him with whoosh of displaced air and roar of engines. The Messerschmitt staggered, right wing dropping as it swept past, smoke streaming from the right engine that swiftly and dramatically was now in flames.

'Crash, you bastard,' came the half-whispered hate-laden voice of James. 'Hit the fuckin' deck.' It sounded like a prayer.

He gave a *tch* of annoyance as the pilot got some sort of control and the ME lost speed; it slowly gained height, and crabwise limped off to the west, one wing belching smoke and flames. It struck James that the rear gunner must have been asleep or dead. The slight annoyance had been replaced by cheerful though limited satisfaction.

James wiped the sweat out of his eyes with the back of his hand. He looked to the quad. It was on fire. The sight hit him like a blow. Dropping the Bren he started to sprint aware as he did so of the figures of his crew, getting up and beginning to run with an urgency that matched his own. As he ran his eyes took in and appraised the scene. It looked desperate. Flames were rising from the ground underneath the quad. One or both petrol tanks had been hit. He was nearly there, and knew exactly what he wanted to do.

Diving through the open door he slid behind the wheel. Praying fervently under his breath and mixing the prayer with furious curses in Arabic and Urdu he switched on, pressed the starter, depressed the clutch, engaged first gear, released the handbrake and accelerated as the engine fired, in one rapid fluent series of actions. The quad lurched forward, picked up speed. He felt the heat decrease and stopped fifty yards away. He switched off and jumped out. His overcoat was in his hands, for a milli-second he wondered how.

Then he was on the ground, under the petrol tank, feeling the heat coming through the cloth and the skin on his face wrinkling in the oven heat. He was aware of the sound of shovels and movement on the other side of the quad. Desperately he pressed the thick material tighter; gradually the heat diminished. A few seconds more and he brought the coat away. The fire was out. He ran round to the other side of the quad jumping the tow tube of the limber automatically with the stench of petrol still thick in his nostrils.

The other tank was leaking petrol, fast.

'Quick! Gerra jerrican an' funnel - catch some of this juice.'

His breathing was steadying. Cockney came down off the roof

with the funnel and an empty jerrican. Swiftly Dodger and he got it under the gashed tank to catch the hosepipe stream of precious fuel. Bell and Rayburn were heaping sand under the other tank and what remained of the sergeant's overcoat. The situation was now under control. James looked back to the former position of the quad. A limited area of desert was still burning furiously. The satisfying gurgle of fuel dropping into the jerrican lifted his spirits slightly.

He walked around to look at the other tank. Flame-scorched paint and a ragged hole where the corner had been told him the bad news. It would never hold petrol again. It was luck that Chalky had been running the engine on this tank. Had it been full? He didn't bother to answer the speculation. The swift gush of petrol could not have been ignited by the bullet or cannon shell that had torn the hole.

He guessed it was part of a cannon shell. A sprinkle of tracer incendiaries from the ME must have hit the ground and lit the petrol the second time round. Whatever or however, it was irrelevant. The quad had not blown up. He was so immersed in his own thoughts that he almost missed seeing the quad's rear tyre. It was flat, in fact half the tyre was missing. It was certain that the runflat would roll no more.

At the other tank they had just got all the fuel they were going to get, a jerrican and a half - about seven and a bit gallons. Chalky, in front of the radiator, was catching a trickle of water in the cooking tin. He smiled ruefully at James.

'Small 'ole, Sarge. Near the bottom.'

James nodded acknowledgement and replied, 'Rear tyre's 'ad it.' He walked down to the gun and limber. All the wheels were intact. There was a cannon shell hole through the gunshield. In the unlikely event that the layer had been in his seat, he would not have been very pleased. There were several smaller holes obviously bullets. Marks of ricochets on the trail and barrel; the trailer was unmarked, He carried on with his careful inspection of the gun. Satisfied at last he turned to have a good look at the quad.

What he did not, could not know of, was a small hole in the compressed air side of the recuperator system, underneath the carriage containing the barrel or piece. The splinter of steel from an exploding cannon shell, minute in size, sharper than the finest scalpel, had impacted at several thousand feet per second. The compressed air cylinder leaked the whole of its contents in a fraction of time.

The recuperator system of the twenty-five pounder field gun, as in most other guns comprised two cylinders, one of oil, the other of compressed air. When the gun was fired the barrel recoiled to the rear on greased steel channels to a limit of, usually, twenty-eight inches. The cylinder of oil cushioned that recoil. The compressed air took over at the end of recoil and impelled the piece back to its runout or normal position. Without compressed air the barrel would not return; it would remain fully recoiled. In that position firing another shell was impossible.

Bell and Rayburn had the spare wheel down from the roof of the quad. The jack was already in position and the wheel nuts loosened. Chalky had drained the radiator. James called out to Dodger and Cockney:

'Get a brew on, lads. When in doubt, brew up, 'an believe me, I'm in doubt.'

'He looked up and saw the prisoner, Karl, standing in front of the quad. Poor bastard, thought James, he doesn't know whether he's on this earth, or Fullers' Earth. He noticed the metal of the quad body, pierced on both sides. It looked like a bloody colander; two cannon shells had gone through the floor. The spare wheel was now on.

'Muscles,' he called. 'Get that tyre off the wheel - we'll need the hub. Tie it on the limber.' Shit! he thought, what a bloody mess. His sphincter muscle relaxed. Like Pavlov's dog, he thought, but it reminded him of his body's needs. He picked up a shovel, some army form blank and headed for where he had left the Bren.

He dug the hole, lit a cigarette, released his slacks and squatted. He took the first rewarding drag on his cigarette down to his toe nails and then relaxed for the uninterrupted and timeless relief of crapping. Here, on his own, he was able to order his thoughts into a semblance of logic. Sequences of thought fell into place as in a jig-saw.

Stiffly he got up, wiped himself and belted his slacks. He might have some answers, possible solutions to their plight. He filled in the hole on the fresh dung, and picked up the Bren to commence his walk back.

Come to think of it, he mused, as he hawked, spat and blew his nose between his fingers, the desert was a vast dustbin. It swallowed the evacuations of hundreds of thousands of men of both armies, their corpses and their discarded rubbish of all kinds. Debris of battles, mines, tanks, guns, trucks and blood, oceans of it and quite a few buckets of tears. The atmosphere sucked up their frantic orders, screams, curses, prayers, hopes and despairing cries like blotting paper.

Back at the quad everyone was drinking tea, except Karl who was spark-out. His chin rested on his chest. He was sitting, legs out with his back supported by the rear wheel. James picked up his tea and contemplated once again, the obstacles to be overcome. Two useless petrol tanks, leaking radiator and an amount of petrol that now had to be conserved. He turned to Chalky.

''Ad a coupla ideas. We can fix the rad'. We'll make some *burgoo*, nice and thick, from the biscuits.'

Chalky's expression changed to one of hopeful relief. it was a glimmer of light in the gloom. Gloom which had turned his brain into, for want of a better word, pudding.

'I 'adn't got that far, Sarge. In fact, I 'aven't got anywhere. It'll work though. Glad someone's thought of summat' to do — this lot,' he grimaced in disgust, 'They're fuckin' 'opeless.'

He thought for a moment. Thought was not one of Chalky's strong points. Finally it came:

'What about the tanks? We could use the autovac -'

He left the words hanging in mid-air.

'That's right,' said James. 'Take the top off -'

Chalky nodded delightedly. Suddenly his mental block and speech had dropped into gear. He groped around in his mind for an idea, something brilliant that no one, so far, had thought of, a dazzling solution. When it came, disappointingly, it wasn't brilliant or dazzling, but it was a method and it sounded practical.

Eagerly he carried on where James had left off.

'Pour the petrol in, through the funnel, from one of the gallon water cans. Burn it out first, eh? Whatd'y think, Sarge?'

James grinned and nodded agreement. He turned to the others and quickly explained what they hoped to do. Chalky drained his mug and moved to the back of the quad. Dodger caught the two packets of biscuits that sailed through the air. Bell, Muscles and Cockney shared the two tyre levers and one hammer. James dusted off the quad floor near the open doorway. Dodger dumped the biscuits there and got the cooking tin out to pour a couple of pints of water in before placing it on the fire.

The crash of hammer and tyre levers on the steel floor echoed over the area as the rock hard biscuits disintegrated under the attack. Ground down into powder, the biscuits did make good porridge. When cold the mixture set like concrete. Chalky was unscrewing the top plate of the autovac.

The autovac system on the quad was a simple vacuum cylinder clamped to the inner front body. The function of the cylinder was to suck up petrol from each tank and gravity feed it to the carburettor. It did this by means of a piston operated by the vacuum. With the engine running, the hiss and sigh of it working was a constant reassuring sound that all was well.

Chalky, having removed the screws, now loosened the two pipe union nuts, one for fuel, the other for air, flipped out the cone-shaped wire mesh filter and laid the assembly on the floor.

He was happy as he worked, started to whistle and hum under his breath. It was all coming together. Minutes later he had the pipe freed from under the stop tap on the autovac, that led to one of the petrol tanks. He threaded it through the floor after removing the rubber grommet.

He laid the pipe on the quad floor as James looked in. The hammering had stopped. The cooking porridge complete with evaporated tinned milk and sugar was bubbling nicely on the fire. Dodger was the chef, stirring expertly.

James saw the pipe and grasped its implications. His eyes lit up. '*Chahbosh*, Chalky. Well done. You're right. We might find another vehicle with a good tank.' Chalky flushed under the praise. James had said it instinctively and it was his way as always, to have a finger on the pulse. To anticipate, use his keen observation and experience to praise or tear off a strip to any or all of them. Privately, Chalky and the rest of the crew thought he had eyes in his arse. To a man, they admired and respected him.

He walked round to the rear of the quad and lifted out the box of .303 small arms ammunition. He split the 100 round drum magazine and reloaded it, six tracers in seven, took the barrel off and replaced that, cleaned the bolt and breech and took the pull through, from his pocket. Threading the piece of four by two striped cloth, through the loop of the cord he pulled it through the breech and barrel from both ends. Cockney poked his head round the back; he had the two drums from the tommy.

'Got some .45 ammo, Sarge?'

James nodded and passed him two boxes. The tommy gun magazines held fifty rounds. For a few minutes they worked in silence carefully positioning the bullets. Finally they completed their tasks. Both fitted the magazine on.

James called out, 'Testing Automatics!'

They each fired a short burst that reverberated crashingly round the landscape. Removing the magazines they each cleared the one up the spout and replaced the magazines. Safety catches were thumbed to Safe and they replaced the weapons in the quad.

'How's the *burgoo*?' James enquired of Dodger.

'Comin' along nicely, Sarge. Gunna gerrit real thick like concrete,' replied Dodger. 'Used to work on a buildin' site - they wus' 'appy days. Not much gelt though. Used to pinch the petrol, siphon it off inta' cans an' floggit. I - '

'You what?' It was Cockney's voice sharp and enquiring. It was also vibrant with suppressed excitement. Dodger found himself the focus of attention, even James looked expectant.

'Why - er - you know - half-inched the petrol - I wasn't the only one,' he said defensively.

'Nah - not pinchin', Dodge. What you said, 'bout the cans?'

'Well, oh, yeah, siphon - that it?'

Cockney nodded, he turned to James.

'Sarge, why pour the petrol? It's goin' be real slow. Couldn't do more than five miles an hour. We've got a tube - the airline - siphon from a full jerrican. That's it - '

The words bubbled out fast. He stopped, looked around at the others.

Like sunshine racing over a clouded field comprehension flickered over their intent faces. Suddenly everyone was clapping him on the back and now everyone was grinning.

The airline, twenty feet of heavy rubber tubing 3/8ths of an inch in diameter, came out of Chalky's tool locker. He fetched it. The quad did not have an air compressor. They were found on most of the 30 cwt and 3 ton trucks. One end clipped on to the compressor pipe, the other on the tyre valve.

James had replaced it before Alamein and it was as good as new. He cut off the tyre valve metal sleeve clip. The sharp blade of his jack-knife severed a six foot length and they were in business. They could put the valve clip back on at their leisure.

'Well,' said James, 'they say two heads are better than one - even if they're sheep's heads - that's one of the problems we don't 'ave to worry about.'

Dodger lifted the steaming porridge off the fire with the shovel. He carried the tin to the front of the quad. They would have to wait for the tin to cool before pouring. Chalky had dug up a pair of khaki woollen gloves, most of the finger ends were missing. He had a charge box ready to stand on. The truncated bonnet and radiator of a quad were high off the ground. Wearing the gloves Chalky stood on the box, took the tin from Dodger and carefully began to pour the still steaming mixture into the radiator.

It was slow work. The tin was still hot and the gloves began to smoulder. He rested it on the upturned bonnet cover whilst he beat out the infant flames. Dodger handed him a cigarette. They waited another five minutes. Soot off the hot tin, transferred to the gloves, was now a black moustache where Chalky had wiped his nose. He tested the tin, much cooler, hefting it up he continued the tedious process. Finally the last dregs were in and slowly trickling their passage down the tubes and fins. Now we wait, he thought, as he stepped down.

It struck him that he had another job to do: plugs and points. Not vital, but necessary for a good start. They would have to crank the engine. It was the best way to avoid flooding the carburettor. Ruefully, he thought, I'm the only bastard working round here.

James sat on the layer's wooden seat. He had removed the firing mechanism from the breech, stripped it down and was now oiling and cleaning it. Satisfied at last he reassembled it and slotted it back into the breech. He thought about the Messerschmitt. The pilot must have had a screw loose. He could only have been on reconnaissance so why do a crazy thing like he did? He hoped he had crashed.

So far, he reflected, the simple task of catching up with the regiment had not proved all that simple. It had almost ended today with a brewed-up quad. Still, that was history. The quad had not brewed up and they were still here, less one. That Me, though, reminded him of June last year on Jock columns. Twenty plus raids a day, the planes concentrating solely on trucks. It was so regular, so predictable anyone would have thought the squadron of Messerschmitts was on the strength of the column. The RSM - he was waiting to get back to Cairo to get his commission as lieutenant quartermaster - five trucks had been shot out from under him. He smiled at the memory. Jack had been really brassed off, he was chewing nails and spitting rust. But he'd finally made it at the seventh attempt. The battery war diary laconically said: 'Attacked twenty-seven times by enemy aircraft today.'

But it didn't stop the columns. Those small formations, under a thousand men, were pirates and they created alarm and despondency in the Italians and respect throughout the Afrika Korps. The desert was their arena. They hit, withdrew and appeared in a different location with bewildering speed. With the enemy having air superiority this was no mean feat, when it happened once. But when it happened regularly (there were three columns operating at any one time) the Luftwaffe showed annoying aggressiveness. The guns were always the main target. One moment you were alive and looking forward to the next brew. The next you were stretched out with your face already drying up, ready to be shovelled into a slit trench. He glanced at his watch. The *burgoo* should be set now: time to get some water in.

IV

James took in the time: 11.30 a.m. Fifty miles to the north of his quad and gun something else was on the move.

Two Panzer Kampfwagons eased out of the unique patch of vegetation that covered an area of six hundred square yards. The leading panzer was a Mark IV armed with the long barrelled 75mm high velocity gun. Twenty yards behind came the second panzer. This was a Mark III armed with the L/60, 50mm high velocity weapon.

Both panzers were girdled, front and rear by spare lengths of steel tracks and sandbags. The beat of their powerful engines rose and fell in deadly waves of sound. Their squat solid sand-coloured shapes bore the black, white-edged cross and identification letters of the 201st Panzer Battalion.

Double track bogie wheels were lashed on the front of both panzers above the spare track lengths. Both panzers bore the scars of battle. The Mark VI had a deep gouged furrow in the armour of the turret. Other ricochet marks and grooves from solid shot were evident on other parts of the panzers' structures.

They carried a menace and an aura of invincibility. Of deadly power that commanded awe and respect. The whole of Europe and most of Russia had submitted to thousands of their counterparts. Today they did not need onlookers to give them awe and respect. Stealth and anonymity would be strange garments for them, but that was their need. One did not escape with flags flying and drums beating.

Thirty yards behind the two panzers a ten ton diesel Lancia truck bounced and swayed. This was loaded with forty gallon drums of low octane petrol, one drum of diesel fuel, spare track lengths, bogies, ammunition for the 75mm and the 50mm, rations, water and machine gun ammunition.

The commander of the Mark VI, Hauptmann Erich Schmidt, perched on the rim of the cupola. His body moved easily to the sway of the tank.

The Hauptmann was a vastly experienced panzer veteran. He had served the Führer and the Fatherland from his wild days in the Hitler Jugend. The Low Countries and France had been times of exquisite enjoyment. He was a natural born killer without nerves and if he possessed normal feelings, apart from complete dedication, one would need dynamite to discover them.

In appearance Schmidt was built like a brick shithouse: six feet six inches in height with wide shoulders, so wide they filled the turret. A peaked cap with exaggerated uplift covered a bullet head. The scalp boasted a one inch stubble of blond, nearly white hair. Eyebrows and eye-lashes were the same, almost white, but he was not quite an albino. A deep scar ran from his left eyebrow along the temple and behind the ear. Against the dark of his tanned skin the contrast was marked. Now it was a pale yellow. In battle or certain other situations the scar would glow, an angry suffused scarlet. His face was hewn from granite, slab-sided cheeks, arrogant bill of a nose whose bridge wavered from previous breaks and a wide, a thin-lipped mouth. Surprisingly, the teeth did not conform to the rest of his features. They were white, perfect, but feminine in size and shape. The eyes were a pale ice cold arctic blue, completely lacking in warmth. They could, and had, aroused terror in many people.

The Hauptmann was a terrifying product of the Nazi master race, the *Herrenvolk*. So far he had had a good war that had brought him several decorations, the last one, the *Pour le Merite*. Early 1941 had seen him aboard an Italian coaster heading for Tripoli. At the end of February he had been part of the reconnaissance in force from Agheila into Libya, under the command of the volatile Erwin Rommel. He had been in Africa ever since, Rommel was his idol. The only other thing he cared about were his panzers. Not particularly the crews who manned them, but his panzers, whether he had fifty under his command or just two, as now.

Hauptmann Schmidt came from Berlin, a city which he had only seen twice in two and a half years. Before the Führer came to lead, to unify and provide work for millions, Schmidt had been a butcher's boy. Mostly he had worked in slaughterhouses, up to his knees in blood. He was no stranger to ripping out the guts of bullocks and pigs. His loyalty and devotion ran on steel rails; the Führer and Rommel.

For three years the Führer had led them to victory. He and Rommel would not fail the Afrika Korps now. Schmidt turned his thoughts back to the previous day. They had been lucky, but then, he assured himself, wasn't he always lucky? When one has been chosen, picked out from millions, one is invulnerable, the gods smiled on one. He was the Herr Hauptmann Schmidt - no one fucked about with him.

He spoke through the intercomm.

'Scholz!' The word rasped in the earphones of the panzer driver. His reaction was instant, involuntarily both legs had flexed, his body stiff, if he could have stood up at attention, he would have done so. The Hauptmann had that effect.

'*Ja, Herr Hauptmann.*'

'Steer one nine oh degrees,' came the sandpaper rasp.

'*Ja, Herr Hauptmann.*'

The Hauptmann slid a cigarette case out of a pocket in the black panzer overalls. He extracted a cigarette and lit it with a gold lighter. The lighter was loot from Paris. The gold cigarette case, a gift from Ilsa. He glanced back to the Mark III and tipped his cap casually to Sergeant-Major Heinz, the panzer commander.

Turning his head back the ice-blue eyes scanned the ground ahead. He dragged deep on the cigarette, the hunter's eyes with unusually wide peripheral vision, roamed swiftly picking up points of reference and automatically registering the range in metres. Nothing. Ahead and around the still damp ground with rocky newly washed outcrops was placid and undisturbed by any form of wheel tracks.

The lighter was still in his hand. The thin lips curled in triumph as he recalled the text book efficiency that ripped France apart in 1940. A country of wide open female thighs. Suddenly, savagely his thought changed. His mind flicked back to the last two weeks. The torment of Alamein. Even his mighty endurance had been tested. The roar of the barrage, night after night, the ceaseless attacks from the air. The incessant ground attacks.

In a day they could have been in Alexandria. He was still puzzled by the enormous amount of new equipment, better anti-tank guns, the American Sherman tanks, the self-propelled guns. Names with religious associations, like Bishop, Sexton, Deacon

- unholy bastards. They called the new seventeen pounder anti-tank gun a pheasant. Pheasant - stupid name, nothing docile about it.

In one day he had lost three panzers. The Tommies had learned fast and steadily the battalion had been whittled down. They had been short of everything. Typically he mourned the two Mark III's and the Mark VI that had gone up in flames, rather than their crews. Like a cavalry colonel who thought more of his horses than of the men who rode them.

The only surplus at Alamein had been the man-eating black flies. Lack of space, life in blasted out dugouts, shortage of water and the sounds of Tommy engineers blowing up brewed up panzers and recovering their own Shermans. That had been the galling frustration.

When the line broke in the centre and north they had withdrawn steadily. Then he had ten panzers but no 88's. Four 105's had been destroyed on the way back. He was left with the last two panzers, his own Mark IV which needed a track repair and the Mark III. Then the heavens opened and it poured.

When they had rolled into Matruh the place was deserted. They had picked up the abandoned Lancia, repaired the track in the tank park, loaded whatever they needed and took off. The little convoy crawled up the steep tarmac road leading out of Matruh and turned west then jinked off south into the desert.

At that time he would not have given odds that they would reach Fort Maddalena in order to head west.

That is, until he had spotted this unbelievable patch of vegetation. The almost jungle greenery was thick and dense and in places over nine feet high. The panzers and the Lancia squelched in, swiftly the branches were cut and camouflage nets draped. Schmidt had walked completely around it. Four hundred yards by two hundred and unique in over five hundred square miles. He thanked the gods of War.

Tensely they had waited. All night the roar of engines, the squeaking clank of tank tracks had gone on as the Eighth Army pressed on. Lines of vehicles and tanks had passed on both sides less than a hundred yards away. Their luck held. No one guessed or looked. The rain was sufficient deterrent, trucks and tanks were dry and warm inside. Bombers had droned overhead to the north. The long night dragged on.

During that wet cold night the Hauptmann had it all worked out. He had six men, half strength because Littner was driving the Lancia. Webber, Braun and Scholz would crew his tank. Heinz, the Sergeant-Major, and Stollenburg could crew the Mark III. He knew only one of his three men well. Webber, a crack gunner. Heinz he knew by reputation, the others, well, he knew their names - how was he expected to remember every little detail? Let the Sergeant Major do it, that was what he was there for.

The slim rocking barrel of the 75mm with its bulbous muzzle brake jutted threateningly and aggressively to his front. Towards the escarpment with its blueish tinge where it faded from sight. Schmidt whistled a few bars from 'Lili Marlene'. The twelve cylinder Maybach engine throbbed powerfully underneath and to the rear of where he sat. As each mile passed, each step nearer to the safety of the south, his confidence increased.

Heinz had acknowledged the casual gesture of his commanding officer. The Hauptmann had briefed them all on what he was going to do, where they were going. It was what he hadn't told them that worried Heinz. The Oberwachmeister or troop sergeant-major jammed his battered *Feldmütze* more firmly on his head.

Heinz was a regular soldier and forty-seven years old. The greyness was barely discernible in the straight blond hair, the blue eyes were quick but warm and set under thick blond eyebrows. Snub nose, craggy chin with a firm full-lipped mouth and good teeth. The facial skin was smooth, the only lines a cobweb of fine wrinkles stretching from eye corners and laughter lines from the base of broad nostrils.

It was a mature face, one that had seen a lot of life, and death. The eyes reflected a lively mind, the normal expression was that of regular soldiers everywhere, cynical amusement and mocking disbelief. He stood, shoulders out of the cupola, microphone at his throat, earphones over his battered sidecap and moved easily to the panzer's motion. His stocky figure looked solid, all muscle.

The sergeant-major was one of the original one hundred thousand men that Germnany had been allowed to keep under the Treaty of Versailles. His first taste of action had been in 1917 on the Western Front. Father of four children in the years since that time, he had married Gaby in 1922. The chaos of the twenties, the reparations, the worthless five million mark notes and the collapse of the Weimar Republic, the starvation and cheerless hopelessness had convinced him of one thing. His life would be the Reichswehr.

He was young, enthusiastic, fit and a good soldier, he knew he needed all the luck in the world to be selected, that and his old sergeant-major's influence had proved successful.

From infanteer to engineer, from internal combustion engines to artillery. From there to tanks, mock up plywood effigies at first. Armoured cars followed: he had enjoyed that before going back to the triple purpose 88mm anti aircraft, anti tank and field gun. Guns! His whole life had been concerned with guns of one sort or another. In the middle thirties he had done two trips in U-boats and in Spain a few bombing raids in Stukas. After the Führer had taken firm control of the German nation, reversed the inhumanity of the Versailles Treaty and given Germany, the Fatherland, a destiny, his role in that grand design was that of instructor in the battle schools.

In the classroom, on the barrack square, in the field manoeuvres, he had passed on his experience. The school boys he had made men. Thousands had passed through his hands, thousands who now still fought on, in the desert and in Russia, thousands more lay dead in an honoured grave far from the Fatherland and their loved ones.

Heinz was one of a fast disappearing generation who still thought of Germany as the Fatherland and not the Third Reich. His brothers in arms called him 'Old Fifty-Seven' for obvious reasons. His birth certificate named him as Rudolph but only his wife used the name.

His posting to the newly formed Afrika Korps had been of his own choosing. After the wave of euphoria that swept the nation in 1940 his pride and a feeling that he had missed out made him yearn for something other than the classroom. Parades were no good. He didn't want to bask in reflected glory behind a military band; he wanted some of that glory personally. He also wanted the frightening, exhilarating and satisfying fulfilment that action alone could bring.

That had come in full measure. Nearly two years later and two decorations, first and second class Iron Crosses, his appetite was gone. He was replete with action, distended by the smoke and flame, the stink and noise of battle. He did not like what he had become, a killing machine, an automaton in action, who only found his real self in the quiet relaxed peace, that followed the crowded minutes of searing exciting flirtations with death.

His nerve was still good although now he was even more cagey, refusing the head on clash, preferring stealth, cunning and a sure kill. Recently even that was losing its appeal. He was sick of killing. A few days before the Alamein battle an old wound in the thigh had opened. Splinters from a mortar shell at Sidi Rezegh had not all been removed. His request for a transfer had been approved and in a few days at the most, he would be on his way home. Until this happened. Still maybe it would still happen. Back to Gaby, the two youngsters, Rudy and Berta. Hans and Karl were still in officers' training school. He could wangle an entrance there with his old contacts.

Three boys, one girl, the Heinz family might not have fifty-seven varieties but what they did have were enough for Gaby and him. He switched his thoughts back to the Mark IV and the Hauptmann. Heinz respected him as a good soldier and a good officer. He was a legend that bore a charmed life. He was also, thought Heinz, a callous indifferent and completely mad glory hunter. The Hauptmann went through panzer crews like the matchbox user discards the burnt matches. He was a destroyer, like the plague.

It was the first time Heinz had been under his command. But as all good senior and long serving NCO's had done since the Romans, he made it his business to find out about the men who led them. The information had only confirmed the rumours. He looked like a rock but he had less feelings. A brilliant squadron commander. If you wanted to stay alive, keep away from the Hauptmann. Rumour had it he drank blood for breakfast.

None of this particularly worried the sergeant-major. But he had to admit he was troubled at the airy dismissal of possible opposition that might lie ahead. They were going into the unknown and the Hauptmann should have said so. What troubled Heinz more was the fact that their leader attracted trouble and if it didn't arrive he went looking for it.

That was the last thing anyone, less the Hauptmann, wanted, particularly on this trip. However, Heinz believed in keeping any reservations he had to himself. He was an early member of the Nazi party (who in Germany wasn't?) but first and foremost he was a soldier of the Wehrmacht, an old soldier who covered his options, kept his trap shut and his opinions to himself. That didn't stop him having opinions or even doubts. The doubts had come during this last year and they refused to go away. Russia, Pearl Harbour and, recently, Alamein.

He took a glance to the rear and the Lancia. They had been lucky to get those ten drums of petrol from the tank park and luckier still to have spotted the hand pump. He caught the gleam of light reflecting off the spectacles of ex-Professor Littner who was driving the ungainly looking truck. An unspoken query popped into his mind, it always did when he saw Littner. He wondered for the hundredth time who the devil had posted Littner to a tank battalion?

Stollenburg, his driver, he knew inside out. He'd bet fifty marks to a frankfurter that at this very moment, he would be taking a swig from the last of the captured rum. He licked his lips for a moment. Not as good as schnapps but good just the same. And it was free, spoils of war from one of the huge Tommy dumps. They were good days, the best. Chasing a beaten demoralised enemy. Well, most of them anyway. But, he reflected, that was then, after July it had all gone sour.

His thoughts switched back to Littner. Who the hell could understand that owl-eyed bastard? Heinz disliked, on principle, any intellectual. In his mind they were linked too closely to the planners and bureaucrats. They would be the ones who would lose this war. For a fraction of a second he was horrified that he, Rudolph Heinz with a quarter of a century's service to the Fatherland, had nearly voiced the thought; it was tantamount to treason. For a moment and to recover from that shocking thought, he concentrated on the desert ahead.

Empty. He took his binoculars and scanned the sky. From there, in his opinion, the danger would come first. Nothing but overcast clouds, but getting thinner. His mind pinwheeled back and grabbed at the name, Littner. He was always talking, arguing, debating. Littner's conversation needed a bloody interpreter to translate most of his phrases into basic German. He forgot that he was no longer lecturing his students. It was a good job that the Gestapo were thin on the ground out here, and detested by the fighting men. Otherwise Herr bloody Littner would have been shopped before now.

Ach, thought Heinz, and spat over the side of the turret. Fuck him, fuck the fucking war and all the fat-bellied Nazi bastards and fuck this fucking desert. Feeling much better in his mind for this mental explosion, he once more settled his eyes on the Hauptmann. Maybe, he thought, with an inward grin, Littner was Gestapo. It'd be just like the devious bastards: they did worse than that at home. He spoke.

'Put that fucking bottle down, Stollenburg. I'll have you on a bloody fizzer if you get pie-eyed on this trip.'

He smiled as the reply came through the headphones. The fervent protestations that he, Stollenburg, was only making sure the cork was in tight enough. Heinz squeezed down inside the turret and took a quick glance to see if the safety was on. Wouldn't want to hit the Hauptmann up the arse with a 50mm solid shot, he thought wickedly. Might shake him - that is, if anything could ever shake that monolithic character.

Other fragments of information about the Hauptmann came into his mind. No one had ever seen him in a foxhole. He scorned usual precautions. Never commented on events outside of his private world. But he handled panzers with masterly skill. His observation was incredibly fast and deadly and his luck a byword. Knight's Cross, first and second class Iron Crosses and recently, the *Pour Le Merite.* Today those decorations were hidden under the black overalls. Normally they were worn for all to see, like a-Heinz searched for the word, not royalty - like a conquerer, a Genghis Khan of the panzers.

Heinz wore his obligatory ribbon diffidently. His sole aim in life now was to survive. His eyes roamed the ground to the front, sides and rear then back up to the clouds above. Nothing.

Hanover would be cold now, the first snow borne on the wings of the sweeping winds from the north German plain. It would slice down the wide avenues like a scythe. For a moment he imagined the rosy glow of the pot-bellied stove with the surround of decorated tiles. The warmth of the cosy room and the comfort of the wing backed armchair.

A small gesture from the Hauptmann, a command to Stollenburg and the Mark III swung left to take up station a hundred yards to the left rear of the Mark IV. He waved to the Lancia to maintain the same course.

Hell at Fuka

The small triangle of panzers and vehicles slipped along at a steady fifteen kilometres an hour. The small wadis and gently rolling desert provided some sort of cover. There was no dust and the Hauptmann used the ground well.

Heinz jammed his elbows into his body and raised the big Zeiss binoculars. Slowly he swept the horizon in a three hundred and sixty degree circle. The powerful scopes brought the dark clefts and cracks of the escarpment into sharp focus. Scrub and sand, camel thorn humps, rocky in places and looked flat but he could detect the rise of the ground, imperceptible as it was.

Steadily but slower they moved on. The small party was rarely on the crests, he took a glance at the Lancia. So far Littner was keeping up well. Just as well for him that he was. I'll have his guts for garters if he lags behind. Maybe I should have put one of the others on it. But what could Littner do in a panzer? Shag all.

Heinz could understand anyone being anti-Nazi, anti-Government - same bloody thing that, the Nazis ruled. But Littner was anti-authority, anti-officer and anti-war. Pacifists like him were a menace. They were a menace because they corrupted their own comrades who were fighting for them as well. Germany had never got anything without fighting for it. They were all fighting for Germany, their wives and families and their girls. All in it together, he grinned inwardly, all in the same barrel of shit. With men like Littner though, the war was lost the moment he donned a uniform. They all mocked him, but like mud, some of his phrases lodged in the illiterate bastards' minds. Every army had its share of nitwits, dumbbells and woodentops. He wondered again at his preoccupation with Littner then realised the simple answer. It was the Lancia and what it carried. Without it they were sunk. It was the key factor in their plan to sweep south of the Eighth Army's advancing front.

Being Italian line of communication transport it was odds on that it had been sloppily maintained by the lazy bastards. Heinz expected trouble; if he didn't get it he would be happy.

Nevertheless his mind was roving and coming up with plans for a contingency: if the engine goes *kaput*, we'll tow it and I'll make sure first, that it gets some maintenance.

He switched his thoughts as his eyes scanned the ground.

Wonder what Rommel thinks about this little lot? It started when he was at home. They say he was a sick man. Don't suppose him being here would have made much difference. No, no one could blame him. The blame lay further away, in Germany. The clique around the Führer grinding their own axes, *ach, yes, mein Führer*, the Afrika Korps is well-equipped, the finest desert fighters in the world. With what they captured from the British they needed nothing from the Reich. Our gallant Italian allies will supply the fuel and they had the ships. The Luftwaffe commanded the skies. There was nothing to cause alarm. They were only thirty-five miles from Alexandria.

Ja, thought Heinz, so we were. Why, with only three divisions and not full divisions at that, they'd advanced over a thousand miles. With two more panzer divisions and another air fleet, they could have been in Persia and into Ivan's back door. To say nothing of India. He day-dreamed for a moment on the alluring but long vanished might have been. For that moment, before coming back to the present, he had relaxed in eastern luxury, waited on hand and foot in white marbled palaces owned by Sultans.

Scholz, the driver of the command tank, was a family man. Unlike Heinz, who was deliberately reticent about his family, Scholz was more than eager to produce snapshots of his four boys and three girls. Whenever the conversation turned to home, he bashed the ears of all who would listen. His family must have been the most talked about and best known in the Wehrmacht. Inside the panzer conversation was impossible. For the tenth time his hand strayed to the breast pocket of his jacket to give a little satisfied pat on the wallet inside. For the tenth time the feeling of pride and security caught at his throat. Dieter Scholz had every reason. Thirty-two years old, he was built like a greyhound, dark hair, brown eyes and regular features that always seemed anxious. He had been in the desert for seven months. So far those months had left little evidence outwardly of the fatigue that constant battle has. Anxious might be the wrong description, it would be more accurate and more in keeping with his maturity, to say concerned.

Dieter Scholz was a well-trained driver and mechanic. He loved engines and machinery. He was the type of man who would always be concerned, about people, animals and other forms of life. Twins ran in both his and Helga's family. Two sets of boys and one set of girls. Where the odd one came from they would never know. In the small town of Duderstadt the family was well known and respected. They were a typically small town German family. Hard-working, industrious and housed, not in workers' accommodation but in a small middle class house on the outskirts. Neither of them had time for politics, family came first, then work. The clever hands of Scholz on neighbours' repairs, his willing concern and desire to help, impressed all who knew him. It also brought in extra marks. They had both signed the Nazi Party forms because it was expected and it was normal.

It was part of the philosophy of Scholz not to initiate or accept responsibility other than to the normality of his family. If he had a view, an opinion, he kept it between Helga and himself. Someday the war would be over, someday they would be together again.

For the hundredth time he wondered what lay ahead for all of them. He turned slightly and glanced at Webber and Braun. He snorted with disgust and returned his eyes to the driver's observation slit. They were asleep. Automatically he obeyed the rasp of the voice coming through the headphones, went through the gear box just as automatically and tooled the Mark IV down the gentle slope into the wadi. A hundred yards further on came the order to halt. The harsh rasp asked how many miles? Scholz read off the mileage on the odometer.

'Sixty-four kilometres, *Herr Hauptmann*. Yes, *Herr Hauptmann*.'

He turned off the ignition, the engine died. Webber opened the side hatch. Scholz heard the Mark III's engine stop. He could hear the diesel of the Lancia clattering away. Bending he took off headphones and wriggled under the hatch before hauling his slim body through and out into the open air. Braun followed him. On the ground they stretched legs and arms and breathed in the cool air.

Heinz climbed up alongside Schmidt.

'Sixty-four kilometres, sergeant major.' Heinz nodded, he had checked the distance too.

'We'll brew up, have a bite. This part I am not familiar with. The map shows good going for thirty miles. When it gets dark, you tow the truck. I want it safe. We fill up now, keep tanks topped up. We travel all night. Nothing must stop us.' The ice-blue eyes fastened on Heinz: he felt the chill.

'Nothing will.' A lift of the cruel lips, snarl of the tiger, thought Heinz.

'Yes, *Herr Hauptmann*. What do you think we might hit, further south?' Schmidt regarded the sober-faced Heinz; he allowed the merest flicker of a grin to cross his stone features.

'Oh.' He gave a short bark of laughter. 'A few odds, a few sods, soft stuff. Maybe the odd armoured car.'

With the main push concentrating along the coast it was clear the Hauptmann expected little of consequence this far south.

'We'll not shoot anything up just yet, but further south, maybe we have a little blitz, warm them up just a little, *ja*?''

Heinz gave a brief smile.

'After Maddalena, a few miles west through the wire?' He waited for Schmidt to reply although he already guessed what the answer would be. The Hauptmann replied briefly.

'Something like that.' His tone and blank expression indicated that he had already dismissed the sergeant-major. Heinz dropped off the engine cover. His voice rapped out orders.

The fuel tanks were topped up quickly and Braun with Littner was filling the empty jerricans from the forty gallon drum. The clamped hand-operated pump made it easy. Scholz and Stollenburg were fastening the jerricans down on each panzer. Webber had completed the brew of ersatz coffee and had cut the cellophane-wrapped black bread in thick slices. He smeared the bread with some of Tommy Tickler jam. Soon they were all eating and drinking, the Hauptmann still sitting on the edge of the cupola.

Heinz finished the last of the jam spread bread slice and took a swig of coffee. Always the bitter flavour reminded him of acorns. He lit a small cigar, it helped. Heinz was too old a bird not to have noticed the sudden drop in temperature that cloaked the normal sounding words, 'something like that'. They had been deliberately designed to put him, Sergeant-Major Heinz, in his place. To underline who would take the decisions, who would be in command.

Jawohl, mein Hauptmann, he thought sarcastically. For the time being we'll play it dead regimental, no advice or comment, utter obedience. Let's see how the cookie crumbles. In his long career

Heinz had met all sorts of officers, but never one quite like this specimen. He had a strong feeling that they were all under the domination of a robot, a machine. I only hope he doesn't flip his lid and think he can take on the whole of the bloody Eighth Army.

'Right, Sergeant-Major. We'll move off when you're ready. If Braun gets the big set working, we may get some news.'

'Five minutes, *Herr Hauptmann* .' Heinz had the official tone in his crisp reply, correct, impartial. He walked back to the Mark III.

The command panzer crew, Scholz, Webber and Braun, slid through the side hatch with practised ease, like seals. Scholz avoided the bulk of the gun, slid past the wireless and wriggled into his seat. He started the twelve cylinder engine, eased it into gear and waited. Stollenburg started the engine of the Mark III. Littner was behind the big steering wheel of the Lancia.

Through the headphones came a crackle, then the rasp of the Hauptmann's voice:

'Advance - 190 degrees.'

Slowly they eased forward out of the wadi. Scholz took a lit cigarette from the fingers of Webber and placed it between his lips. He accelerated and the Mark IV picked up speed. Webber, a thin dark-stubbled good-looking man of twenty-five, settled himself comfortably in the gunner's seat and closed his eyes.

He was known as 'Deadeye', a tribute to his skill as a gunner. Braun sat on the co driver-operator pad and made a small delicate adjustment to the inter-panzer radio set, lips pursed in a soundless whistle. Satisfied he got up and moved over to the gun telescope, bracing himself against the pitching of the perforated steel turret floor. His forehead against the padded rest he looked through the graticuled Zeiss lens.

They were approaching the crest of a gentle ridge about a thousand metres away. One of thousands, maybe millions in this endless, everlasting wasteland. Braun felt restless. Unlike the others, who seemed to take everything in their stride, the uncertainty was affecting him. His nerves felt like overstrung piano wires. It had built up over the past month. He tried to shake it off, this presentiment, this foreboding of disaster. He moved back to his seat and took a quick glance at Scholz. He envied him, calm face, really nice disposition, easy to get on with. None of them knew each other well. But they all knew of the Hauptmann. He didn't know about the others but when he was ordered to report to him after the usual shambles, his stomach had become a void; he had felt like sausage meat about to enter the mincer.

Before the war Braun had owned a small radio and gramophone shop with jewellery repairs on the side in Brunswick. He was thirty-three years of age and looked every minute of it. The thin intelligent face was deeply lined, telltale lines etched deeply. Lines that told of a vocation that required deep concentration.

It was a worried-looking face at best. Now it reflected the apprehension and torment of his thoughts. Had Braun ever been at the scene of a crime, the police would have arrested him, just from his appearance.

His memories of Herr Hauptmann Schmidt went back a long way, to France and the panzer regiment they had both served in. Lucky for him he had been in Headquarters. He admired Schmidt as a brave man; who wouldn't with all those decorations? Otherwise he thought him a fool. By some genetic freak the Hauptmann had been born without nerves, at least the type of nerves that Braun understood.

In Braun's opinion the Hauptmann's unusual attribute was no excuse for wantonly tempting fate and actively inviting and scornfully accepting, every challenge to his apparent invincibility.

Braun had known many of the men in the crews of the Hauptmann's panzers. Had watched them fry and die in agony. They had all died for an ego. He didn't relish that fate. He didn't want to die at all. At least not until he was eighty. Why hadn't they all been captured at Alamein? Brunswick was a nice place. He wanted to see the city again, wanted the chance to marry some sweet dark-haired girl. Dark because he wanted no part of the Herrenvolk myth.

His thoughts returned to the future, that is if they had any future. If - *if* there was the faintest chance of the Hauptmann avoiding trouble, if - it was all bloody ifs. He knew, bitterly, that was out of the question. The mad bastard would go looking for it and when he'd finished, they would all be six feet under or fried to a crisp. There might be a full regiment of Shermans lying right across their route. Or a brigade, even a division. Then they'd be in it, right up to their bloody necks. If they had any necks left.

Braun by this time was bearing a screwed up ball of panic, like a lead weight in his guts. He could, in his imagination, almost feel the shells hitting the steel around them. Feel the white hot heat, smell the sweet pungent odour of burning flesh and feel his skin cringe as fingers of fear raced over his body.

Braun was intelligent enough to know what was wrong with him, yet also realised how impotent he was to control it. Feverishly he wiped the dank sweat from his face and neck. He was no good to himself or any of the others in this state. The dirty piece of cloth had once been known as a handkerchief. Desperately he tried to think of a way out. A way to preserve his life.

Scholz glanced away from the green-tinted vision block to his front and took in Braun's anguished face. Quickly he looked back. That type of anguish was private. He had seen it many times, on the faces of men and women, coming out of flats, escorted by the black suited Gestapo. Faces drained of hope recognising the inevitability of their destination. He cleared his mind and concentrated on his task.

Braun was unaware that he was grinding his teeth. His brain was exploring and his mind lashing around in all directions, searching, searching. Combat for any length of time has startling repercussions on the central nervous system. The seeds sprout from the first moments and they grow insidiously.

Combat fighting efficiency commences at one point, the point when the fighting man accepts that there are several levels of danger. Close, near, fairly near, and it doesn't matter. That noise in itself cannot kill. Rapidly growing experiences add their own quota to his conditioning. At the same time his mental and physical reflexes undergo a jolting wake-up process. Before the first combat all are innocents. Like chameleons he adapts, some quickly, others more slowly. There is no set period of time, there are certain averages but those are a rough guide, nothing more. What is certain is that they all reach a peak of efficiency where the time taken varies widely.

The decline in fighting efficiency is also certain. Again there are no set patterns or times; sometimes it is a gradual process over many months or sometimes, years. A day can crack and destroy, or a week, a month and longer periods. The phrase to screw up one's courage is more accurate than many people think.

The pre-battle screwing up of courage, the endless waiting require tremendous fortitude and endurance. Even the best twitch a little under these requirements, become irritated and angered. To the General, this is by no means a bad thing.

Braun had reached a certain stage in his decline of fighting efficiency where self-preservation became the one and only sane answer. Wildly he thought, I'll desert; up with the hatch and out to safety. No, that was no good. What about Old Fifty-Seven back there? He'd be sure to spot him as he bailed out. So would the Hauptmann. A chill ran through him. No way there; the Hauptmann would cut him in two with his Schmeisser. He wouldn't even slow down.

He made an effort to calm his fears, to get some order into his thinking. Slowly his brain took command of the jumble of irrationalities that filled his head. Calmer, he concentrated with all his technician's ability to blot out the surges of panic. He realised suddenly that Webber was awake and regarding him with mischievous sardonic eyes. He gave him a shaky grin. Christ! Has he guessed?

He fumbled for cigarettes, quickly lit two and passed one to the gunner, cursing inwardly at the tremor in his fingers. Webber nodded his thanks, Braun turned to the radio. Scholz had flipped the binocular eyepieces over the vision block. The Hauptmann's dangling leather boot tapped a rhythm. No, how could he? I don't even know myself. The mental reassurance brought the answer. Tonight, that was the answer, that would be the time. After they had heard the news. But that wouldn't be tonight. The big radio was kaput. No spares.

Still that would not bother him. All he had to do was head north-east. Grab a couple of water bottles and some bread to last him until he met up with the Tommies. He could soon disappear. The desert was a big one and the weather was in his favour. Life in a prisoner of war camp was better than certain death out here in this useless wilderness.

Having made his decision he relaxed. Once he got away, the tensions, the fears, the shrinking inside would be over.

Braun had spent too long in the company of the brave and the stupid. He longed for a world of sanity, one without war where opinions and conversations were free. Where the knock on the door in the early hours never happened. A normal world, a return to start up his own business, have a home graced by the welcome and softness of a woman. It could happen. It need not be a fairy tale. Men like the Hauptmann and Heinz would soon be forgotten; anyway they would both be like ducks out of water.

Littner would fit in, he wasn't as screwy as they thought. Scholz and his family, he imagined, could live and survive in any kind of world. He was, well, not jealous exactly but envious of Scholz and the years he had enjoyed his family. He could have been like him. There had been times and he might even have had a larger family than Scholz.

'Halt short of the crest.' The clipped voice brought him and the others back to the present.

'*Ja, Herr Hauptmann.*'

'Three o'clock - four kilometres - below us. Smoke - just slight. See what it is.' He ignored Heinz's reply. Already his clipped orders to Scholz had resulted in the Mark IV edging closer to the crest, still hidden from the valley but with the long 75mm barrel now pointing in the direction Heinz would take.

The Mark III roared off behind him running parallel to but below the crest. Two miles further on Stollenburg crept up the low slope and stopped just short. Heinz scanned the area from where slight whispers of smoke were rising. It was a crashed aircraft.

'Stollenburg! Carry on.' The command was brief. It was also blizzard cold. Below him Stollenburg rolled his eyes upwards and the flicker of a grin twitched across his face. Old Fifty-Seven had been rubbed up the wrong way by the fucking Hauptmann. His hackles were still up. Stollenburg knew him of old, knew how far to go, sensed his moods and always played it cagily. Stollenburg was not one of those who had been vaccinated with a gramophone needle; indeed he could have played the mute's part without effort.

Heinz had slid down from the turret and tapped his shoulder. Stollenburg raised his right hand and accepted the peace offering of a lit cigarette. They were back on terms with an unspoken apology. Heinz climbed back into the gunner's seat and picked up the wrecked aircraft in the lens of the powerful telescope. They drew nearer and stopped twenty yards away. Heinz dropped off the rear of the Mark III and walked over, the panzer's engine rumbling contentedly.

It was a Messerschmitt 110 twin-engined, twin-ruddered fighter bomber armed with cannon and machine guns and mottled sand in colour. The right-hand engine was completely burnt out and the main wing on that side had collapsed. The fire had been confined to the engine, the smoke he had seen was now a mere trickle. Couldn't have been long, thought Heinz; bloody miracle the whole lot hadn't gone up. Might still do that. He moved back hastily, his native caution in high gear.

The perspex canopy had been neatly stitched with small holes on the side furthest away from him. He moved back to the rudders; they were a lot higher than he had realised and he felt dwarfed. Moving along the fuselage at a safe distance, he focussed his binoculars on the cockpit. The three occupants were dead, the black red blots of dried blood making grotesque features that had, not long ago, been alive and probably laughing. Heinz cleared his throat and spat. The small holes were obviously small arms fire, from an automatic. He turned away to walk back to the Mark III.

The ME had left a wide swathe for a distance of over two hundred yards in the flat surface. If that was the line, it had come from the east, in trouble with the pilot being the last to die. Heinz did not think it was possible that the plane had landed unaided by human hands. So, that meant troops, the enemy. How many, and how far away? He reached the panzer and swung up to pick up his headphones and drop his legs into the cupola.

'Command!'

'*Ja?*'

"'ME 110 three crew - all dead - shot down by small arms fire. Fire now out. Do you, *Herr Hauptmann*, want us to do anything about the crew?' The report was crisp and concise.

The Hauptmann's reply was already sounding in his ears as the last syllable dropped from his lips.

'*Nein*! We are not undertakers. Return.'

He switched back to intercomm and before speaking, remembered, just in time, that he was speaking to Stollenburg.

'OK, let's get back. Go down the valley. We'll have to let

the desert take care of those poor bastards.' And it would, he thought, in three months they would be mummies, without the winding cloths. Desiccated effigies. Fly on, fliers, and the best of luck.

The command tank came over the crest to be followed shortly afterwards by the Lancia. Heinz slipped in a hundred yards to the left rear. Steadily they advanced across the valley. Not a valley in any other country; more a slight, imperceptible flat dip in the rolling derelict landscape. Reaching the other side, the Mark IV halted. The Hauptmann scanned the ground ahead and swore. Heinz had moved up to the same line a hundred yards away. What he saw did not exactly boost his morale.

As far as the eye could see ahead stretched broken country. Splintered rock surfaces, camel thorn humps, wadis, banks of scree and what amounted to cliffs. The Hauptmann felt rage rise within him. Trouble was, he could think of no one to blame. Heinz felt mild disappointment but then again he had never thought it was going to be easy. Littner was too far back to see anything. Webber gave a snort of disgust as he focussed the telescope. Scholz didn't much like it. Stollenburg, eyes glued to the binocular periscope, allowed lips to curl in a wicked grin that revealed tobacco-stained wide-spaced teeth. His thoughts at that moment would have got him shot. That's buggered it, was his first reaction which was followed instantly by, well, Herr fucking Hauptmann Schmidt, you arrogant bastard, what are we fucking waiting for? Orders. Oh I see. Yes, from the Führer, your personal friend Adolf. Better still, you're big enough, carry the fucking panzers across.

He reached down beside him and brought up the dark pint bottle containing the captured rum. He took a large swig, wiped his lips and returned the bottle. The permanent ache within him subsided minutely. In July Rheinhart had been alive. By August 31st he was a piece of roasted flesh. Left in a brewed-up Mark IV. The Hauptmann's command tank. Stollenburg's eyes were like flint. He leaned back automatically producing cigarettes and lighter, face scowling as he lit and sucked down the satisfying nicotine-laden smoke.

Four days ago and quite by accident, he had learned the truth about his brother's death. Now, quite simply, he wanted the Hauptmann dead. If he got a clear chance he would kill him.

Panzer crews were dependent on each other, an interlocking close-meshed team who shared everything. When the worst happened and the panzer was knocked out, humanity took over regardless of rank. Too often there was no chance to get anyone out. In the case of Rheinhart, one man could have rescued him and that was the Hauptmann. Instead he had turned his back; only one without a spark of humanity in his make-up could have done that.

Stollenburg came from Hamburg. He was a docker and the son of a docker. The family were real socialists, as was the area, it was tough in dockland, a hard life in the tightly knit community. But they all shared solid beliefs and held a wary cynicism of the Nazi party. It was hard to find a party card. But they were loyal Germans. They gave the Führer his due; he had provided them with work and restored pride.

Heinz waited for the Hauptmann's instructions. He knew what course he himself would follow. There was only one way, go east, skirt this type of impassable ground. To get to the west looked impossible. And certainly the Lancia couldn't make it. He chewed on the unlit cigar between his lips.

'Sergeant-Major! New bearing. One one oh degrees.'

Heinz acknowledged briefly. Understood.

The Hauptmann had been unable to hide the suppressed rage in his voice. Heinz thought he detected a massive frustration behind the command. Christ, I could do with a drink, then resigned himself, that would be the last thing in the mind of their leader.

The Mark IV passed behind him on the new bearing. He told Stollenburg to take up station and waved to Littner.

Twenty miles to the south-east they turned back onto 190 degrees into an area that had good going intermixed with dozens of side wadis. The thoughts of Scholz had turned back, inevitably, to home and his family. His reverie was sliced into by the knifelike voice in his ears.

'Action! Action! HE - load! Driver right, down this slope, left at the bottom. Sergeant-Major, halt the truck. Take up station to my right.'

Heinz gave rapid instructions to Stollenburg. The Mark III turned in its own length and headed for the truck. He pointed out a small side wadi off the main one and Littner slotted the big Lancia in. The light was fading, in another hour it would be dark. Stollenburg headed down the wadi.

Five minutes later they were tucked into the wadi side eighty yards to the right of the Hauptmann and almost invisible. The sand mottled camouflage blended into the camel thorn bushes and crevices. Heinz traversed left, set four hundred metres on the circular scale and waited for the target to appear.

Stollenburg had checked the co-axial machine gun and had two rounds of 50mm high explosive shells ready.

Braun slid the 75mm HE shell in to the breech and closed the block with a satisfying clang. He tapped the shoulder of Webber and clasped another shell in his arms.

Webber was lining up, range scale set to four hundred metres. Whatever was approaching would travel from left to right. At this range, tanks, trucks, armoured cars, it wouldn't matter. They were kaput.

The Hauptmann had caught the tell tale sign of movement from the top of the wadi, small convoy, one armoured car. His head was now below the cupola rim. They waited, no one speaking, licked lips that had suddenly become dry.

The only sound, the chuckling of the powerful Maybach twelve cylinder engines. Even those were drowned by the huge orchestra whose swelling Wagnerian music filled the Hauptmann's head. The light was fading imperceptibly under the brooding clouds. The time was 5.30 p.m.

V

James walked from the limber against which he had been leaning. He took a water can out of one of the lockers, stepped over the legs of Karl, the prisoner, grabbed the petrol funnel and went to the radiator.

Chalky steadied the funnel and James poured just over a gallon down the uncapped pipe. Anxiously they both waited. Years later the water reached the lower fins. Chalky got underneath. The rest of the crew had crowded round the front of the quad. Now they all waited. His head reappeared, his expression told them nothing. He stood up to face James and suddenly his face split into a delighted grin.

'It's OK, Sarge. Not a drop. Dry as a bone.' The expression on the sergeant's face relaxed, softened. It was one less problem.

'Fill 'er up,' he said.

Chalky had taken off the pipe and union from one of the useless petrol tanks. He laid it on the quad floor. If they were lucky and found a derelict truck with an intact tank the pipe union would fit. The tank could stay on the quad floor.

James, deep in thought, looked at the German. Yet without seeing him. The chalk white blood-smeared face suddenly impinged on his vision. His mind came back to the present. Karl was dead. He felt a quick pang of disappointment. All right, he was the enemy, he knew almost nothing about him. But he was a young man, a lad, a stranger, but not quite. Contact had been made between them and somehow it made it all different.

Quickly he stifled his feelings and called Bell and Rayburn over. Their reaction was akin to his own. They took shovels and walked to a point thirty yards away. All, in *their* own way felt that because their prisoner had died, they had failed in some way to do all they could to save his life. They were in the same age group and it made them, for an instant, conscious of their own mortality. The last of the wood made a cross. They marked it simply.

'Nov 1942. Karl Schwarze. Paratrooper. 90th Light.'

By the time they got back to the quad, Karl Schwarze was just a fading memory. Out of sight, out of mind. Briefly he had been a part of their existence, already hardly any of them could remember his face. Like the ruined tyre he was now a discard.

Chalky fastened the bonnet clips.

'Rad's full now, Sarge.' His look was confident.

'OK, Muscles, get round to the front, ready to swing 'er. Cockney, get that full jerrican on the roof, next to the hatch.' James looked at the other, his eyes fell on Dodger.

'Right, Dodger, you're elected. Get the tube we cut off and show us how it's done. Another thing, important, an' I mean that. Stub out your fags. No smoking from now on. OK, let's get movin'.'

Cockney gave a wicked grin as he sat on the hatch side gripping the jerrican. Dodger fed the tube into the can. His expression said it all. He was not looking forward to a few mouthfuls of petrol.

'Come on, my son. You're the fuckin' expert,' quipped his mate.

'Bollocks!' came the reply. Sometimes Dodger felt he could cheerfully kill him. He emptied his lungs, put the tube in his mouth and sucked - and sucked - and sucked. He sucked until his eyes were popping out like chapel hat pegs. Until his ears were ringing and his heart beating a mad tattoo aginst his ribs. Finally he had to give in. He let the tube fall from his lips and stood, chest heaving as though he had just completed a marathon.

'Bit difficult?' asked Cockney considerately. Dodger was too busy whooping air into his lungs to attempt a reply, his face looked like the man in the Turkish bath. Cockney took the tube from his unresisting hands, and took three quick powerful sucks removing his lips for a fraction of a second after each suck. As quick as he was, he was not quick enough. The jet of petrol filled his mouth as in one swift coordinated movement he emptied his mouth and pinched the tube hard holding it down for Dodger to take.

Dodger's eyeballs were returning to their sockets. His irritation now admiration. Tinged with it was suspicion as he tried to work out how Cockney had done it.

Cockney grinned. 'You didn't hold your mouth right.' He raised his voice. 'Chuck us a water bottle up 'ere before all me teeth drop out.'

Dodger passed him the water bottle, then bent to hold the tube over the open top of the autovac. He released his finger pressure to let the stream of petrol flow.

'Half full - that's it - keep it at that level,' said James. He pushed the petrol stop to 'on', nodded to Chalky, who shouted to Rayburn to start turning the starting handle.

The engine caught as Chalky switched on the ignition. It settled down to a even rhythm. Rayburn got in the quad. He looked as though he had won the Irish Sweep. He settled in the seat next to Bell. Half turning he opened his mouth to speak, saw Bell's closed eyes and decided against it. He knew it was deliberate. One of these days I'll knock his fucking head off. He is, he searched for a word, he's a standoffish bastard. He caught James's eye and grinned; less one, they were all jubilant. They were going to move, an hour ago that had seemed unlikely, even impossible. Rayburn found it difficult to be put out for long; his placid nature reasserted the pattern of years spent in farm work.

The front of the quad was pretty crowded, James half kneeling on the rubber pad seat, Cockney on the roof with legs braced across the hatch, Dodger with his back to the windscreen directing the flow into the autovac. They waited, James wanted to be satisfied that the system would work, he gave it three minutes. It worked.

'OK, Chalky. You'll have to drive like an undertaker. Ten miles an hour. Pick the flattest bits, if there is any. Move off.'

The quad moved forward slowly, picked up speed. The right-hand door fell off with a clang. It had been open and clamped back to the body. They had all missed the fact that both hinges had been severed.

'Leave it,' said James quickly at Chalky's instinctive move to slow. 'We don't need the fuckin' door.'

'Fuckin' drivers,' yelled Cockney. 'We've lorst 'alf the 'appy 'ome. Thinks he's at Brooklands.'

Chalky and the others grinned at the jibe, any slower and they'd be in reverse. The miles went by, nothing in front, nothing anywhere, sky full of greyness, through wadis, down slopes, up rises and jinking slowly and carefully around camel thorn and rocks. James had aching knees, Dodger thought his neck was broken, Cockney wished he had a cushion. Rayburn dozed. Bell looked wearily out of the open space where the door had been. Chalky was humming the 'Dead March'.

Nineteen miles and over two hours of discomfort for most of them they saw a graveyard of six vehicles scattered widely to their left. The nearest one was a 15 cwt Morris truck. It bore the black white rimmed cross on both doors and bonnet. They stopped ten yards away and James got out. Rayburn jumped out and walked across with him. Rayburn got in the driver's seat.

'Touch nothing!' came the crack of James's voice.

James had looked at the truck through his binoculars previously and something had caught his eye. Something unusual. He was trying, without success, to remember what it was. Dropping flat he squirmed underneath. His first glance told him all he wanted to know.

'Muscles, get a pair of pliers - *jildi*.'

Rayburn slid off the seat and went back to the quad. On his return he passed the pliers to James. He took them and clipped the wire that ran from the dynamo to the concealed mine. He scraped the sand away from the base of the metal. It was a Teller mine holding about twelve pounds of explosive. He could detect no more wires. Gently he uncovered the mine, unscrewed the detonator and dragged the Teller out. Wriggling underneath, he checked along and both sides of the vehicle length. It was clear. He got to his feet.

'Was it booby-trapped, Sarge?' Rayburn asked nervously.

'It was. Starter or even handle would have blown you sky high. Me too. They're crafty bastards. Can't take anythin' for granted. Right, we'll take a look at it now.'

'Thanks, Sarge. Good job you stopped me. First thing I was gunna do was get it going.' His big open face wore a relieved slightly puzzled expression. Relieved because he hadn't blown them all up, and his own narrow escape. And puzzled because he nearly had; one simple reflex action and he had nearly - he ground the thought from his mind. That was why he was still a gunner and Geordie was a sergeant. He liked it that way. The Army way.

James grunted. 'Hang about a bit.' He called to the two who

had got out of the quad, Chalky and Bell. 'Hold it, you two.' They stopped, the engine of the quad murmured softly. James wanted to think. Something was wrong, uneasily he lit a cigarette whilst he tried to concentrate. He had missed something, but what?

He recalled Rayburn's words, tried to remember what he had said in reply. What had he been thinking of then? He had only grunted. A normal playing down of an incident. Another one, that over the years had become part of their lives. Not normal by ordinary standards but accepted. This acceptance and tolerance of the unusual was a factor that had grown from their experience. He had often thought that had he come across a battleship firing broadsides at all and sundry, he wouldn't have been surprised. He looked at the derelict truck again. His eyes fell on the Teller with the unscrewed detonator he had placed on the top.

His skin contracted on the back of his neck. The cunning sods. His brain clicked into gear. Can't see wood for trees. He had missed the obvious. Find one, fairly easily, assume that's it and relax. Exactly what the Jerries wanted him or anyone else to think. Well, we'd better start looking. He took a careful slow walk around the truck. The tyre tracks between the front and back wheels were clearly marked. Two feet in front his eyes spotted a discernible but faint difference in texture of the sand.

He knelt and examined the ground closely; it confirmed what he had suspected in that first glance.

'Get a couple of bayonets, Muscles.'

Rayburn turned and went back to the quad. By now all instincts sharpened, James was tuned to danger, his brain clearer, eyes sharper, nerves tensioned like violin strings. He stepped back, lifted binoculars and from various angles checked the ground through the lens. He found what he was looking for just a foot behind the dropped tailboard.

He glanced back, Rayburn had stopped fifteen yards away lightly holding two bayonets.

'Chalky, that small tin - in the tool box - let's 'ave it over 'ere.' He continued to look through the lens, and released breath he didn't realise he was holding. Finally, as satisfied as he could hope to be he dropped the binoculars on his chest and turned to take the small tin box from the driver. From it he took two split pins and handed it back. To Chalky's enquiring look he said:

'S Mines - two of 'em, back of the tailboard.' Chalky's eyes widened as James continued:

'I think there's more Tellers in front. I'll do these bastards first.' He unslung his binoculars and handed them to Chalky.

'Right, get round the other side of the quad. Tell 'em all. Switch off the engine. Get Dodger and Cockney off the quad and all of you flat on the deck, *mallam*? Understand? If I get blown up, keep the glasses. *Yallah-egri owam*. Now get out - and quickly.' James waited until the engine stopped and they were all under cover.

Dropping to his knees he lowered his body on to the ground close to the tailboard. All that could be seen were two sets of vertical prongs three in number. Each set was slightly off the vertical and spread; they looked like thin twigs, innocuous, innocent, part of the desert fauna. James looked at the prongs and knew he was looking at death. Tread on one of these and they could be set to explode at various weights and that was it. The canister was packed with steel balls; one explosive charge sent it up in the air to about six feet, another charge exploded the canister. Over three hundred steel balls with the velocity of rifle bullets then tore the air and anything in the vicinity.

Slowly his fingers started carefully to remove the sand from below the prongs, all around the tube of steel and the container below. Removing the sand to bare the mine was not a difficult task. The sand had only recently been dug; it was soft. He paused for a moment, rolled over and took the first split pin from his pocket. Sweat dropped off his eyebrows. His fingers felt like bananas. He took a short breath and let it trickle slowly from his mouth as he inserted the split pin into the small hole in the tube.

He felt carefully around the base for wires, it was clear, unlinked to the other. It had taken about three minutes. He was shaking, not from muscle strain but sheer fright. He sat up. Fuck this for a game of soldiers, he thought. One thing's for sure, I'm not putting in for a transfer to the sappers. He lit a cigarette and inhaled deeply. Slowly the shaking reduced and his heart recovered to a steady beat. He waited another two minutes before lifting the once deadly cylinder. About nine inches from the prongs to the base and four inches in diameter. Shrapnel mine, the 'S' mine. Feared and hated by all who were unfortunate enough to tread or nearly tread on one. True shrapnel in that container, round steel balls.

Men who were wounded often used to say they were hit by shrapnel. James knew the difference; as a gunner pre-war he had fired true shrapnel shells. Anything else that hit you should correctly be termed splinters, whether bomb, shell, mine or grenade. The Medical Corps had a blanket name for wounds GSW or gunshot wound. It didn't matter to them what had caused the holes, GSW said it all.

He turned his attention to the other mine. This time he was more confident with less shake in his fingers, more his normal self. Five minutes later he stood up and shouted to the crew. If they had been worried about their number one it was not evident by their expressions. Cockney and Dodger were the quicker to show relief.

Always the practised mimic, Cockney, in his best public school accent, drawled. 'My Gawd, Sergeant James, hi had no ideah, no ideah at all that we had a mines disposal expert in hour pahrty. Jolly good show. Absolute first clarss effort. Remind me - ' turning to Dodger, ' - must have a word with the Commanding Orficah. Must be something we can do - '

'Ha bloody ha,' replied James with a tight-lipped grin. He bent swiftly and retrieved the two bayonets.

'There is - ' handing the two comics - 'one each. Get stabbing with these. Start about eight feet in front and in line with the front wheels. Nice and gently. At an angle. Got it?'

The pseudo-major and his adjutant looked at each other in dismay. Dodger made a brave attempt at Stan Laurel, telling Oliver Hardy that 'it's another fine mess you've got me into,' Rayburn's grin slowly split his face, even Bell gave a tentative smile, Chalky couldn't restrain a giggle that grew to a laugh. James grinned, a wicked grin. He beckoned to Bell, Rayburn and Chalky.

'Right, let's 'ave a look in the back, under that cover, be careful. If you find a wallet, keep your fingers out. I've known of razor blades fixed cross-wise. I don't want anyone losing a finger. Muscles, take a look at the engine, Chalky, there's two undamaged petrol tanks an' they're the same size pipes and unions. Get up there, Bell, be careful. See what else might be useful.'

James left them and went to see how the amateur mine lifters were going on. Both faces were a study in concentration.

Gingerly they were slipping the bayonets at an angle into the sand before them. They were still six feet away from the front wheels.

'Hold it a minute,' said James. He took Dodger's bayonet. 'Look - in about six inches or more - four feet in width.'

He demonstrated exactly what he wanted then went back to the rear of the truck.

Rayburn lifted the bonnet. The engine looked OK. He checked the plugs and leads, unclipped the cap of the distributor, checked the contact segments, the points and carbon brush. The high tension lead looked good. It seemed a well maintained and clean engine.

'Looks OK, Sarge.' He fastened the bonnet cover down, and joined the three at the tailboard. Bell was chucking clothing out of a battered suitcase. The covering tarpaulin was on the ground. Rayburn was curious and loot-conscious. So far in this war, he'd nothing to show for it, a camera, pistol, binoculars, a few million lira, anything would do really. He looked over Chalky's shoulder just as he was lifting the lid of a steel box. Heard the whoop of delight and craned closer.

'Corn in Egypt, ' Chalky breathed. In the box, laid out in meticulous teutonic order were all the tools, a complete fitter's tool kit. Rayburn gave a sniff of disappointment and moved away. James took a look and smiled. The anxiety that without proper tools the fitting of amother tank might prove extremely difficult disappeared. Chalky had thought about it, so had James.

'Sarge.' It was Bell. James swung up and moved to the front of the truck. Bell indicated his find. It was a light machine gun, a MG 34 with two boxes of ammunition.

'Useful,' James commented. 'What's in the big box underneath?'

Bell passed him the gun, raised the lid of the large wooden box.

'Christ,' James exclaimed. 'This is a bloody arsenal, keep on lookin'. We might finish up with an eighty-eight or - ' reflectively, '- the *Scharnhorst?*'

The large box contained eight Teller mines, all with detonators and twenty or more potato masher grenades.

'Sarge!' The hail came from Cockney and was immediately followed by Dodger's shout. James dropped off the side of the truck and walked forward.

'Lissen,' said Dodger. He slipped the bayonet in and out and they all heard the metal to metal dull thud. Cockney said:

'Same 'ere.' Both bayonets were a foot from the front tyres.

'Leave yours,' he said to Cockney. 'Come over 'ere an' I'll show you. You start like this.'

He demonstrated the whole of the method that revealed another Teller mine and lifted it; this time he left the detonator in.

'Right, now you two can 'ave a go. Careful, don't rush it.' He moved away to watch.

Both started hesitantly, conscious of the eagle eyes that regarded their efforts. Soon, within seconds they had gained confidence and five minutes later the Teller was lifted out of the hand-scooped hole. Both Cockney and Dodger were aglow with their success. Willingly they carried the mines to the rear of the truck. Leaning the mines against the rear wheel they took in what had been found.

It affected them all, this manna from heaven. Morale, that intangible vital ingredient, shot up like a thermometer in a heat wave. Six jerricans, all empty and three water cans painted with a white cross completed the total.

James called Chalky over. Together they discussed the practical aspects of the situation, as it was now. Before sighting the derelict, the only thing on their minds was a petrol tank, nothing else. Now, all sorts of other avenues concerned with their gift horse, needed consideration.

Firstly, to cannibalise the truck, taking what they thought would be useful, would be a waste. Unnecessary waste was anathema to all of them. They were scavengers with an innate, highly developed acquisitive jackdaw flair for picking up articles. A knack for scrounging, for themselves, the troop, battery and the regiment. In this they were completely amoral. Like all desert rats they were proud of their ability to adapt, to manage with what they had and what they could scrounge.

If they could get the truck going, just take one tank off it, they had a useful addition and one that could tow the gun if needed.

' 'Ere - ' handing Dodger his binoculars. 'Take a walk. Up

to that rise in front. Keep a good lookout and *bolo* - shout - if you see anythin'. We're goin' to be busy.'

James and Chalky walked back to the quad. They checked what petrol and water they had. Thirty-five gallons of petrol and fifteen gallons of water remaining, should be sufficient.

'Get the autovac put back together, Chalky 'll get the tank off. Put it on the floor behind my seat. We'll only need a short length of pipe.' He left Chalky to it, picked up the funnel and a jerrican and walked over to the truck.

Muscles and Cockney were smiling and chatting. Bell was leaning against the truck-side smoking. James thought, have to have a word with him, on his own, when this lot's sorted out. His mind dwelt on possible reasons for the aura of dejection and worry that seemed to hang, like a cloud, wherever Bell was. Might just be his bint in blighty. One never knew with men; sometimes it was simple and at others so bloody complicated as to be insoluble. Nowt' so queer as folk.

He dumped the full jerrican by the truck.

'Right, Cockney, you and Rayburn put four gallons in the left-hand tank, the rest in the right. If none of 'em leak, we'll use the right hand one for the quad. First we want to get this goin'. I 'ope we're lucky. Can't tow it wi' the quad, not at the moment anyway.'

The two men soon had the fuel poured. They waited, James ran his palm underneath both tanks, he got to his feet with a relieved grunt.

Half a mile away Dodger was flat on his stomach with the binoculars to his eyes scanning the ground ahead. Clouds hung like wet balloons overhead and the desert held a cheerless atmosphere, lonely, empty with no welcome. Miles and miles of sweet fuck-all. He lit a cigarette. His mind searched around for something, any topic to relieve the boredom of what he was doing. Nothing came, his brain seemed to be in suspended animation. For a while he hummed a tune under his breath. That didn't do any good either. He swung the binoculars on to the truck and quad. Well at least, everyone seemed busy, Geordie should have sent Bell up here, suit him down to the ground. Well, I don't want to think about him. Wish I could think of something, anything, something cheerful.

Been a right ta-ta of a day so far. Sooner we get back to the troop the better, Don't like being on me Jack Jones, roll on the chuffin' boat, get back to Blighty, sink a few pints, 'ave a night out, up west. Pick up a bit of skirt. Get married, 'ave some kids ah, that'll be the day. Felt sorry this morning, what with Lackery getting knocked off. Fancy that poor bloody Jerry kicking the bucket. Just goes to show. His stream of consciousness faltered; he turned back to the monotony of watching the uninhabited wasteland without any enthusiasm.

Cockney switched the petrol on, waited twenty seconds, then switched off.

Muscles had the fixed starting handle in the grip of his powerful right hand. He looked at Cockney, saw him nod and commenced to slowly turn the handle. Cockney counted the turns and switched the fuel on again.

'I'm switching the ignition on at three,' he shouted. 'One - two - three.' The red light came on the dashboard. Muscles slowed the turns, stopped then gave a sharp upward pull. The engine caught, fired, Cockney eased the choke, it burst into throbbing life. His right foot blipped the acclerator. He was grinning like a Cheshire cat. James came round, tapped his shoulder, Cockney inclined his ear. James said clearly, 'Reverse - along the truck tracks. OK? Then take it up to the quad, six feet away - your right side, the quad's left - all right?' Wells nodded. James wasn't taking any chances.

Cockney listened to the even rhythm of the six-cylinder Morris engine. Satisfied, he depressed the clutch, engaged reverse gear and moved slowly back along the previously made tyre tracks. He went back twenty yards before moving forward to come up alongside the quad. Setting the hand throttle he slid off the seat.

James with Bell and Rayburn close on his heels arrived at the quad.

'Let it run for ten minutes, Cockney. It'll do the battery good.'

He looked at the others. 'Right. Plenty of tools in the box. Let's get cracking and get this tank off.'

They set to with a will. The newly acquired hacksaw went through the truck pipe like butter. They cut it off four feet from the tank union. Bolts holding the petrol tank bracket proved easy to unfasten. In ten minutes they had the tank in the quad and behind the number one's seat.

Chalky had been thinking about pipes and unions as he

reassembled the autovac. He thought he had an improvement on his original idea. Now he cut off a six-inch length of rubber from the tube used to syphon fuel from the jerrican. He paused for a moment, then jumped out of the quad to rummage in the fitter's kit on the tailboard of the truck. His hand came out bearing two small jubilee clips. He flashed a grin at James.

'This, this is the answer, Sarge. Does away with all your bloody unions. Piece of cake now.'

He dashed back to the quad. He could hardly wait to get the pipes coupled together. The pipe from the bottom of the autovac lined up with the new tank pipe. Working quickly, he soon had the rubber pipe over both ends of the two pipes. Straining hard he pushed them, millimetre by millimetre together. He tightened the jubilee clips. A sigh of relief escaped him. Right, petrol. Jumping out of the quad he grabbed a full jerrican off the trailer, carried it round, while Cockney held the funnel. The five gallons gurgled into the tank. Chalky screwed the cap in, the autovac he had already filled. Shaking with excitement he slid into the seat, switched on and pressed the the starter.

The quad engine burst into life. He increased the power. Anxiously he watched the join in the pipes as ears listened for the hiss of the autovac. It would show that the petrol was being sucked up from the tank. The hiss came. So, suddenly, did the leak from the joined pipes. He switched off, pushed the pull-push petrol tap off and slumped back in his seat.

He had been so sure. That had suddenly changed to despair and bafflement. That petrol had literally pissed out. Under the rubber pipe at both ends. Yet the only pressure was the suck of the autovac. He felt like the crossword fan searching for a word, stymied. Wearily he lit a cigarette. His brain felt like a seized-up engine, useless.

Cockney looked in the door, saw the dejected expression on Chalky's face. His quick mind grasped immediately that here was more trouble. He reached over to take a light from the driver's cigarette. Took a quick drag to let smoke trickle from lips and nostrils.

'What's up then, mate? Got a problem?'

Chalky explained in disgusted tones what had happened. His listener *tck-tcked* his sympathy. He took the pipe in his fingers.

'Tell you what, my old son.' Chalky gave him a despairing

glance, the look of a tradesman at an idiot. Cockney knew the look; he carried on.

'What you want, mate, is another pipe. No, not another petrol pipe, but a pipe inside the bleeding' pipe. Get it ? Then the rubber pipe goes over the top. Then you clamp it.'

He waited, impatient for the light of understanding to show on Chalky's features. Chalky was absently prying the centre bakelite boss of the steering wheel off. It came free.

Thoughtfully he turned it over to look at the inside. Someone, unknown to him, had written inside the bakelite cover in indelible pencil. The words said simply, 'Now put the fucking thing back.' He grinned then started to laugh. Cockney looked in amazement.

'Well, mate, it's not as funny as all that. All I said - ' The words trailed away as he read the inscription. Laughter bubbled up and he was soon outdoing Chalky who was gradually attempting to regain some sort of control. They sounded like a couple of hyenas. The laughter attracted both James and Rayburn. Their curiosity was confined to their eyes; both men's lips were primed by the always infectious waves of mirth. They were ready, eager to laugh. The written words released that now uncontrollable completely unrestrained, hoots of glee.

It was over a minute before the laughter turned to chuckles and even then Cockney had the last word.

'Cor, I ain't laughed so much since Ma got 'er tits caught in the mangle,' he observed.

The chuckle came from Rayburn; the others had heard it before.

'Can't win 'em all, I suppose,' said Cockney. James turned away with Rayburn following. Cockney looked at Chalky. The laugh had done them all good, lifted spirits, released tension. Now it was back to the present, to the problems. They hadn't changed but in some way, the little interlude had imbued them all with optimism. Not if, but when.

'I've got it, what you said.' Chalky's voice was confident. 'A smaller diameter rigid pipe joining the petrol pipes first, then the rubber. You're a fucking genius.' Cockney spread a pair of deprecating hands. He grinned.

'It's nothing. I do it all the time.'

Together they walked over to the truck and brought James up to date. He thought they had as much chance of finding a length of pipe as a needle in a haystack. Bell held up a pair of tin shears and suggested they cut some tin from a petrol can. Rayburn was delving in the bottom of the German tool box. No one else was taking much notice; they were all thinking and Bell was feeling ignored.

Rayburn's fingers felt a hard object wrapped in cloth. Slowly he brought it out and unwrapped the cloth. It was a tin box eight inches by four and two inches in depth. His powerful fingers clawed the lid open. Inside were bits for the hand-drill that was part of the kit. They ranged from two inch down to a quarter, underneath the larger bits was a division of plywood covered in green baize cloth. Rayburn eased it up. The recess contained much smaller and finer bits. Some were protected in metal tubes.

Well, it was an idea, he thought. The tubes were too big anyway, Nevertheless he lifted them all out and gasped. A small tube, rubber caps at either end - could be! He took one cap off. Inside it nestled one spring. He put the spring down and walked round slowly to the truck's missing petrol tank. Hardly daring to hope he brought the cut off end of the pipe to the small two-inch long tube in his fingers.

He walked round to join the others. He felt their incurious gaze, waited for a break in the discussion. A discussion that was now floundering for lack of new positive ideas. It seemed to Rayburn that he had waited all his life for the moment that was to come. The opportunity to take the centre of the stage. When it came he could not have timed the occasion better.

'I think - ' He paused, then went on, 'This is what we are looking for.' He kept his face straight, he liked to think that it was impassive.

The astonished faces now looking at him were his biggest reward. James reached forward and took the small tube from his fingers. 'Christ! 'Ere we are all talkin', out of ideas, thick, stupid. Muscles, take a bow.' As an afterthought, 'Hey, I hope it fits?'

'It does - perfect!' rejoined a happy Muscles. Chalky grabbed the tube from James. He had work to do. Thirty minutes later the repair completed and both truck and quad filled up, they were ready to go. James looked at his issue watch. It was 3.30p.m.

'Right, we'll 'ave a brew. Do another hour or so, have some

connor and bed down for the night. Bell, nip over and fetch Green, will you.'

They sat aroung drinking the welcome thick brown tea, The conversation was on an optimistic level, the atmosphere relaxed. Later as they moved along at a steady twenty miles an hour the sky had lifted slightly, the desert had a newly washed look and the sparse camel thorn a tinge of green.

They were approaching the limit of the belt of rain that had flooded the coastal strip. The gun and quad were followed by the 15 cwt Wells was driving and Bell his fellow passenger. The MG34 - Bell thought of it as a Spandau - leaned against the front of the cab. The gun was cocked and loaded with the safety catch on. Bell stretched out his legs luxuriously. He lit two cigarettes and passed one to Cockney.

There was very little privacy in a gun crew and certainly none in the quad. It suited him, yet there were times when he wished he could talk, really talk to someone, privately, man to man, without the eternal skitting and slow timing that communal living invariably encourages.

Their eyes followed the quad; they watched the head and shoulders of James protruding from the hatch. There was no dust and they were thirty instead of the normal hundred yards distant. Bell deliberately and with considerable effort cleared his mind. Pushed the dark cloud of depression to the back of his brain.

'Good job Geordie spotted that booby trap,' he remarked.

Cockney grinned, fag and bottom lip joined. 'Yeah, Muscles could 'ave lost muscles. Get it?'

Bell smiled, the first time for days, his physical discomfort quiescent. The truck engine seemed in good fettle; at this speed the usual roar and wind noise subdued. Cockney's left hand was automatically slipping the gear lever through the gears as his left foot double declutched. He made it look easy Bell thought, but then everything Wells did, he did with ease. He wondered sometimes about his background. He wouldn't have said so but he admired him, both for this ability and more, for his unquenchable optimism and humour. The only time he had seen him devastated had been this morning after Lackery's death. That hadn't lasted long though. And that took character.

'Look at old Geordie there. Looks like a bloody pirate. Come to think of it, I wonder what 'e did before he joined Kate Karny's?' Cockney's voice cut into his musings.

'I don't know,' he replied steadying the Spandau. 'Maybe he was born in it.'

'Yeah, might 'ave something there. Imagine - he popped out when 'e was born, wearing three stripes an' a gun. Nah, I think 'e wus a miner, somewhere in Durham, wherever that is. He's a real tough nut though, proper Geordie but wi'out the accent. Remember when Jenkins deserted with that three-tonner full of ammo?'

Bell smiled, he was beginning to enjoy Cockney's company. 'Yes, I remember that. Waited for nine months until he came out of detention, took his shirt off and knocked him all round the leaguer.'

Cockney smiled at the memory. 'Poor old Jenkins, he didn't find out until he'd been battered senseless, that he'd got the hidin' not for desertin' but for takin' three ton of ammo with 'im.' He peeled the cigarette from his bottom lip and flipped it into the desert.

'Yeah, nearly dropped us all innit. We ran short. Never seen Geordie so livid. I'm glad he's on our side. No bull about 'im, a good bloke, best number one in the regiment. Do your job, no problem. If you get in trouble, he'll back you up. 'Eard from that bint of yours yet?'

Cockney knew the answer, it was an open secret in their small world. Out of the corner of his eye he saw Bell's expression resolve into the more familiar lines of despondency. Mentally he kicked himself. Was it the wrong approach? Would Bell clam up as he always did? He waited, kept his expression sympathetic.

Bell looked across undecided, maybe this was the time? Just the two of them, no one else. Looking at Cockney's profile, he made up his mind not to brush aside this genuine enquiry and, he was sure, it would go no further than the front of this truck. He winced as the front wheels bounced off camel humps. His vertebrae protested for what seemed the millionth time in the last two and a half years. This country boasted millions of these common obstacles. Cockney fought the uncooperative front wheels. They started to dance and weave around the humps as did the quad in front.

'No,' he shouted, 'it's been six weeks. I had a letter from her sister. Full of hints, innuendoes, spiteful gossip. Still, you don't want to listen to my troubles.' He broke off, trying to relax his stomach muscles to the increasing bouncing of the truck. His mournful gaze fastened on the twenty-five pounder gun bouncing like a rubber ball in front.

Cockney's voice came clearly over the engine noise.

'Dinga, don't be so bloody stand-offish. No one's goin' to take the piss. We're all mates in our crew, you know that. You can tell me. I might be able to 'elp. In any case it'll do no 'arm to gerrit off your chest.'

Bell spat a mouthful of phlegm over the top of the canvas door. He turned to Cockney, haltingly at first but fast gathering confidence, he started to explain.

'Her sister says she's been seen with a Yank boy friend. We're supposed to be engaged. We haven't seen each other for three years. It's not knowing, the uncertainty. If I could see her, it might be different. I want to believe that her sister is stirring it up. You see, the sister, well, she fancied me, but I - well, she wasn't my type, jealous little cat. She might be right - could be two-timing me. It's driving me up the wall. I can't stop thinking about her and this Yank. Maybe he's a negro. I can't do anything here - might as well be on the moon. It's so far away and so long ago, and other people get letters, don't they?'

He fell silent, aware the question was rhetorical. What he'd said was only a part. He could not talk about the main ordeal that was haunting him. The malevolent inner claws that were ripping him to shreds, that never left him, for one second. For want of something to do he lit two more cigarettes and passed Cockney one.

'Ta,' Cockney acknowledged. He had waited before making a reply. What Bell had said was nothing new or even serious. It was like a child begging for sympathy. Instinctively he knew there was more to Bell's problems than he had admitted. Even that admittance had been blood out of a stone, unwilling, reluctant. If there was ever going to be a time when Bell would really talk, it wasn't here, at this time.

He began a rambling story concerned with mail that had been lost, ships sunk, letters finishing up in India and ending with the encouraging remark that six weeks was considered normal. He told him not to worry, knowing as he did so that no worrier takes any real notice of other people saying that.

Shufti, in front, Dinga. Musta bin in June - Christ, it's a right mess.'

They were approaching a former battle area. Under the leaden sky it was as cheerless and forlorn as an East End cemetery on a rain-filled day. The hulks of burnt-out tanks, British and German armoured cars, trucks and guns littered both sides of the track they were now on. An 88mm gun, its muzzle flared like a woman's pleated skirt, pointed bleakly to the lowering clouds. Paper, thousands of pieces, lifted and fluttered like butterflies amongst the debris. To see paper, so long after this kind of skirmish was unusual. The sand was snuff dry and lay thickly around wheels, full and empty ammunition boxes with brass cartridge cases from the larger calibre guns, poking up from the ground. Off to the left stood isolated lonely groups of makeshift wooden crosses, rifles reversed, helmet on the butt, bayonet deep in the sand.

Bitter relics of forgotten men. Had Cockney been on foot, he would have walked on tip-toe. Scenes like this were common enough. Yet in some strange way the desert took over, began to hide the torment soften the outlines and cloak the scene with silent dignity. Like wrecked cathedrals. Cockney heaved a sign of relief as they left. In June many things had happened on the way back to Alamein.

His natural ebullience and cheerful optimism took over.

'Sooner them than me,' he said.

Bell nodded and agreed. He had been about to resume the conversation but decided not to. It was rarely that conversation lived for long travelling in a bouncing truck. It was always a strain to catch what the other said over the sound of the engine and mouths soon got dry after the first few words. One usually sat in silence, half dozing or reading a paperback that had gone the rounds of the regiment. He didn't feel like reading. Anyway, he'd nothing to read; it was on the quad.

It was queer how the mind worked. Take this morning. Even now it had a dream-like quality. Now why think about that? Got to think of something other than that. Unconsciously he was watching the progress of the quad and admiring the deft touch of Cockney's movement. He closed his eyes. Happy days. Yes, four years ago had been the best days of his life. Lily and he were in love, thinking of marriage. He had been the proud owner of a 100 Ford 8 with real leather seats. The family business had provided that as it had the job of under-manager in one of the five provision shops owned by his father. How he had prided himself on being a good driver, knew all the hand signals, steered correctly, never broke the speed limit and could even double declutch. He smiled as he thought of the picture he must have presented. A pompous prig.

Until he had driven, for the first time in the desert, he had been smug. The desert brought him down to earth with a bump. There were no roads, no policemen, no traffic lights, no driving on the left. No syncromesh gear box and no leather seats and apart from some canvas protection, open to the elements. The trucks were primitive, the desert surface brutal. He learned, as they all did, by experience. That experience took a full year to gather.

Lily had posed the question in one of her letters. What was the desert like? He could think of nothing else to say but, it was like the sea. Miles and miles of utter loneliness. No features, no landmarks, an arid empty wasteland. He had failed, he knew, to describe it, knew it was much more than that. That was his viewpoint and that had been in 1940. Since that time, the months and years had revealed a bewildering multiplicity of moods. Dark and threatening, overwhelming with its discomfort in the *Khamsin**, hateful with the hordes of black, biting flies. Unyielding as it bounced the largest trucks around, like peas on a drum. Absorbing with the rise and setting of the sun. Bitter in the winter months, blinding in the savage heat. A chameleon of thousands of square miles.

No birds to sing a dawn chorus. An arena with thousands locked in gladiatorial combat. A killing ground and a ground that killed. He hated it. He could never come to terms with it. His thoughts flicked back to the morning's events. For some reason he had not been conscious of fear. His movements had been as quick and urgent as any of the crew. But in his own capsule of time even the burst of machine gun fire had been slow. He had felt a curious confidence that had he got up and moved around, nothing would have hit him. Afterwards he was

---

* *Hot Desert Sandstorm with high winds*

impressed and awed but uncomprehending. Usually things moved so fast that it was all over before one realised it.

Time was relative. Crushing an insect underfoot takes only a fraction of a second. But how long did it last to the insect? A fraction, a month, year, a lifetime, or even longer. No one knew.

VI

Cockney whistled through his teeth, past the cigarette that hung limply from his lower lip. He was watching the quad, having dismissed most of what Bell had said. Quite simply, to him, it was not the real reason for the picture of misery that had been Bell over the past three weeks.

Maybe it was a bint? Not the blighty one. Maybe he'd met one in Cairo - maybe. He dismissed the speculation. Not Bell. Anyone else, yes, including himself - might as well accuse the Pope. Still, who knew what went on in the bleeding nunneries - they had vestal virgins, didn't they, temple harlots. Monasteries and nunneries - stands to reason, they'd be bound to get together. There might even have been orgies. He licked his lips at the thought, felt a stirring in his groin. For a brief fleeting moment naked male and female bodies writhed across the screen of his mind. He felt an erection; the old saying was true. A standing prick had no conscience. They're all the same size in bed and the same colour inside. His agile mind switched to another topic. That ME this morning.

I hope the bastard crashed. It had been quite a day, so far. His imagination began to soar as he visualised the tale he could relate, back at the troop. He gave it his attention. The headline came up in bold black type. He couldn't help grinning.

Attacked by a squadron of Messerschmitt fighter bombers. Escape from German Panzer Division. Ordeal of valiant gun crew. (From our special correspondent in Cairo.)

Today's story once again underlines the valour of our troops in the Eighth Army, led by General Montgomery. I was privileged today to meet the guncrew of Kelly, the twenty-five pounder gun that took on the armoured might of the Afrika Korps - and won. Not only did they send the panzers packing but in the process shot down six Messerschmitt 110's

Hell at Fuka

I interviewed these men. All of them are sun-bronzed veteran Desert Rats of the ? Regt Royal Horse Artillery. Gunner 'Cockney' Wells modestly related his part in the drama that unfolded in that desolate windswept wasteland we know as the Western Desert.

Suddenly the grin became a giggle then a laugh. Bell looked at him with surprise. Cockney caught the look.

'Just bin thinkin', makin' up a story, I should 'ave bin a bleedin' war correspondent. I'm goin' to pull their legs rotten when we get back. You know - author's licence. The truth by Cockney Wells. Maybe I'll send a bleedin' letter to *Crusader*. You never know, they might even print it.'

Crusader was the Eighth Army newspaper. Bell smiled briefly. There were times when he just didn't understand the humour of his comrades. Or didn't want to make the effort. He and Cockney were opposites. Cockney was a gregarious extrovert and what was he? Tell the truth for once. I'm an introverted, moody, miserable bastard and I should feel ashamed. He realised suddenly, the tactfulness of the crew. They had left him alone. Seemed to have a clearer insight into his behaviour than he did. If he could only see a way out, I can't go on much longer. He closed his eyes.

Cockney was having second thoughts about the tale he was going to tell. Might be a bit much, a panzer division, make it a battle group and cut the number of aircraft to two shot down. The thought struck him that even if he told the truth, would any of his mates believe him? Knowing the cynical bunch, he doubted it. He sighed inwardly - couldn't bloody win, could you?

His eyes rested on the figure of Geordie in front. He felt an affection and admiration for the quick-thinking tough gun sergeant. Geordie could be a real bastard when he wanted; mainly it was with the enemy. Rode the crew on a light rein. Never needed to say much, he could joke with them all, call them by their nicknames and never had to repeat himself. He was Geordie, behind his back. To his face he was Sarge or in the presence of an officer, Sergeant. None of them would have dreamed of addressing him as anything else. Like the gun, he was solid, reliable with a controlled aggression that exuded confidence. It took a lot to shake him and he would not be beat.

Christ, I'm glad he's in charge and not me, thought Wells.

He glanced at Bell, felt a wave of sympathy, smothered it quickly. He'd never been one to easily understand. Different class, I suppose. They're never the same when they retreat inside themselves. He began to pursue another line of thought, humming softly to himself. For him, formal education, if one could term it that, had finished at the age of fourteen. He considered now that the only useful advice from the hard-as-nails headmaster had been contained in one sentence:

'Read, Wells - anything and everything.'

He had not needed any persuading. Whether by chance or design the head had picked on the one subject that he loved. Cockney did not pick the books, they picked him. His memory was good, got better and his mind soaked up the knowledge like blotting paper. Inevitably his taste improved as his mind expanded. His appetite was insatiable and his discards grew as he became selective.

Sometimes the local librarian pointed him in another direction. Always the change bore fruit, made him think and admire one more author to add to his list. In the library he could read for free the daily newspapers and, if he was lucky, the periodicals. As one dead end job followed another his scant pocket money counted in coppers, bought second hand books which were sold back to a different shop.

The streets of East End London, the dockland community, the wide boys, later called spivs, had taught him survival. He was a professional class fighter and naturally adept at any sport. He retained his cockney manner of speaking deliberately. It was camouflage in a wartime army. Like a true Londoner he merged into a completely new pattern of life. Quick to mimic, to see the funny side, there was more, much more to Wells than met the eye.

His new line of thought had fastened on the last leave in Cairo, shortly before the Alamein battle. Dodger, himself and Bell. He and Dodger had picked up two belly dancers from the Sweet Melody Cabaret, on Sharia Emad El Din. Cairo was submerged under thousands of troops all looking for the same thing, bints!

The competition was intense with no holds barred. It seemed that Hollywood had released thousands of 'Robert Taylors' and their doubles. Queues stretched from one end of the Sharia Wagh

El Berka to the other, outside the brothels and all the way up the stairs. Cockney had not fancied their chances; he was already thinking they had made a mistake in coming to Egypt's capital city. But Alexandria would be worse and Suez or Port Said were out of the question.

Chance brought a glance from two sloe-eyed dusky beauties. Svelte nubile females in high heels and fashion dresses. Their glances met and Cockney had grabbed Dodger's arm and dragged him across the wide crowded street. Chemistry, he thought, a fraction of a second and they were set for the next four days.

One gold bracelet for each of the girls from the Mouski; that set them back ten quid each. The girls lived in an 'out of bounds' part of Cairo. Zenab was his, Zena was Dodger's. The 'out of bounds' notices worried neither of them.

Both girls were skilled in the subtle arts of the dance. It turned out that they were descended from a long line of famous dancers. Their home was one large room with kitchen and bathroom in small separate cubicles. The lavatory was a tiled hole in the floor of another cubicle.

For four days and nights they relaxed, they drank Pilsener Biere and Zibib but never got drunk. The girls were happy, unrestrained in their affection and the room full of laughter. Four days sped by. Tears were shed but to no avail. They were both a little overcome when they joined Bell at Cairo main railway station, Cockney remembered, too wrapped up in what they had enjoyed to take much notice of him. But, when he thought about it he had noticed a change in Bell. He actually seemed happy. Wanted to talk but neither of them felt like talking, the memory of the two girls was too close. He had rambled on about the number of good films he had seen, the Majestic with its sliding roof. One of the films had been *The Four Feathers*. And yes, Bell had enjoyed his leave. Now that was unusual. Suddenly, he had it, or thought he did. It could not be anything else. Bell had met a bint. And, Cockney thought, the length of time was about right. Bell thought he had a packet. It fitted. He glanced at Bell's face, his eyes were shut. He felt confident that he was right. Poor bastard, making a mountain out of a molehill. Better wait and see; it has to come from him. He's got to unbend, trust his mates. If we're good enough to die with, and surely he knows that, we can understand and try to help.

Bell shouted: 'Glad I wasn't there.'

Cockney turned a puzzled look on him.

Bell went on, 'That lot - where they got caught, a few miles back. Wonder what happened?'

'Me too, Dinga. Too bloody dangerous. They'd probably 'ave some 'air-brained bastard leading them. Someone who didn't give a chuff, 'ad a charmed life an' was lookin' for a bloody gong an' glory. Looks like he got the glory anyway. Give me our lot anytime. No one believes in dead 'eroes. Keep your bleedin' 'ead down, let 'em keep the medals. 'Alf of them who get 'em are a bit whacko, got a tile loose. There's a lot more who should have got 'em, but there was no officers 'anging about at the time.' His voice was flat, a monotone of cynicism.

Bell nodded agreement. It was the view of all those who survived. Sorry about blokes like Lackery but glad it wasn't them. Basically no one was braver than anyone else. He recalled the OP officer at Beda Fomm in early '41, dashing across fire-swept ground to get to a closer position from which to observe.

'That was a bloody good shot of yours this morning.' It was rarely, so soon after frantic actions, that they were discussed. Usually it was the next day or days after. Cockney darkened under his tan slightly embarrassed.

'Thanks. Wish I'd bin a bit quicker. That fuckin' Spandau wouldn't 'ave got a round off. It was Lackery's time - he was a real good bloke.' He brooded for a moment.

The might have beens. Normally it was a pointless exercise. Still, sometimes out of the blue, when things had calmed down, out of the subconscious would pop a question. If the brain was cool and fertile enough something would emerge. An inkling of an idea that might save a second, in their isolated world of the gun and their speeds in handling it. Today though, no questions came to mind. He wondered idly what the rest of the crew were thinking.

*

In response to Dodger's tap Chalky reached back and took the lit cigarette from his fingers. He was still thinking of the graveyard of mixed casualties, of the eyeless sockets that had regarded him with impersonal tolerance. No matter how often one saw the aftermath of savage clashes you never got used to it. At best you tried to ignore, pretend it wasn't there.

He slipped through the gears imperceptibly as they moved slowly down the slope of another wadi. He noticed a faint trickle of steam from the radiator cap. Have to keep an eye on that. The cloud seemed heavier, hadn't really been light all day. In less than two hours I'll bet it's dark. Like India, don't get much dusk. Those bodies back there, the shitehawks and vultures would have stripped them clean in a matter of hours. Here, the process was slower, the winds and the dry heat would desiccate them eventually.

After the war, if there was going to be such a time, it would take decades to clear up the mess of the desert. Scrap iron could become a major industry in Egypt. Crafty sods, the gyppos, all they seemed to have contributed in this war was an empty desert, a rented arena for us to fight in. They could and did sit back and collect the ackers. Devious bastards, the Arabs. Still - he felt a surge of amusement - when they collected the scrap, they might get a shock. Quite a few would get blown up on mines or booby traps. The desert would exact a price. Usually it was blood.

Of course now, after the victory of Alamein they would be staunchly pro-British although the departure of the Army from the Delta meant the end of easy profits. The palmy days were over for the Pashas, the cabarets and the bars; they would all be back to Egyptian customers. All the whores would have some explaining to do. Shouldn't think we'll see Cairo again. Next it'll be Tripoli, then Tunis. Then what? France? Maybe Sicily, Italy. Could be Greece. Another five years and we could be in Berlin.

Who knows? We could even end up in Blighty? The thought made him happy. Wonder if they'd let us in? Naturalised Genu*ine* Bedou*ine* A-*Rabs*. Turn out your daughters. We've got something for them - been saving it up. Don't all rush, this regiment has plenty for everybody. He grinned inwardly at the fantasy.

*

His placid face outwardly calm, Rayburn was still feeling odd tremors of unease. He knew what it was but could not explain it. Either to himself or anyone else. His countryman's calm acceptance of life and death had been rudely dented a few hours ago. He looked at his fingers. Fingers that had nearly pressed a button that could have blown them all skyhigh. He thought about the moment, a glimmer of understanding flared in the recesses of his mind but was snuffed out by fingers of incomprehension. He had been asleep for the last hour; Dodger still was.

His attitude was the same, one minute you're here, the next someone switches off the light. Simple, acceptable, inevitable. We renew the cycle with our seed. Well, maybe not me. Not yet. But wait a minute. I could have. Bibis in India, bints in Egypt - yeah, I could have fathered a dozen chickoes, brown skins, blue eyes and fair hair. He asked himself the question: So why was I worried this afternoon? I wasn't bothered this morning. Bullets, bombs or shells, what's the difference? What's all the fuss about mines? You're dead, that's it.

He pondered the questions. Why hadn't he forgotten or at least dismissed, what was, after all, just another experience? It wasn't the first with mines and no doubt would not be the last. But this time - illumination came in a blinding flash of understanding - this time, it had not been just him. Most of the detachment could have suffered. His would have been the responsibility and the guilt. Guilt, I'm feeling guilty. Tortuously his mind turned the word over and looked at it grimly. He sighed with relief. Nothing happened, I nearly made a mistake, that's all. Forget it - and this time, he did.

*

Dodger came awake quickly, eyes open registering the scene, the rattle of cans, groan of body structure and purr of the engine's beat, rising and falling as Chalky negotiated the varying ground. He felt hungry, more than that he was bloody starving. He tapped the legs of the sergeant. James bent and looked.

'Sarge, how much longer? If I don't get some nosh soon I'm gunna waste away.'

James looked at his watch. Quarter to five. He said, 'Another ten minutes, Chalky. Pick one of the wadis. Get some grub. Have a wash and shave. We've about an hour before dark.'

Dodger relaxed and turned to Muscles.

''Ow about you, Muscles, me old china. Fancy a scoff?'

'Too true. Belly thinks me throat's cut.' His mouth twitched in anticipation; he rubbed his chin. 'Could do wi' a shave. Got any razor blades less than a year old?'

'Got a Gillette, nearly new. You can use that. Tell you what, innit queer? I woke up bloody starvin'. You'd think that all I could think about would be steaks, fish an' chips. Instead I'm thinkin' about a bloody poem - one me mum used to tell us.'

Muscles, who knew, only vaguely that poets were creatures with long hair, tortured expressions and weedy physiques could only remember snatches of the standard poems they were taught at school. Things like 'A bumping pitch and a blinding light, an hour to play and the last man in, play up, play up, and play the game'. Or Mini-Ha Ha, Horatio, the boy stood on the burning deck. Gunga Din, yeah well, he knew that Kipling wrote that. But he was an author not a bloody poet. His thoughts raised a gleam of interest in his eyes.

''Ow's it go then? Don't leave us in suspense. Let's be 'earin' it.'

Dodger grinned, slightly embarrassed. In a crowd with a couple of pints under his belt, it was no sweat. With two of them it was just a little bit different.

'You really wanna' 'ear it?' Rayburn nodded.

'*Saheeah*? - True?'

'Course I do. Could do wi' a laff.'

'Right, mate, here goes.' Dodger concentrated, opened his mouth and in the dulcet tones of Whitechapel began.

Epitaph for a Biby

> A muvver was barfin' 'er biby one night,
> The youngest of ten an' a tiny young mite.
> The muvver was pore an' the biby wus thin,
> Only a skeleton covered in skin.
> The muvver turned roun' for the soap orff the rack;
> She wus but a moment, but when she turned back
> The biby wus gorn; and in anguish she cried:
> Oh, where is my biby? - The angels replied:

Chalky shouted, 'Come on, Dodger - a bit louder.' James was kneeling on his seat listening hard. Dodger's voice rose, he was getting into his stride and relished two more in his audience.

Yore biby 'as fell dahn the plug-'ole,
Yore biby 'as gorn dahn the plug.
The pore little thing wus so skinny an' thin,
'E oughter'bin 'barfed in a jug.
Yore biby is perfectly 'appy,
'E won't need a barf any more,
Yore biby 'as fell dahn the plug-'ole,
Not lorst - but just gorn before.

Grins that had dawned as he recited the old Cockney ballad had blossomed into titters, giggles and, as he completed, unrestrained belly laughter. Chalky had been leaning to the rear and side, one eye on the ground ahead and one hand on the wheel, was shaking like a jelly. James had his head down, shoulders heaving and Muscles, half recumbent was gasping like a stranded seal. To cap it all, over the barks and shrieks of laughter, Rayburn who was laughing like the dummy in the fun fairs, let go a tremendous thundering King Emperor fart. For a split second its volume and sheer majesty half drowned the laughter. Then it triggered another burst of glee. Rayburn smiled contentedly.

'Gas masks on. Stop the fuckin' quad. Abandon ship. Muscles 'as blown a bleedin' 'ole in the floor. We're sinkin'. Every man for hissen', Dodger cried.

Still laughing Chalky followed the pointing finger of James across a well defined track to turn into a small wadi. The fifteen hundredweight went past, turned and stopped ten yards from the quad.

'Drop the gun into action rear.' James shouted. In seconds the gun was unhooked, on the gun platform, unclamped and ready, pointing across the track that ran from north to south.

Brew can, cooking tin, fire tin. The sand fire lit, the brew can on, another fire tin doused with petrol on the tin's sand, lit with a thrown lighted match and the cooking tin holding a couple of pints of water, placed on top. Tins were being opened by active jack knives. Tins of stew, potatoes, peas, beans and a tin of bully beef. The last of the bread came out; it just managed six thick slices now being spread with Oleo margarine. Cockney opened two large tins of peaches and a can of evaporated milk. All the messtins were ready with the six enamel mugs arrayed on the quad floor inside the door.

Dodger was stirring the stew which was steaming. The appetising aroma twitched his nostrils; he looked like one of the Bisto kids. He added half a handful of flour, the stew bubbled as he worked it in with the spoon. Bell threw a handful of tea into the boiling brew can. Chalky had filled up the quad petrol tank, found a small drip in the radiator and placed an empty brass cartridge case underneath. James had taken hot water in his mug from the brewcan and was already half shaved. Cockney had topped the 15 cwt petrol tank up, checked the water and dipped the oil. Rayburn and he had unlashed bedding rolls and taken small haversacks belonging to the crew, out of the lockers.

It was a long practised routine. One in which the jobs they did rotated, not in any particular order, more by unspoken agreement that depended on where they were, when the quad halted for the night. In everything they did they were a team, no one a spectator. One might say they had grown up together, the past two and a half years had packed in more incidents, more personal danger than two or three lifetimes. All of them shared more than the dangers, the discomforts, fears, trembling fright or sheer misery, shortage of water and inadequate rations, desert sores and boils. They shared mail, parcels, even toothbrushes at times and shaving gear.

James cast an eye from time to time on the activity. He wiped the last of the soap from his face, rinsed the shaving brush and cleaned the dismantled razor. He placed them, with the small steel mirror on the off white, nearly grey towel and rolled it up. Refreshed by the shave, he felt clean and alive. The act of shaving could be a bind and was sometimes utterly impossible in battle conditions, yet it had the greatest single effect on mind and body.

It would not go unnoticed. The crew would all shave after the meal. It was like so many things that James did, not an order, more an indication. What he knew of psychology he hadn't learned from books. With him it was an instinct, highly developed, of anticipation and empathy. The knack of understanding, the tolerance and sometimes sympathy of one who had seen and experienced the unfairness of life.

None of this ever showed in the sergeant's expression. Like

all regulars with years of service behind them he had developed, as a recruit, the wooden expression. Then for the next two years came the eager, the willing look. Followed at the end of three more years by the neutral blank-eyed wary expression. Three years on the North-West Frontier of India added maturity and confidence, awareness of the frailties of his body and how to survive. Two and a half years of war in the desert, the majority of the time in action, had completed the layers that time had engraved.

His eyes were green. Few people noticed the colour because that changed from light to dark, even to hazel. Deep in them a sardonic cynical humour seemed always to lie waiting. They could reflect the cold bleakness of northern oceans, the twinkle of warmth and also the neutrality of the observer. The hair was black and cut short, it bristled, the nose, short and straight, lips mobile over strong slightly misaligned teeth. The jaw was pugnacious and split by a strong cleft. A small white vee on the wide forehead marked the limit of the forage cap peak and contrasted sharply against the dark almost black skin. With his stocky muscular physique the impression was one of durable impressive competence, a latent authority, someone not to be trifled with.

He ran a comb through the short hair, banged the faded red and blue sidecap on the front wing of the quad and jammed it back on his head. Dodger pronounced the stew ready. He doled it out with aplomb. James took his turn, a word of praise to Dodger, a quip to Rayburn not to expect seconds and walked to the other side of the quad to sit in the open doorway.

In one way this was symbolic, the difference in rank, always marked by subtle or not so subtle boundaries. This evening it meant simply that James wanted to be alone for a brief time. At other times it was a recognition from him that they needed their privacy, their opportunity to talk freely without the inhibition the mantle of authority evoked. It was too, an empathy, unspoken but freely exchanged.

Used, as they all were, to eating with one eye on the sky and ears cocked for orders they ate swiftly and to a pattern, with the messtin held close to the chin with the left hand whilst the right spooned in the food. The spoon sufficed for everything, the knife and fork rarely used. In normal conditions the flies, sun and breeze-laden dust laid down the rules. As everything in this desert did, they had adapted.

Each man had an obligation to leave no food uncovered at any time and to kill flies. The latter pursuit needed no encouragement. The most placid and inoffensive developed a massive hate for the big black constantly biting bearers of disease. Their success could be judged by the results. The regiment had not had a single case of dysentery reported in their time in the desert.

But here there were no flies. Hallelujah! If they were here in the morning, by ten o clock the first outriders would have arrived. At noon there would be thousands. They all knew this as they concentrated on the immediate task of filling the inner man.

The stew disappeared, so did the peaches, bought from the battery canteen truck. Water was already heating in the brew can and each helped himself to some for a shave and skimpy wash. The badinage went on all the time, good-natured taunts, veiled references to officers they had known and not liked. Threats to the female and nubile population of England interspersed with comical and lurid encounters with the bints of Cairo.

Now they sat on bedding rolls smoking cigarettes and relaxed, remembering the day that was slowly slipping away. Each occupied with his own thought, in the interval before the desert night came in on silent wings. So many desert evenings, over eight hundred of them yet always slightly surprised by the quality, the peace and stillness. At these times conversation was superfluous. It was as if the desert folded comforting arms around them, the lonely vastness shrinking to the confines of this small wadi. It affected them all, this brief period, softened their cynicism, created a yearning for home, for love and understanding and lightened the load, the burden of sorrow that each carried within him.

Many of the men they had known had gone, some in a fleeting second, some obliterated leaving no evidence that they had ever lived. Only the memory remained and at these unique interludes sentiment reappeared and affection, happy memories. It was a prelude to what would follow later on, the normal period of reminiscence. The nightly recounting of episodes that at the time were full of horror and despair but in the telling took on the cloak of humour.

James leaned against the ammunition limber and regarded the peaceful scene from under lowered lids. He sucked gently on a cigarette. He had been remembering too; first Lackery; he had been the closest, a real mucker, closer than any brother. Then other faces had flitted across the screen of his mind. Some from 1940, though it never seemed that long ago. His thought came back, to the quad, the truck and the next day. Tomorrow should see them back with the troop, at Bir Khamsa. He was feeling more confident now, food in one's belly made a difference. Today had been unusual but now it had gone, tomorrow should be plain sailing.

Well it should if, his cautious nature interposed. Maybe it was too soon to assume, better to wait, play it by ear. I'm not clairvoyant, wish I was, but - only sometimes. He looked at his crew. Nice to see clean faces. Otherwise they could have passed for Arabs, all they needed was a *jellabiah** and *burnous*, a few mangy goats and sheep and a tatty old tent.

They were dressed in a variety of styles that would have broken the heart of the stoutest Guards sergeant-major, in more ways than one. He looked at Rayburn, he was still chewing a rock hard biscuit covered with grapefruit marmalade. He wore a woollen balaclava the face part rolled up, a scarf around his wrestler's neck, tatty drill shirt with a khaki cardigan (gansy, Muscles called it), battle dress slacks tucked into grey socks and beetle crushers. Unconcernedly he was crushing the biscuits between large white teeth. Dependable and an easy man to live with, not always as slow in his thinking as he wanted people to think.

Bell: he looked at him. He wore a khaki forage cap fore and aft. A long overcoat flapped around skinny calves in the wisp of a breeze that brought the promise of a chilly night ahead. Well worn battle dress slacks and blouse liberally loaded with sand over canvas gym shoes and no socks. Reserved - you could certainly say that.

James had seen that type of reserve at the training depot. A smouldering revolt against Them, the faceless ones who had transplanted him arbitrarily from a safe sheltered civilian way

---

* *Bedouin gown worn by most followers of Mohammed*

of life and into the hurly burly. The do-as-you're-told, masculine and totally alien world of the military system. Intelligent though. Surprised he hadn't applied for a commission. Must have that word with him.

Chalky had drill slacks and shirt, battle dress blouse, desert boots and small tropical Bombay 'Topi'. Good bloke Chalky; not a lot shook him. So long as he got his fags, bottle of beer, the odd booze up with the old stagers of the battery, he was happy. He looked skinny but that body was a steel spring, tireless. He would still be soldiering in another twenty years' time, if they let him.

Cockney's garb was the most bizarre. Drill slacks and shirt, silk neckerchief, black tank corps beret with the RHA cypher in white metal, leather jerkin and an old sheepskin coat. The ensemble was completed by suede desert boots. With his talent for mimicry and East End humour there was never a dull moment. James was determined, eventually, to persuade him to accept promotion.

Dodger looked like Dodger; khaki shorts that were too long for his short legs and hence had been folded and rolled above his knees. Rhodesian khaki wool stockings gartered firmly below the knees, army boots and webbing gaiters, battle dress blouse and a much ripped jerkin. The Cockney sparrow, his dark matted hair covered by a cherished 11th Hussars pink beret.

Like a bloody fashion show, including me; jerkin, battle dress, suede boots and red and blue side hat, but at least, he did have his stripes and brass gun of the full sergeant on both arms.

James was not a sentimental man. The softness, feelings of concern had largely vanished in the purging of hundreds of actions. When this lot is over, he thought, it was going to take him and thousands of others years to rediscover gentleness, loving concern and true emotion.

It did not mean he had no concern for his guncrew but it was a different type of concern. It was devoted to one objective. Get them all back to the battery in one piece. Any affection he felt for the men under his command was held firmly in control, like a father, rough but scrupulously fair. Tears and feeling were wasted in this place.

Suddenly he heard it. So did the rest of them. The sharp whip-crack of a high velocity gun. It shattered the calm peace, enveloping them all and galvanising the crew into rapid movement. The instinctive reflex asked no questions as their bodies responded to a propulsion beyond their control. They were on their feet and at the gun muzzle almost as quick as James and none remembered just how they got there.

A second gun opened up and as the sound carried on the slight desert breeze from the north-east, James recognised a deeper, heavier note: two guns and both sounded like anti-tank. Between the reports came the faint fast chatter of machine guns in short bursts. The gunfire was coming from the north-east. Eyes strained to the higher ground that rolled to the distant blue-black horizon. Ground that they had covered a few short hours before. As they watched a mushroom of flame grew and expanded. The sharp thumps of the high velocity guns ceased. The flames cast a red and white glow that spread to reflect the flickering oven like fire from the low massed clouds. A long burst of machine gun fire cut off suddenly. Then silence. They stood there. No one spoke.

The glow grew less. Now intermittently came the faint jumping jack crackle of exploding ammunition as the horizon merged into the blackness of night. All they could see now was the faint reflected flickering on the clouds. Finally that disappeared.

The first crack of that far-off high velocity gun had affected more than James's ears. A sudden lead weight had dived down the elevator shaft of his stomach. All his instincts, his gut feeling, informed him in a flash that what he had heard was trouble and it could be with a capital T. He felt a finger of fear that danced over suddenly shrinking skin.

The feelings lasted no longer than a second. Then his brain took over. Rapidly his thought clicked into some sort of organised pattern. His brain was now asking the questions. He hoped it also had some answers.

Did he know, accurately, where they were? No - not to within ten or fifteen miles.

What was in front of them? Don't know.

Why did you think they were Jerry guns? Not sure, but sure about the machine guns. Can't mistake that rate of fire.

How far away? That's difficult. You know how sound travels; slight breeze, dampness coming in - could be ten maybe fifteen miles; my guess is about ten.

Do you reckon it's panzers? Yes -I just know, maybe two, a different note from one of the guns, maybe a 75mm and a 50mm.

What do you intend to do? Stay put, no moor, be like blind men.

A picture flashed into his mind. An 8 cwt wireless pick-up travelling in uncharted country at night. Disappearing over a rocky ledge, turning over to land on its side. The wireless set still chattering away as they reached it. 'Can hear you clearly - strength five,' repeated endlessly. The picture went. Hobson's choice, he thought.

Cockney's voice at his elbow penetrated his thoughts.

'What'd you think it was, Sarge?' he asked. James's voice as he replied was deliberately impersonal, even offhand.

'Could be anything, I suppose. Difficult to tell from this sort of distance. It didn't sound too 'ealthy. My guess is 75's. Tank guns. Could be ours - '

Dodger completed the sentence. 'Yeah, an' they could be theirs, Sarge.'

James looked at them. Saw the tenseness of features dimly and sensed the aura of apprehension. For a brief moment he felt uncertain, his former confidence of tomorrow's plain sailing, shot down in flames. There were no easy answers to their problems. All of this, the day that had now gone, the unseen threat that lay to the north and their separation from the troop, were new experiences. He wondered for a moment, whether or not there was an unseen malevolent presence determined that they would never reach their goal. His practical mind laughed it off. They don't have albatross in the desert.

'Yeah.' He answered Dodger's observation but was speaking to them all. 'They could be, most likely are. It's on the cards - two maybe three panzers 'eading south before goin' west. They musta' met up with some of our lads. I'm just guessin' an' I'm 'oping they're goin' west.'

Bell's voice cut in quickly.

'What do we do, Sarge? If they're a couple of Mark fours, on their way south - don't stand much chance, do we?'

'We've always got a chance,' James answered easily. Other angles had popped into his mind. 'I don't think, if they're Jerry tanks, that they'll move at night. Too risky. Their maps aren't any more accurate than ours. They don't show bloody great 'oles you can drop into.

'They don't know, any more than we do, what is concentrated to the south or west. But at least we're heading into an area more likely to be friendly. Brigade or Division could 'ave leaguered only a few miles away. Anyway, we've only about sixty miles to go to Khamsa.' He paused, half expecting a comment, realised he was talking mainly to convince himself and decided to bring his talk to a close.

'We'll start as soon as we can see in the morning. No brew. Tonight we stay here. One man on guard from ten o'clock. No sweat.' He delivered his favourite quip, 'Don't panic - *remembah! You are British*!' The appreciative snigger came from all but Bell. He waited for the snigger to subside before asking. He was unable to keep the tremor from his voice.

'What about tonight? What if they - ?' James cursed himself for not covering the point. He suddenly felt irritation flare within him, asked himself was it because Bell was asking the nit-picking question. Or was it because of a certain pique, disappointment that, particularly after the crowded events of the day, his judgement was being questioned.

'If they attack us 'ere,' he answered calmly. 'That's a good question, Bell. One that a clever chap like you, an intellectual, should never 'ave asked. As you all know, me being gifted with second sight, you might be sure that the solution is obvious - even to you.' He turned to face them squarely. By now they all had their night sight and could see his face.

'Would any gentleman like to enlighten Mister Bell on what we are goin' to do in those circumstances?' James knew what he was doing. Holding Bell up to ridicule, sarcastic mockery. He had also sensed that Bell in these conditions could trigger a panic. All of them knew what blind unreasoning panic could do. It was not going to happen to his crew.

'So,' he said. Back came the throaty reply.

'Get the fuckin' gun in action - quick!' James gave a tight-lipped grin, satisfied. He went on.

'For the benefit of anyone who is bein' rather thick - I can't dot the i's or cross the t's - if they move tonight, we'll 'ear them first an' a long time before they get 'ere. If they're close enough, an' only then, we'll know what to do. Right, we're in the right position. Get two rounds of HE out and one AP - two charge threes an' one supercharge. Stand fast, make that two AP's an' supercharges. *Do not load.* Get your beds down. We've plenty of time for light 'earted conversation before kip.'

Cockney had a German self-lighting palm torch in his hand. By constant squeezing, the small dynamo inside the casing provided a faint beam of light. They were made by Phillips in Holland and were useful loot. He directed the beam as Dodger with Rayburn extracted the rounds and their charges from the limber.

James had unclipped the handspike, depressed the small pedal on the trail and now slipped it into the socket. He did not seriously expect their unseen opposition to come rolling down the track. But he was keeping his options open. The night was as black as the inside of a sweep's ear. Later on it might be different. If the cloud lifted, or dispersed there would be starlight.

Before entering the wadi earlier he had automatically checked the distance to the wadi mouth from the track. A hundred yards, not more than that. At the moment they could see about three feet. If they got starlight later that could vary from fifty to one hundred and fifty yards.

At Alamein even with the artificial moonlight created by searchlights on the clouds, it was still almost impossible to read.

Eye retinas retained muzzle flashes, sometimes for minutes. They might let them pass if they hadn't been spotted; that was chancy. He realised he had not too many options. If they engaged and were lucky they could knock one tank out with certainty at this range. Then, well then, they were blind and if there were three tanks, they were sitting ducks.

Could do with a welder's eyeshield for the layer. Or maybe we could use the Jerry grenades, and we've got mines, their own Tellers. He patted the handspike and turned to walk to the quad. His mind was now full of possibilities. Ideas came and went but under it all rested a confidence and optimism that had been absent. It could be done.

VII

The music of a gigantic orchestra pounded in the ears of the Hauptmann. Wagner - he recognised it instinctively. It flowed irresistibly through the whole of his being. The joy was unbearable. Inwardly relaxed he felt the familiar surge of invincibility sweep through his veins.

Peaked cap on the back of his head, eyes clamped to the turret ediscope, their future target slowly approaching. As targets went it was pathetic. Three British Bedford trucks, mud spattered and desert scarred, all three-tonners. They were led by a Marmon Herrington armoured car. The ice-blue eyes behind the lenses regarded them with contempt.

'Sergeant-Major, take the AFV. Let it pass you. Out.'

'*Ja, Herr Hauptmann*,' acknowledged the cool voice.

'Webber, let them come to us. Take the last truck.'

There would be two to three minutes yet. Come into my parlour, my friends. For you, *der Krieg ist kaput*.

In the Mark III Heinz chewed irritably on the stub of the small cigar. Let it pass you - who the hell does he think he is? Am I a fuckin' recruit on the range at Paderborn? Tell your Grandma how to suck eggs. Sometimes I think the Hauptmann thinks he's bloody Siegfried, riding into battle on a bloody great charger. This situation I do not like. We're not far enough south and west to play games.

His eye followed the armoured car. The bereted black head disappeared from the turret, the 50mm tracked slowly right. Heinz thought sourly that the Hauptmann needed his head examining. Three lousy trucks, probably carrying surplus gas capes, some ammunition and petrol and one bloody armoured car. We knock them out. Then what? We achieve exactly the opposite of what we were supposed to do.

Instead of stealth, anonymity, caution, we advertise. It did not make sense, who knew what was in the area? Could be a regiment of Sherman tanks leaguered up over the next hill. We could let them go, we're virtually invisible - they'd never know. The Hauptmann is a fine soldier, probably the best, but he scares me half to death, the bastard. Maybe he thinks he's God.

The Hauptmann held both hands fingers stretched in front of his eyes. Steady as a rock, the mark of a warrior, the scar along his temple pulsed red, livid in the fading light. The orchestra had ceased. The thought crossed his mind that it was only recently he had become aware; maybe the recurrent dream had something to do with that mighty music. Ah, the dream.

It was always the same. He led a thousand panzers that stretched to the three horizons. The *Pour Le Merite* and the Knight's Cross in Diamonds graced his impressive black uniform. In his hand, the baton. The wide avenue choked with the roars of 'Sieg Heil!' The banners, flags, admiring faces, stiff forests of saluting arms. The saluting dais, the Führer, all waiting - for him. Always the music, martial in the dream, military bands with the solid beat of marching boots.

Idly he watched the armoured car jinking around the camel humps. Ten o'clock, the trucks following in a rough triangle, the last one the apex. The analytical half of his brain summed up rapidly the plan of attack. Behind him the Maybach engine burbled contentedly. He looked through the ediscope towards the Mark III. Dimly he just saw the faint outline, almost invisible and detected no vapour from the exhaust. The orchestra began. His fingers stroked the livid scar. In his mind, back in the dark recesses a soft flickering glow burst into flames in the very core of his being.

It was a flame of doubt, of unease. The two halves of his brain in conflict. The music was taking over, seeping over the defensive dam. He conjured up the slogan, 'Clench your teeth and endure', the creed of the Hitler Jugend. He realised his own molars were grinding, grinding. Pictures of the 'Strength through Joy' camps, unlimited sex, nude bodies. Ilsa - their coming together had been that of the lion and the lioness. A clash of Titans, brutal and angry. The bed, a lair of ferocity, of rutting that satisfied only briefly.

During the tumult of thoughts and emotions two faces, those of his parents, gazed at him with surprise and horror. The icy half of his mind regarded them briefly, without regret. His casual betrayal had meant Officers training school. Weak vessels, both of them unfit to be a part of the *Herrenvolk*, the Master Race.

His brain commanded his mind to clear, a trickle of sweat rolled in a globule, reached the scar and ran along the depression in the skin. Behind that skin, within that skull a massive subdural haemorrhage pulsed and throbbed. The Hauptmann, a man of steel that now, was distinctly flawed. The exterior would look the same only the bubble in the brain would grow. Soon the iron will would be impotent. The splinter from a British shell lay somewhere near Arras. From the moment it carved a ridge in the skull of the Hauptmann the fuse had been lit. At any time that reservoir of rage would implode.

*

One o'clock, the angle was perfect. Heinz pressed the tit, the high turreted armoured car squarely in the centre of the serrated telescope sight. The gun bucked, tang of cordite fumes, essence of battle swirled in the turret. In the same instant the armoured car burst into flames and turret off, careered wildly with gouts of flames and smoke mushrooming from the wrecked superstructure. Ammunition was exploding rapidly accompanied by Very lights and the searing white hot fuel explosions. For a brief moment the armoured car was hidden; it came to a halt draped with curtains of fire, already the rubber of the tyres was ablaze, the thick black oily smoke a funeral pall.

Heinz had seen the hit, the tramline of tracer from the 50mm armour piercing shot as the armoured car was torn apart. He was, in that same instant lined up on the truck, the HE shell clunked in the sound smothered by the clang of the breech. His mouth a thin taut line he fired the HE. It was a hit but not a mortal one. The truck was still moving. The breech clanged shut, tap on the shoulder.

'Right! After the truck. Get movin'.' Stollenburg slid into the seat, the panzer lurched forward and in the direction of the errant vehicle. The Mark III sheered around the outcrop to attack from the flank. The last thing we want, thought Heinz, is for a truck to escape.

'Move!' he snapped.

Stollenburg accelerated. The truck, still being steered by frenzied hands suddenly turned right. Stollenburg stopped. Heinz was lined up; he fired. A sheet of flame billowed out as the petrol tank exploded. He heard the familiar chatter of the MG 34 as Stollenburg raked the truck. Heinz tapped him on the shoulder as he murmured:

'Cease fire!' Nothing moved in the mass of flames and black smoke that billowed slowly up. Stollenburg was back in the driver's seat, the Mark III turned in a half circle left. He clambered back behind the co-axial MG34, muttering to himself. He was feeling like a jackrabbit, up, down, up, down. He looked through the sights.

Webber's first round of 75mm HE had sent the last truck up in a balloon of white hot heat that was spectacular. He grinned, face illuminated briefly in the flare. His targets did not always provide such satisfaction or such immunity. His next round took out the second truck. It halted suddenly, the awkward bulk of it lit only by the dancing reflected flames of its companions.

A sharp command from Schmidt and the Mark IV ground forward and stopped twenty metres from the silent shape. The only movement, that of the flapping canopy cover, instantly a derelict.

Heinz noted without surprise that it was nearly dark. He felt a stab of apprehension as the Mark III turned to face the second truck. These flames could be seen for miles in this near darkness. He saw the the Hauptmann had slid down from the command panzer. Luger drawn, he was walking across the few metres separating victor and vanquished. Dimly, in the half light he thought he saw a movement.

Through his sights Stollenburg caught the same slight movement, near the rear wheel. His finger tightened on the trigger. The tall figure of the Hauptmann, arrogance in every line of his body, the executioner ready to put a bullet into the head of any survivor. And thought Stollenburg, he would enjoy it. The sights of the MG34 rested squarely on the Hauptmann's back. His figure in the line of sight. Was this the time? An unfortunate accident, trying to save the life of their leader. A tiny minute pressure, a pulse thumped in his neck, that was all; he would leave no more men to fry. His finger exerted the tiny pressure.

Heinz had been slightly surprised when the Hauptmann slid off the Mark IV. There was no valid reason unless - he felt disgust and knew there was only one reason: to shoot the survivors. Serve him right if - his question hung in mid air - the tall arrogant figure suddenly stopped, appeared to stretch momentarily, then crashed, like a riven oak to the ground. He was aware of the chatter of the machine gun; it had seemed simultaneous. The Mark IV joined in, the prone figure he could just make out close to the rear wheel jumped in convulsive agony. The swathe of bullets crucified him to the damp earth.

Heinz slid down the armoured steel and, pistol drawn, ran across the intervening few metres. He flung himself flat as the truck exploded, the wave of heat enveloped him, passed. He drew a deep breath. Kneeling beside the dead Hauptmann, he turned him over with an effort; it was like rolling a heavy log.

Herr Hauptmann Schmidt now had a third eye. Little good it would do him, in this world or the next. Hardened as he was to all the horrors of war, Heinz shuddered. Not at the neat circular hole directly in the centre of the forehead. Or the mass of blood-drenched grey cellular matter oozing like sago pudding, under the massive head.

It was the expression, frozen in a rictus of rage and terrible hate, he sought for a word, demoniacal and utterly evil. He remembered a phrase of Littner's: the evil face of Nazism. He closed the sightless eyes quickly. Better get this bastard six feet under. An inner flash of cynicism mocked him - get a stake too and drive it through his heart. Heart, the last thing this one had.

Kaput, Herr Hauptmann. Your unbelievable luck ran out, and for what? He felt no sorrow, a tinge of regret, perhaps, but that only because they were another man short. They would manage but it would be more difficult. Panzers did not have a five-man crew for fun. Every man in a crew had a job to do. Now we have five, one crew for two panzers. The thought crossed his mind to dump the Mark III, he dismissed it. He needed a better reason. Maybe he would be forced to, at some time, before they got back but not yet.

He took a quick glance around. The armoured car still blazed but the flames were subsiding. The filthy black smoke from the burning tyres swept an acrid stench that was stifling to his nostrils. He turned to find Webber and Braun beside him.

'Get a couple of shovels, you two. We'll bury the Hauptmann now.'

Webber nodded and they both went back to the hulking outline of the Mark IV. Heinz heard the Lancia drive up, the engine stopped. He signalled to Stollenburg to cut the engine. Scholz had already done so. The scene was macabre and like so many he had seen at Rezegh, the Cauldron and Alamein. The flickering flames of the burning trucks, the denseness of the smoke, the smell, the desolation. The red hot hull of the armoured car and their own elongated shadows. The crackling of exploding small arms ammunition sounded muffled, like the crackle of dry wood on a campfire. The half reflected glare bounced off the death's head insignia on the Hauptmann's collar. The battledress blouse of the dead Englishman reflecting the blood that still gleamed wetly in the dancing light.

Heinz walked over to the truck. The heat was still intense. He stopped ten yards away, looked at the body, drew himself up and saluted. You were a brave man Tommy and a bloody good shot. He turned away, in a few more minutes the truck would cremate the body when the superstructure collapsed.

Webber and Braun returned and started digging. After a few shovelfuls they hit rock. Stollenburg came over with a pick. He motioned curtly to the two shovellers to get out of the shallow trench. He had ignored the body. He attacked the rock layer with regular strokes of the pick stopping to lever the flat slabs up and toss them out. The powerful body of Stollenburg, muscled like a weight-lifter, carried out the task effortlessly and automatically. His mind occupied by one question. Had he killed the Hauptmann? He could not be sure.

He hoped he had; he could feel no guilt, just satisfaction. He would spit on his grave. So far consequences had not entered his thoughts. He levered up another slab nearly forty pounds in weight and tossed it out. He stepped up, the trench was still shallow, needed to go deeper. His breathing was even, untaxed. He lit a cigarette, took the first drag and turned to look at the body.

I knew it, he thought, when he saw the expression; he was fucking mad. Evil-looking bastard, and that's not my bullet through your skull, more's the pity. It'll have to do, Rheinhart; it's finished. Heinz came back from the Mark IV, in his hands a blanket belonging to their late and very dead commander.

Stollenburg went to help; they shook the blanket out. Heinz

taking the huge shoulders, Stollenburg the feet. They eased the body into the centre of the woollen shroud. Wrapped it around the corpse and covered the head.

Heinz got to his feet and lit a small cigar from the tin case he carried. Felt the soothing influence of the smoke ease the tautness, begin the relaxation. Well, that's that, he thought. Out of all the tons of red hot steel that had been flung at the Hauptmann, the thousands of bullets, all it took was one with your name on it. A little tinpot skirmish, if you could term it even that, a needless action in which the enemy only fired one round. We gained nothing, only a cadaver.

Angrily he kicked the ground as he walked away. Cigar clamped between his lips he started to think. The situation had changed. He was sure the armoured car, even had they been in radio contact, hadn't had a cat in hell's chance of reporting the attack. On the other hand the gunfire and the flames weren't exactly a secret. They could have been observed and correctly interpreted by stronger forces than those now under his command. My command! That's a laugh. Two panzers, one suspect truck and six men. I'll bet General Montgomery and the Eighth Army are worried. Ach, fuck it. The only question at the moment was whether to move or not.

The Hauptmann wouldn't have given it a thought. He would have pressed on seemingly oblivious to what might lie in front. But, I'm not the Hauptmann. I haven't that massive confidence, that colossal conceit. Mad? Nearly certain that he had been. But what a soldier, out of my class. He couldn't help feeling slightly inadequate.

Heinz had been in the Wehrmacht too long not to know the limit of his own capabilities. He was a competent soldier and used to command but without the flair or intellectual ability that might have seen him wearing officer's epaulettes. He could fight with the best of them. Was just as crafty, as artful and equally, if not more deadly. Always though, from above had come the orders. They may have been stupid, clever or just mediocre. But in nearly twenty-five years he had always obeyed.

Now he had to decide, that blanket-wrapped recumbent figure had given his last order. As he stood there idly watching the gravediggers his brain felt curiously sluggish. His normal active mind half asleep. Confusion to his enemies, now where the hell have I heard that saying? The answer eluded him. He was used to dealing in blacks and whites, relatively simple issues and using his initiative in strictly limited fields, backed up by the system. Two panzers, one truck. That was nothing; but it was very much something in a situation that, ten minutes before, had been crystal clear. Now and quite suddenly that clarity had become obscure. No manual he had ever read could provide a set of rules to follow.

It occurred to him rather belatedly that the Hauptmann had made it all sound too easy. Bash on at night, regardless. It had daring, verve and audacity. Six months, a year ago he knew he wouldn't have thought twice. Now the Hauptmann's intentions sounded bloody silly; they were still too far north. The time to press on at night was after they had covered another hundred and twenty kilometres further south. And avoid trouble. We don't want another repeat of this lot. He dismissed firmly the slight feeling of disloyalty that crept into his mind. He was now in command, the King was dead and - the afterthought came unbidden - we might all be better off. He walked over to the three toilers.

'Here,' he said to Webber, 'gimme that shovel.'

Webber handed it up to him and clambered up out of the trench. Heinz dropped in, spat on his hands and commenced digging. The exercise cleared his mind. He concentrated on the feel of the shovel as it bit and slid into the earth. He worked fast. The sweat dripped into his eyes, his hands started to feel the beginnings of a blister and his shoulders ached. He continued to dig until his shoulders were below the lip. Swinging himself up he dusted his hands and looked at Webber and Stollenburg.

'Okay, let's have him in.'

Webber and Braun walked over to the blanketed hump and gasping at the weight, carried it over. The trench was not wide enough or long enough for anyone to get in and still leave room for the corpse. At a signal from Heinz they swung the bundle and dropped it down horizontally. The solid thud set Braun's teeth on edge. Heinz stood back. They were all there, including Littner. He paused to gather his thoughts.

'Well, there's not much I can say. The Hauptmann had no religion. He was maybe the same as the rest of us. Anyway, there it is. If anyone wants to say a prayer for his soul, they're welcome.

You may not have liked the Hauptmann very much.' There was a muted murmur of agreement, he couldn't tell from how many. 'He was not a likable officer; he had no friends -- none that I know of -- so, rest in peace, Herr Hauptmann Schmidt, you were a good soldier.'

Heinz stepped back and motioned to Webber and Braun to fill in the grave. He took out the wallet that he had removed from the Hauptmann's pocket earlier. In the dying light of the flames he saw there were just three articles and a wad of Reichmarks. A Nazi party card and two photographs. One of a blonde girl in revealing negligee. Provocative and sensual beyond belief. The expression one of unquenched naked desire, built like an Amazon with rampant breasts, large erect nipples, inviting thighs and a pubic mound framed by the blonde bush. The sheer sensuality twitched his groin. Heinz had seen thousands of photographs of this type. But never one like this.

'Bloody hell.' The exclamation escaped unbidden from his lips. He bent closer to read the message written in a bold hand. 'Come and fuck me, Erich, again and again. Ilse.' On the reverse was an address in Berlin. Despite himself Heinz had an erection. He looked at the other photograph to take his mind off the sexual stirrings.

This showed a young dark-haired boy in the uniform of a paratrooper. On the back, in pencil, a short message. Heinz strained his eyes to read it. 'Dear Uncle, Am now in desert with 90th Light. Respectfully, your nephew, Karl Schwarze.' He slid the card and photographs back in the wallet.

Littner came over with a roughly fashioned and wired wooden cross. Webber wrote the simple information: '*Hauptmann Erich Schmidt. KIA Nov. 1942.*' Stollenburg volunteered to put the cross in. The others moved away and gathered around the sergeant-major at the Mark IV. Stollenburg knocked in the cross with a tank crowbar, turned with his back to the others and deliberately spat on the grave. He took a swig from the bottle of rum, swallowed it gratefully, grinned and in a flat hate-filled vicious snarl, said.

'Roast in hell, fuckin' Nazi pig. Fry, you bastard, fry.'

'Stollenburg!' Heinz shouted. He turned and walked to the group. 'Did you get the cross in?' Heinz enquired.

'*Ja,* Sergeant-Major.'

'Took you long enough.'

'Just saying a prayer for the dear Hauptmann, Sergeant-Major,' Stollenburg replied in an unctuous tone.

He passed the rum bottle to Heinz. Someone stifled a giggle. Heinz took a swig, passed it to Webber.

'Right, Webber, you're in charge of the Mark IV. Braun, double up as loader. You'll lead -- 185 degrees -- we should hit a track soon. Littner will follow me. Our objective has been slightly changed now.' There was an audible sigh of relief from the shadowy figures around him, he went on:

'Slightly. We move out from this lot maybe a couple of miles. Tomorrow we move off at first light. One man on guard.'

The voice of Scholz broke in.

'Sergeant-Major, sir,' Heinz stopped what he had been about to say and cocked an attentive ear.

'Some work on the engine, Sergeant-Major. Got to do it, ignition and the *Feifel*, the air cleaner, sir.' Scholz had got it all out in a rush. He couldn't help but look uneasy.

'How long?' The question was calm.

Scholz blamed himself. The big twelve cylinder Maybach had been spitting; he had felt the loss of power. He had also been aware that the Hauptmann could have hauled him over the coals for his dereliction of duty. He had, as he was sure most of them had, been scared shitless by the terrifying Hauptmann. One of the side effects of this dread was a reluctance to report that anything was wrong with the panzer. He was blamed anyway.

'Three hours - maybe more? Can't really tell until I take a look, sir.'

Heinz regarded him for a moment.

'Okay, you've got till morning. In the meantime break out some grub. We'll have a meal. Another fire doesn't matter and we'll hear anything that comes before they see us.' His mind felt clear. Already the Hauptmann was half forgotten. Something else occurred to him as he stood there.

'Littner, how's the truck? Will it start?'

The thin face, eyes hidden behind the steel framed spectacles, turned to him. The cultured tones answered defensively:

'This morning, sir, we had to tow it. The battery is very low. Sir, shall I -?'

'No.' His eyes fell on Stollenburg. 'I want it towed over here.'

Heinz walked forward and indicated where he wanted the truck and the Mark III.

'Get the tarpaulin off it and stretch it over - like a workshop, Scholz. Inspection lamp?' He caught the nod of agreement and carried on.

'Stollenburg, you help Scholz. Littner and Webber, you're the cooks. Braun, how's the big radio?'

'*Kaput*, Sergeant Major. Needs a new part. Intercomm and tank to tank, okay, but -.' He shrugged his shoulders.

Heinz nodded. Braun knew his job, if he said a set was *kaput*, it was.

'Right, let's get organised. Truck first. All of you give a hand with the cover.'

The Maybach of the Mark III burst into life. Ten minutes later the three vehicles were in a tight little group, the Mark IV facing south-west, the radiator of the Lancia ten feet away from the rear, the Mark III backed up facing south-east. The large canopy cover draped to floor level. Scholz had the inspection bulb lit and his toolbox open and ready to start. They sweated as they removed a length of track off the engine cover. Webber and Littner had the two small stoves going and nostrils twitched as the stew got under way.

Heinz swung himself up and inside the turret. The dim light inside was sufficient for his purpose. He opened the mapcase and studied the meagre information. He traced the route they would follow. About twenty-five miles, or forty kilometres ahead, the ground rose on both sides, a gap in the escarpment. It looked like a valley. More likely to be a fairly wide wadi. Past the gap was more broken country, wadis and ravines, places to hide. Further south the going improved. That was the target; then they could turn west. Satisfied he replaced the case. Coming up through the cupola the smell of the cooking food reminded him that he was hungry.

'Grub up,' Webber called.

The flap of the cover faced west, the direction of least danger. One by one they ducked in with the variety of mess tins and tin plates they individually preferred. Webber shared it out. It was good, Italian veal, sausages, tinned vegetables and potatoes laced with tomato puree and split peas. They sat on the ground wolfing the hot food and drinking the ersatz coffee. Tastes, like always, thought Webber, like bloody acorns. The black bread helped to fill their stomachs.

The atmosphere was relaxed, in some way subtly different. Each had their own thoughts, none had discussed the recent loss of their commander, yet it seemed that something, unseen but dark and terrible had gone. They had all felt it. As though they had been unwilling passengers on a runaway juggernaut, helpless, puppets of events controlled by one man. Twigs in a stream whose current whirled them down to a river.

That rapid current was there no longer. A beaver called Heinz had replaced the dam. From now, the twigs would march in orderly fashion. Somehow confidence had, for the moment, returned and a joint hope that they would, in time, reach a safe harbour.

Scholz cleaned his eating irons in the sand, packed them into the locker and looked around for Stollenburg. Braun joined him.

'He's gone for a piss.' Answering his unspoken query: 'I'll give you a hand, nothing else to do.'

Scholz grunted his thanks. Between them they got the engine covers off. Heinz and the others had gone. The flap parted and Stollenburg ducked in carrying two five-gallon drums of oil and a stout three feet by one wooden board.

'Need something to stand on,' he explained. They worked steadily, fell easily into a team intent on their particular tasks. Braun was there more as a link to pass the required tools. The other two were the experts. Conversation was minimal as they worked. The big Feifel filter was finally persuaded to disgorge a mixture that was more mud than sand. It was heavy and took three of them to handle it. Stollenburg had the plugs out, cleaned them all with a wire brush and set the gaps.

The tarpaulin rustled and Webber slid his way in.

'How's it going?' he asked cheerfully.

'Not bad,' replied Scholz. 'I shan't be far out, about three and a half hours. Been a bit of a cow, so far.' He glanced at his watch. 'Been at it for over two hours. Time for a break - got a fag?' He wiped his hands on a piece of waste.

Webber obligingly took a tin of captured Players cigarettes from his overall pocket. He lit three and passed them over, then lit one for himself. Gratefully they sucked smoke into their lungs. It was warm in the improvised canvas tent. For a few moments they sat silently enjoying the British cigarettes. Scholz was the first to break the silence.

'Must admit it shook me, you know, when the Hauptmann copped that bullet. Was bound to happen, I suppose, sooner or later.' He shook his head dolefully before he went on,

'But in a silly farting tin pot effort like that. Just shows, my wife always says that, you never know.'

'Bloody good job we don't,' said Webber drily. 'If we did, we'd never move out of a foxhole. Ach! His luck ran out. It only takes one to kill you. He was living on borrowed time, from the first minute he got in a fucking panzer. He was a mad bastard though,' he said admiringly. 'Mind you, he didn't give a fuck for his crew; self first, last and always. Maybe,' he added, 'we might be better off with Old Fifty-Seven?'

'Maybe, you could be right,' agreed Scholz. 'One thing about him, he doesn't go looking for trouble. More cautious, if you see what I mean. Course,' he said, a little smugly, 'we're all the same, us married men with families. We think about them but, in action, well, we're there, just like you single blokes.'

Webber nodded in sympathy. Braun smiled, it was more a sickly grin. He had been shocked by the sudden demise of the Hauptmann then reassured by the change in plans outlined by Heinz. But he felt, still too near the surface of his mind, that undercurrent of panic. The thought of what they might meet.

It was all right planning, he thought, if you knew what you were planning for. Out of the lot of them no one had any idea. Even Heinz would be whistling in the dark. They were out of touch with events, with information as scarce as snow in the Congo. As the radio expert, Braun regularly listened to the BBC and compared the news with Herr Doktor Goebbels' version, then made up his own mind. He was far better informed, hence, far more worried.

Wherever he had been Braun had acquired a certain unique reputation in the troop, squadron and in the battalion. All at ground level. The surreptitious act of imparting fairly accurate information was not for officers. Officers could believe what they liked, the men had changed since those early 1941 days. Probably because they had more downs than ups. Morale was like elastic, too much stretching and it broke. Ground into them like the sand they rode over was a hard shall of sardonic cynicism. They all had it to a greater or lesser degree.

Braun felt trapped in a web that grew ever tighter. The forlorn hope that he would be able to desert seemed pathetic to him now. One couldn't desert in a jumble of smashed and burnt out vehicles with only the dead left to surrender to. The only thing left, was to wait and that was hard. But he had to. Wait for the opportunity to get out and that wasn't when the odds were stacked against them. That would be suicide. The change of plan, the caution of Heinz, more sensible to the others, complicated and added to his own hopes and difficulties. The conversation between Scholz and Webber flowed over and around him without touching, even scratching the surface of his mind. He moved over to help the two drivers reassembling the Feifel.

Scholz was talking again, about his family. Webber interrupted him deftly and regaled all and sundry with the lurid details of a night spent in Tripoli. Scholz listened despite his natural reservations, unwillingly at first, began to chuckle at Webber's vivid description of a dusky Italian wench. His fingers were busy, screwing and tightening screws and bolts but his mind was fantasising. A picture of smooth brown skin, jutting breasts and eager loins. For once Helga was forgotten. The wantonness of his thoughts and desires at this moment made him envious of Webber. Jealous of him being able to enjoy, in the flesh, what he had only known in dreams.

Helga, the kids, the ties of home and his deep love for all that, always made him feel ashamed of lustful unrestrained desires that culminated in wet dreams, afterwards. Now at this moment and feeling as he did, faced with the reality of his thoughts, he knew what would have happened, given the chance. A thought struck him.

'How many women d'y reckon you've had, Deadeye?'

He waited, slightly awed by his own frankness, halted his busy fingers, his lower lip trembled and his eyes shone. Stollenburg grinned silently. Even Braun started to take notice. There was an air of expectancy. Webber and his women were notorious in the regiment. The scene seemed to invite secrets, warm, lit and with just the four of them, just four men with similar hopes, desires and starved of feminine company. The titbit that Webber had revealed had whetted appetites yet normally Webber was taciturn. It was unusual to find him so expansive. Maybe he just felt the need to talk or was talking to prevent Scholz.

His blue-visaged countenance looked swarthy in the reflected light from the caged bulb.

Smiling lazily he looked like a Spanish gypsy, he was starting to enjoy the situation. Actually relishing it and come to think of it, no one had ever asked before. Not directly, more casual enquiries to which he had replied with hints and an odd suggestive innuendo. Why not? Tomorrow, if they lived that long, was only a few hours away. Give them all something to smile about, lift their spirits. They could all die laughing. The names and faces he shuffled in his mind like a pack of decorated playing cards.

'Hard to say,' Webber said deadpan. 'Twenty, fifty, a hundred. Who knows? The times I've nipped out of bedroom windows, down drain pipes, catching my boots and trousers thrown after me. And the fathers - whee! Four times I can remember sprinting like hell and beating the shotgun pellets. Once I got a dozen in my rump. Had to get one of my mates, picked them out with tweezers, missed my wedding tackle though.' He paused for a moment letting the memories flow, the faces and bodies appearing like developing photographs.

'Let's see, there was the first. You never forget the first. And if she's a virgin, man, she never forgets you, even after she's married. They can never refuse you, see. The first one in gets a permanent pass.

'Marlene? - Berlin, blonde, buxom; she nearly bit me to death - I've still got the scars - couldn't straighten my back for a couple of days. I was new at it, hadn't had the practice. I daren't even sneeze, it was agony. The next - let's see - it was Hilde in Dresden. She was small and dark, lovely eyes, ah, lips like cherries and perfect teeth. I loved her, true.'

He looked at them, the growing smirks disappeared, his face was serious.

'Not for her body. Just, well, she had a beauty that was perfect, but, she was a cripple, and she wanted me to - I'm a callous bastard, I know - fuck anything with a hole in it. But it wasn't like that with Hilde. It was pure and lovely. I would have married her. Still, water under the bridge.'

'Why didn't you?' asked Scholz, softly.

Webber looked at him, gypsy eyes soft. 'She died - bastards

took her away. She was a Jew. Someday, someday, I'll - anyway, it's over.' He lit a cigarette, rubbed the smoke from his eyes, gave a grin.

'Now Paula, that was in Munich, she was an actress. No acting with me though. No, sir. She had a flat. I lived like a lord. All free. Ah, they were happy days. Then, when we started, when we went into Austria, there were two sisters. They were both blondes, built like - not Venus, no they were more - Junoesque. They were all for Strength through Joy. We all got the joy - but I lost my strength. They rolled me between 'em like pastry, broke the bed.'

There was a gurgle of laughter, Webber smiled.

'I had a farmer's daughter on the Polish border - that was short - called her Wanda. But it was - sort of special. And after all, well, there's just too many to count. In France, Paris, boy! the women there, they eat you. True!' He paused and whistled slowly, his bright animal eyes mocking Scholz, before continuing.

'Italy, what a time I had. The Signorinas. All the men must have been in Africa. I tell you. They were queuing for it. Sicily too. The further south you get, the more passionate the women. I could kick myself over the ones I missed. I mean, you're only here once, should make the most of it, you're a long time dead. Come to think of it, I could just do with a chance to get the dirty water off my chest - preferably dark, sloe-eyed, big-titted and tight arsed. It doesn't matter whether she speaks the tongue of the Fatherland. My language is universal.'

He lounged back comfortably against one of the bedding rolls they had chucked off. Watched them work. None of the three knew whether to believe him or not. He knew from the expression of the silent Stollenburg that he was the sort who wouldn't believe the sun would rise, until he saw it. Braun was only half here, too preoccupied with his own problems. But Scholz had drunk in every word. Some of what Webber had related was true, some was fiction.

Scholz looked up from his task for a moment. He wore a puzzled expression. His total experience was limited to Helga. He knew how it had been for them in their courting days. Plenty of kissing, plenty of squeezing but hands off the rest. Until their wedding night.

'How,' he asked Webber, 'how did you manage to have all

those women, and still stay single? It beats me.'

Webber laughed. 'Find 'em, fuck 'em, and leave 'em - the soldier's farewell. Never fails. They want it more than you do - well, more times, anyway.'

Scholz gave a small embarrassed grin and resumed his work. He was still thinking, unwilling to let it go. His voice came again.

'I'll bet you'd have been all right, if we'd have got to Cairo. You know, belly dancers, mixed races. They say you can't beat 'em for looks.'

Webber gave a sardonic laugh. 'If, *if* we'd have got to Cairo, he says. My dear Scholz, how the fucking hell do you think we'd have got there?'

Scholz was taken aback by the sudden change in direction. Braun woke up. Stollenburg paid him the compliment of turning to look.

Braun said, pleased at the question, because it hinted at criticism and he sensed a possible ally. 'Well, we nearly got there,' paused, then flew his kite, 'all we needed was a few - a few more - ' He let his voice trail away, and waited.

Webber's tone was cutting.

'A few more - Christ! A few more what? Panzers, guns, planes, rations, water, petrol, transport. Oh sure, we needed all those - and a lot less miles behind us.' Now he had their full attention. Suddenly he felt reckless. Even the chance that Heinz might hear him seemed unimportant. The flap of the cover lifted and a figure ducked in. It was Littner. Bodies that had tensed, relaxed. Stollenburg said.

'Where's Old Fifty-Seven?'

'Examining the wreckage and digging a latrine,' Littner answered in his precise manner. Eyes turned back to Webber. Stollenburg said. 'Go on, Deadeye, tell us where we went wrong. It'll be a change from Signal and, who knows, all of us might learn a bit.' It was the first time any of them had heard a complete sentence from him, and his tone was not exactly discouraging. Webber went on as if the interruption had never happened.

'Once we'd left Matruh, even with all the captured stuff, we'd had it. Just the same as on the Ostfront. You mark my words. Ivan 'ull be back, just the same as the Tommies came back. They'll have more gear. We'll get the shitty end of the stick there, just as we've had it here.

'Tell me Scholz, or any of you, have we ever put down fire like that constant barrage at Alamein? Of course we haven't. We never will. They've always relied too much on these babies.'

He slapped the side of the Mark IV then continued in the same calm flat voice devoid of emotion. All his voice betrayed was an accepted cynicism; he was not even trying to persuade them.

'They've always thought that these - the panzers - were the answer. But they aren't. If there is any answer, it's guns. It doesn't matter whether they're towed, self-propelled or in a panzer. It's guns that count. You can build the biggest panzer with the heaviest armour. It doesn't get you very far if the other side produce a gun of larger calibre, greater range and a higher muzzle velocity, whose shells go through your armour like butter.'

He dragged deeply on his cigarette, removed a shred of tobacco from his tongue, gave a wicked grin.

'So, you see, my friends, it gets you nowhere. Well sited guns. Guns with muzzle velocities of over six thousand feet per second will always be the masters in any armoured battle.

'Yeah, the gun is king. We don't really need tanks - just need low down tracked transport, recoilless guns on hydraulic platforms, hollow charge shells and air observation - air OP's. I reckon people like us could invent and design exactly what I'm talking about - better than those cretins in Berlin anyway.'

Scholz and Braun by this time were looking a bit stunned. Stollenburg was enjoying it all. Webber had put into words many of the things he was incapable of expressing. Littner had listened with quiet satisfaction. Seeds were growing; it was reward enough that other people had begun to question.

'But,' Webber went on, 'why go on? I'm no intellectual like our Herr Professor here. We all saw what happened in the last few weeks. The Tommies caught on. They still can't handle panzers like our lot, but they're learning fast, got better equipment - six and seventeen pounder anti-tank guns - and they'll get even better. Wait until we meet the Yanks. They've got kit running out of their ears. When you think back to Alamein, Christ, I've never seen our blokes so low. Just like old Braun here - scared shitless. Give him a chance and, boosh! he'd be in Cairo tomorrow - as a bloody POW - and I can't say I blame him.'

He smiled at the embarrassed expression on Braun's face and knew that his shot in the dark had landed right on target. He felt the same kind of satisfaction as when he had scored a hit on one of the 'Tommy Cookers', the new Sherman tank.

'You what?' Braun queried. 'I didn't hear you, I was thinking, here, if you think I want to be a bloody prisoner, you've got another think coming.' His voice was heated with fervent denial.

'Come off it, Brauny boy,' Webber's tone was gently disbelieving. 'We're all friends here. You can trust us. Nobody's going to split. Anyway, it won't make any difference - we'll all be in the bag in a couple of days. That is, if we're not six feet under, like the bloody *Hauptmann*'

'Why?' Scholz said in an alarmed tone. 'Don't you think we're going to make it?'

'Make it?' Webber really held the centre stage, they were hanging on his words. 'Come to, Scholz, where've you been for the last three days? Asleep? If we get twenty miles without anyone spotting us, I'm a fucking Dutchman. We'll be lucky,' he said sardonically. 'They didn't all go up the coast road, y'know. I'll bet there's an armoured brigade, if not a division somewhere in front. We can't get far enough south to miss 'em. In a few more miles we've got to head west for the good going. That's when the fun 'ull start. I'll bet all my back pay on that. For us, it'll be *kaput*.'

Braun, watching Webber's face and listening closely, now tried to define exactly what Webber's attitude would be in the future. An uncertain future that from Webber's description, now seemed blacker than ever.

'I don't get you, Deadeye,' he said curiously. 'You sit there, calmly tell us we haven't a chance, which incidentally is my own opinion, I agree with you, but then, perhaps I'm different, I want to get home, in one piece if possible. But you - you're just the opposite, you don't give a fuck. You're not bothered, even concerned, about the prospects. You take it all as it comes. You even look as though you enjoy it. So, what about you? Are you going to pack it in? Try to escape?'

Webber said dryly, 'No, not me. Don't get me wrong. I didn't say I'd stopped fighting. Far from it. I shall be firing this baby as long as I'm in one piece. But it doesn't stop me thinking, or facing facts. Come to think of it, our friend the Herr Professor might just have got it right. We're all suckers. But,' he went on, 'first of all, right or wrong, we're all Germans. I'll take my chances with Old Fifty-Seven. Can't really see myself as a prisoner. Anyway, if I get knocked off on this little jaunt, what's the difference - here, Italy or trying to stop Ivan. I'm easy. Come to think of it, we might even run across a Bedouin caravan. Might even get myself a bint, you know, with the tattoos and the yashmak.'

He flashed a sarcastic grin at the others and rubbed his groin suggestively, closed his eyes in simulated ecstasy. Scholz looked across at Braun in bewilderment. As he worked his mind was trying to come to terms with Webber's philosophy and finding it difficult.

Braun passed a spanner, tightened another screw and wondered. Not at the content of Webber's spiel but surprised it had been the gunner who had voiced it. If what Webber had said was a true reflection of his feelings then his attitude was illogical. At least to Braun. He could have enlarged considerably and backed it all up with facts and history, opinions and views, but the last thing he wanted, was to be the focus of attention. Leave that to Littner or, at the moment, Webber.

Scholz, now that was different, he felt sympathy there and if anything, Scholz had even more reason for trying to stay alive, get back, eventually to his family. With two of us in the same mind, we could work something out. Let the Webbers fight to the last round. The war had been *kaput* since June '41. Maybe they would have had to fight Russia at some time but in '41, the only fly in the ointment was the Brits. Russia could have waited. They should have got them out of the way first. Then this lot in the desert would have withered on the vine. India would have packed in and South Africa were closer to Germans than English. June '41 was suicide for the Reich. Now the writing was on the wall and it was ten feet high.

Stollenburg and Littner had gone outside. Webber had his eyes closed. Scholz looked meaningly at Braun and tapped his forehead. Braun shook his head. No he didn't think Webber had a screw loose. He had only put into words what most of them must be thinking. Scholz fastened down the covers of the engine and packed his tools away. He ducked out and went to find

Heinz.

Heinz had not meant to but had been unable to ignore part of the conversation on his return to the Mark III. He was not too surprised. It took a lot to shock or surprise him. Even the ragged tear of bullet holes almost invisible across the broad black overall covered back of the Hauptmann. It was not new in his experience. The Western Front, Spain, and here, it happened. The hole in the forehead just made it easier. He knew why and felt the relief of not having to ask questions of someone whom by now he considered a friend.

So the conversation provided nothing new although it was a change to find that Littner was not the instigator. It was in some ways an advantage to know what men were thinking and even better that they articulated those thoughts. Out here of course. Back home they would be shot. Back home - it wasn't often he could afford the luxury of thinking about it.

Gaby and the children flitted through his thoughts in brief flashes, sometimes, nearly always at inconvenient moments.

The wider picture, since 1933, he tried to ignore. They were not the sort of memories he unlocked the gate of his mind for. For those years he had kept his head down, bent like the bamboos under the wind of change that had transformed Germany.

Duty and Honour; he had followed the creed. But the meaning of the words had changed. It reminded him of a saying, something about liberty. Give me Liberty or give me death. No, that wasn't it. He thought for a moment. Liberty oh, what crimes are committed in thy name. Duty and Honour - same thing.

The most difficult time for Heinz had been when he and Gaby had realised they could no longer really talk. Hans and Karl were both in the Hitler Jugend, Rudy and Berta already wide-eyed devotees in the school version. When they talked, they talked outside.

Out of the minds of babes. They both remembered that, always. In the Third Reich it paid to be ultra careful, a word from a child was enough for the Gestapo. Their exchange of letters were models of loyalty to the Führer. Survive until the iron grip relaxed, if it ever did.

'Sergeant-Major.' He realised it was Scholz.

'Ready to start up, sir. To test.'

'Right,' he replied. 'Go ahead.'

Heinz called to the others to remove the tarpaulin and stow it away in the truck. Five minutes later they were packed and ready to move. The engines burst into life with the deep throated roar so familiar to them all. The Lancia, towed by the Mark III and led by the Mark IV, nosed its way south into the darkness. Fifteen minutes later, having covered two miles they halted, nose to tail. Silence reigned as the engines deep throb ceased.

Scholz and Braun slid out of the front hatches. Webber out of the cupola. Scholz tripped and swore as he landed, a misjudgement in the inky blackness. Braun was more careful sliding slowly to the ground.

'Think I'll take a leak.' Braun's voice was loud enough for the others to hear.

'Me too,' said Scholz.

They walked off together counting the strides. Fifty paces on they stopped and relieved themselves. Night vision was returning. By common consent they squatted to face the tank. From this distance it showed dimly as a hump of more solid grotesqueness. Faintly they could make out the Mark III and the Lancia. Braun turned to face the dim features of Scholz. He commenced to speak in a whisper.

'You're the family man, Scholz, aren't you?'

'I am, proud of it too. But what are you getting at?'

'Well, you want to see them again. No matter how long it takes, don't you?'

'Of course, that's obvious. Mind you, the sooner the better, Helga will just - '

'Yes, I know,' Braun broke in quickly. 'Look, I've been thinking this over since last night. I want to get home too, in one piece. How about it?'

Scholz pondered for a moment.

'So, Webber was right, hein? You want to give yourself up?'

Braun's whisper was urgent, pleading, he hoped he was right about Scholz.

'It's the only sensible thing left to do. Of course Webber was right, though how he guessed I'll never know. I can't work him out. D'y know him well?'

'No,' Scholz whispered. 'I'm the same as you. The panzer gets knocked out, I'm told to get my gear over to the

Hauptmann's tank. Webber's a stranger really, never worked with him before. He's been with the Hauptmann for over a year, like Stollenburg with Heinz. He's a bit weird, unpredictable. Maybe he had more in common with the Hauptmann. Anyway, tell me, have you got any ideas, about giving yourself up?' Scholz was unable to utter the term, desert. Giving up didn't sound anything like as bad.

'I mean, how're you going to do it?'

'Well,' Braun said slowly.' It all depends, on what happens, after we get going tomorrow. It's all a bit hit and miss. First, we've got to meet up with the Tommies. It all comes down to that. If we don't, then we scrub it. Anyway, if we lead, it might make it easier when we see them. I could wave a towel out of the turret, reverse the gun. If Webber cuts up rough, well, I'll have to take care of him. You know, a tap on the head with a spanner. It'll be for his own good as well as ours. You can stop the panzer when we get near enough. Then we can walk over. We'd have to put on a burst of speed when we see 'em. It's not really a plan. We'll have to react to the circumstances, seize the chance. It's better than dying. I think we should manage. What do you think?'

'Sounds all right,' Scholz said. His voice held a quiver of doubt under the hope, his thoughts jumping the gun, already accepting the future life of a prisoner.

'What about the Lancia?'

Braun grinned in the gloom. 'Littner? Don't worry about Littner. He'll have his own ideas, and he'll keep his head down.'

Scholz came to a decision. 'Right! I'm with you. We'll just have to play it by ear. And you - don't forget Webber.'

'Never fear, he's priority when it comes. Mind, not a word, right? Let's get back.'

Braun held out his hand, they gripped firmly. Rising to their feet they walked back to the little leaguer, Scholz talking about his family, Braun passing the appropriate murmurs of agreement.

He felt calmer for having confided in Scholz. Even though the intended action tomorrow was sketchy and uncertain. A decision had been taken. Now it remained in the lap of the gods.

Heaving himself up on to the panzer he reached down inside the turret to take the commander's Schmeisser machine pistol.

'I'll stand first watch,' he said briefly to Scholz.

Scholz grunted his agreement and climbed back into their travelling home. Webber was curled on the floor of the turret on the loader's side with a blanket wrapped loosely around his body. His eyelids flickered for a brief instant as the figure of Scholz passed. His mouth twitched for a fleeting second then, once again was firm and almost cruel. The mouth of a fighter, relaxing.

VIII

James leaned against the gunshield and watched the sky to the north. Not that he could see much further than his nose. It wasn't quite the stygian black of a coal cellar but it was trying its best. The last four hours had been nostalgic and at times wildly funny. A flood of reminiscences, mostly from Wells and Green assisted by Chalky and Rayburn, was the reason.

When the duo of Cockney and Dodger really got into their stride depression and apprehension faded into insignificance, they cocked a snook at anything and everybody. Laughter had taken the place of gloom. James had been relieved to hear it. A sense of humour was essential in this empty land. Without it you were lost. To laugh was to renew your faith in yourself and your comrades. It belittled your fears, raised your hopes and boosted confidence that was beginning to slip away. Laughter was a tonic that needed no bottle to contain it. The crew were coming back to normal.

James had to admit he was not wildly happy. Experienced as he was, the strain of the past twenty-four hours and what might happen tomorrow, were putting pressures on him that were new. They were all used to it, conditioned. None of them welcomed or liked it. It was just desert life. He missed the organisation of the troop, probably more than they did.

Here and now, he had to make the decisions - all of them. So far and until they rejoined the troop they would be decisions of a different type, to the normal pattern expected of him in the troop. Up till now, he hoped he had been right. Later, if they survived he knew he would be questioning, thinking and remembering. James was feeling the loneliness of command and he didn't particularly like it.

The cool breeze from the north laid light fingers on his face. Suddenly, he heard it. The sound of a powerful engine breaking into life and immediately followed by a second. Sound in the desert at night travelled incredible distances, he reminded himself, and the breeze helped it along. A short while ago he had heard heavy guns from the north-west. Probably the fleet and that could be over sixty miles away. The initial blips of acceleration merged into a deeper throb, now much fainter. There was suddenly the close proximity of bodies around him. Two or three minutes later, borne on the breeze, across the vast silence of the desert they heard the throb and whine of engines in low gear.

'Load the HE!' James ordered.

The thunk of the driving band of the shell, the clang of closing breech settled his thoughts. This looked as though, very soon, some of his questions were going to be answered.

'Get the Teller mines out and the detonators.'

Vague darker shadows moved to the back of the truck. Rayburn put two mines at his feet. Soon he had the eight from the box. Two of the self-lighting hand torches played beams of light on the black round shapes. James put the detonators in each, straightened up.

'Just a precaution. If they come any further, we need all the help we can get. Let's have those grenades out.'

Eighteen potato masher grenades were swiftly added to the lethal pile at James's feet.

'Right,' came the crisp voice, 'pay attention. I think we've plenty of time, that is, if they come. I think we all know now. Two panzers. If the worst comes to the worst, we have enough here to give 'em a hot reception - if we do it right. The mines we can lay across the track. Rayburn and Bell, you'll be with me on the gun. I'll lay. Cockney, Dodger and Chalky, you'll be out there with the grenades. Up on the tank from the rear, pull the string, drop it down the turret, two if you can manage it. You three are the fastest, you can also lay the mines.

'I'll be ready 'ere. Soon as I see one, I'll open up. That's about it. Just 'ope it doesn't 'appen. We'll keep listenin'.'

They remained in a group lighting cigarettes from the others' glowing butts and cupping them in half-closed hands, backs to the potential threat and all listening hard. For what seemed hours but in reality was fifteen minutes, they heard the rise and fall of sound that betrayed the levels and drops the panzers were moving over. Finally the throbbing died then stopped.

'Leagured,' breathed James. 'Make safe!'

Cockney flipped the safety catch to safe on the firing mechanism. He let go a long sigh of relief.

'Phew - hit the top of me 'ead, someone . Get me 'eart back in its proper place. What about the mines, Sarge?'

James looked at his watch. 'Leave 'em - just in case - ummm, another 'alf 'our and' I'll get me 'ead down. Muscles, you're next, then Dodger, Chalky, Bell, then Wells. We're not 'anging about in the mornin'. Soon as we can see, we're off - no brew.' He commenced his lazy stroll around the gun and the two vehicles the Tommy gun slung over his shoulder. The rest moved back to their bedding rolls.

He eased the Tommy gun on to his lap as he sat down on the gunlayer's polished circular wooden seat. For now, he thought, I can rule out a night attack. The desert was a big place. Only those that lived in it knew how big. The panzers would follow the track had they continued. That was safest. Have to get out of their way in the morning.

He tried to put himself in the position of the commander of the two tanks. It was odds on he was trying to go south and then west. The panzer's range, he guessed, was about a hundred miles. They could not carry enough fuel for much more than that. They had to have a truck with them. Agheila was a long way. His mind was working smoothly as he sat. He hadn't solved any riddles, reached any brilliant conclusion to the problems that might, almost certainly, lie ahead. But the thoughts had clarified his mind and in some way, lifted his spirits.

He looked at his watch again. It was time. Getting up, he moved over to the quad. Rayburn loomed up in front of him. The sheer bulk of the man suggested confidence. It occurred to him that the night seemed lighter; he glanced overhead, the clouds were breaking slowly.

Rayburn said, 'Okay, Sarge?'

James handed him the watch. 'Yeah, you're on. If you 'ear anythin' particularly tank engines, wake me, even if it's a false alarm. Got it?'

'Yes, Sarge.'

James walked over to his rolled-out bedding. Going to be a long night, brain too active. He slopped off his boots, slid down beneath the blankets, pulled one over his head. In less than five minutes he was asleep.

The night wore on; it got colder as the clouds lifted and faint starlight cast its faint glow over the land. Bell came to as Chalky gripped his shoulder and uncurled from the comforting foetal ball his mind and body had adopted. He slipped boots on, jammed forage cap over lank hair, got up and took the rifle from Chalky.

The dream had vanished. So had the comfort of his mother's breast and the support of her arms. He was aware immediately of his acute physical discomfort. It was too much. There was only one way out. His mind mocked him. The coward's way. Other voices clamoured in his mind. Taunting, sarcastic and pitiless. His sheltered upbringing had not prepared him for this. He would be an outcast and the details entered in his paybook, on his army record. Contracted venereal disease 1942. Type: Syphilis.

The word horrified him, gnawed at his sanity; his brain had branched out from the word. Blindness, paralysis, tertiary insanity. You can't marry. Any children could be affected, born imbecilic. He wandered over and sat in the passenger seat of the truck. Lit a cigarette, drew the smoke in. This would be the last. He hoped his mother and father, Lily - yes Lily - just forgive me. He slipped out of the seat, stood for a moment his mind made up. He walked over to the gun, slipped his right boot off, sat down, removed the sock, opened the bolt of the rifle, slipped a round into the chamber. Right, he was ready.

Now he lowered himself to the ground under the muzzle of Kelly. He felt calm, almost relaxed, looked up from under the recuperator saw the slightly flared muzzle. A few stars just visible. The steel of the rifle barrel cold and metallic to his tongue, gripped the barrel of the rifle with his left hand, felt for the trigger guard as his right hand steadied the length of it. His big toe found the guard. He closed his eyes. The searing shock of pain as the foresight ripped his lip coincided with strong hands wrenching the rifle from his grip.

'You bloody idiot!' The epithet was whispered bitingly; he had never heard such venom in a whisper. He struggled to his feet. Sobbing, he said:

'Why? Why didn't you let me do it?' He saw now that it was Cockney. He lunged for the rifle. Cockney put off his little boy rush with contemptuous ease then slapped him quickly, twice across his face. The slaps were light, tremendously fast. They stung the cheeks of Bell like a whip.

'Easy now. Stop acting like a tart an' keep your voice down. 'Ere, 'ave a fag.'

Cockney lit a cigarette behind the gunshield. Bell took a light off it. He had the cigarette in the corner of his mouth, both lips were raw in the centre. Wearily he sucked smoke into his lungs. Cockney looked at the wretched hunched figure. He was perplexed and seething with anger at what he had discovered. He also felt an enormous wave of pity.

Bell sat, the picture of dejection, drained of emotion and feeling utterly empty. Cockney moved over and sat beside him. He squirted a stream of saliva between his teeth into the darkness.

'Now, Dinga,' he whispered forcefully. 'You're not kiddin' me anymore. It's a lot more serious than the bint in blighty to make you want to blow your fuckin' brains out, that is, if you've gorrany - which I doubt. You're in trouble, bad, if I'm any judge. Open up, tell us wharrit's all about.'

Bell was weeping. 'I can't, it's too horrible. Just leave me alone.'

'Not on your bleedin' nelly.' Cockney thought for a moment. Oh well, in for a penny. 'What's up, mate? Think you've got a packet?'

Bell's head shot up. Right on target, Cockney thought. He gave a soft whistle of disbelief.

'An' that's what you wanted to blow your head off for? Stone the bloody crows. Don't you know that medicine 'as come a fair way since the Crimea. No worse than a bad cold nowadays. Keep your shirt on. Look at Muscles. He's 'ad one. Fit as a bloody fiddle. None so pure as the purified, mate. Your bint 'ull never know, 'an there's no after effects for kids. An' that's the bleedin' truth.'

Bell's whisper came. 'You - you don't know what it's like. The pain, the bloody pain, it's awful: a bit longer and I'll not be able to pass water.' It was typical of Bell that he felt he could not say piss. Cockney studied him in the faint light then decided the conversation was getting nowhere.

'Right, you think you've got a packet. You're scared shitless. First things first. Let's see if you 'ave. Let's take a look. Come on, get up. Grab that gun cover, I'll get a torch.'

He moved away and was back quickly. He moved like a cat with smooth sure control. Together they lifted the gun cover off the limber and walked a few yards away. The cover was stiff and heavy but once Bell sat inside his head acted as a tentpole. No one would see them from the quad. Cockney knelt down.

'Come on, open your flies. Let the dog see the rabbit.'

Bell, in darkness and curiously unembarrassed, even fatalistic, undid his buttons and took out his penis. Cockney took a long look in the light of the torch.

'Any discharge, Ding?' Bell whispered in the negative. Cockney stood up. Bell readjusted his flies and stood. Anxiously he said. 'Is it - is it bad?'

'Well,' Cockney said judiciously, 'you've not got a dose. Far from it. Your cock is not going to drop off. Listen to Doctor Wells, my boy. You've got Bellonitus or something that sounds like that. Actually,' his low tones took on the plummy tones of a vicar, 'actually, the correct medical phraseology is Phimosis and that is not too serious.' His tone returned to normal, well, normal for him.

'All it means is that you have a constricted foreskin, irritable, itchy and painful. It could cut off your water in time, and if left long enough, could be quite nasty. Soon as you can, get it soaked, often, half a dozen times a day. Then you want vaseline, cotton wool and a supply of matches. Got to get behind it. After a bit, you'll be able to get it back. Then for a time tie a bandage round it to keep the foreskin back. Keep it clean after that.

'Dodger an' me, we've 'ad it. We should all have been circumcised when we were born. Wouldn't 'ave bin any of this lark then.'

Bell thanked him effusively and then told Cockney the whole story liberally sprinkled with apologies. Cockney let him get it out of his system. He didn't want thanks; he was satisfied with the warm inner knowledge that he had saved a life. He would keep all this to himself. Bell had been lucky, so had he. A bint, a packet, nothing new.

He cut off Bell's story as diplomatically as he knew how. The floodgates had burst and he had started repeating things and getting maudlin. Cockney did not relish being a wailing wall. Over two years of taciturnity and aloofness could not be forgotten in a matter of minutes. Anyway, he did not want to be bosom pals and that was more a matter of class, working class opposed to middle class. Bell, at home, lived in a different world. The haves; it was a world of prigs, money, good homes, mannered, aloof and so bloody sure of themselves. They all seemed to forget in that world before the war, how much it was going to change. And change it would. It had already begun, the march to equality was not to be seen. Invisible, it moved in the hearts and minds of all who fought, this war's aftermath was going to be different from the Great War. In the meantime, get some kip, first light was close.

To the north the day's pursuit was over. Somewhere overhead, beyond the mass of cloud a homing force of bombers roared back to the east. There they would refuel, bomb up and once again take off and head west. They would have plenty of company as the shuttle service continued throughout the night. From the escarpment and beyond came the rumble of guns, the bursts of Very lights and offshore the sky was split by the flashes from the fleet. At Halfaya Pass night fell on the old concrete pill boxes that had once held the 75's and 88's in 1941. Some were old panzer or Matilda turrets. The same positions had been held till dusk. The job of delay was complete.

Further south and ten miles to the west, the Shermans, armoured cars, guns and motorised infantry had leaguered for the night. Further south still, beyond Maddalena and thirty miles inside Libya, light forces had leaguered too.

The night and the desert had enveloped the Eighth Army spearheads like a rough blanket. The brewfires were out. Now the only illumination came from the knocked-out tanks and trucks of both armies. Weary men, drained by the previous days of stress, carried just one thought in their heads. It took priority over food, drink, even a smoke. Mucus dust rimmed eyes whose lids weighed a ton demanded and got their insistent need; sleep, blessed oblivion.

The degree of weariness varied with individuals. They were all tired and all at the sharp end. Some needed just ten minutes' cat-nap. They would sit, not talking, just relaxing as they waited for the inner shriek of nerves and tensions to subside. The horrors of the day burnt on the retinas of shocked eyes. Each knew their personal horror pictures would fade and disappear. But none knew when. After the cat-nap they would get up to wander around the leaguer, talk to other men, share fags, listen to the nine o'clock news, anything to avoid the sleep they so desperately needed. Because for these unfortunates, the cine repeat performance of the day, in colour, would unroll on the screen of their minds.

The others were maybe the lucky ones. Their bodies huddled in the rough blankets embraced the earth. Their minds, memories and all consciousness plunged through that same earth at terrifying speed, through the core into the deepest pit. Their sleep was akin to death. They did not dream. Their log-like figures would require a hefty kick to drag them back into another day.

By eight o'clock the wireless traffic had been reduced to a trickle. The incoming reports from all formations, the situation reports, SITREP, armoured fighting vehicle strength, AFV, ammunition state were in process of being collated. Talc on maps covered by fresh, new symbols. Problems of logistics, operating distances, replenishment points had all travelled down the airwaves, back along the increasing tail of an Army that stretched to the Delta. RASC transport was still being towed out of mud that was slowly drying back to its original texture, sand. Slightly west of the old Alamein line, now history, waited the Italians who, herded miserably together, waited anxiously for the next day. Tomorrow they would be on their way to Cairo. In a vastly different way to what they had expected. Not as conquering heroes but as prisoners of war.

At DAK, Deutsche Afrika Korps headquarters the headlong rush from Alamein had been slowed to a planned withdrawal. The points along the long road back had been selected. These key points would be defended in the well tried and successful method with minimum forces inflicting maximum damage. Engineers under the command of General Karl Buelowis, were obeying the genius whose sophisticated devices in explosive warfare, were to cost the Eighth Army engineers many casualties. Already the ingenuity of this wizard in booby traps was taking its toll. Not just along the coastal route but in other wide flung areas over which the scattered Afrika Korps had passed. A certain large British minefield south and west of Matruh had warranted the full attention of six engineers for the better part of a day.

The greater part of the remnants of the Afrika Korps through these delaying actions, had now got a chance to reach Tunisia. Cyrenaica was untenable, even El Agheila would cause little delay. To this end the few well-sited guns, the scarce panzers, would make the enemy cautious. They already had a cautious general. Anything to slow him still further gained precious time. Time to recover, to refit, to fight again as an army. The first defensive line seemed to be the position at Mareth; it could even be further back at Wadi Akarit.

Before then the enemy would pay, in blood for every mile.

*

Remarkably for Heinz, he felt no desire to sleep. He sat with overcoat on in the commander's turret seat, head resting against the pad and cigarette between his lips. Another three hours before first light. He heard the soft pad of boots outside, Littner's boots, as he passed along the length of the Mark III for yet another circumambient tour of his charges. The feeling he was experiencing was only strange in its rareness. He recognised and accepted it. The peculiar loneliness of command.

Stollenburg slept, snoring slightly, curled on the iron perforated grid of the turret floor. The sky overhead cast a faint gleam of starlight. The flames from the scene of their early encounter, directly behind them had vanished. He felt, for a moment, as though he was alone on a place like the moon. The chill of the night seemed to attack the very marrow of his bones. Getting too old for this lark, he thought, bones get stiffer, feel the cold more, not soft physically but well worn. On the way to the knacker's yard. Tomorrow, no, he caught himself, today in another three hours we shall be on our way. Then what? His attempted projection of thoughts into the future that lay so close, bounced off the wall of uncertainty in his mind.

Then death, mocked the grim skeleton skull of the late Hauptmann. Heinz willed himself to think of something else. Kicked himself mentally and reminded his apprehensive inner being that this sort of situation was what he had been trained for.

The soft footfalls approached, passed, the sound diminishing to disappear finally as Littner reached the rear of the Lancia. Heinz dragged deeply on the cigarette as his thoughts centred on the Reich and the conduct of the war.

In normal circumstances he had little time to think of anything other than survival. Rations, fuel, ammunition, ranges and maintenance. Reading the ground, identifying targets and speed, of thought, of movement, split second decisions. And control, of himself and others, iron self-discipline always to set the example, the standards of conduct. That he would always do. Despite the doubts that recently had been allowed to creep in.

Another voice mocked this last declaration. Would you honestly do that in any circumstances? If for instance the Gestapo took Gaby away. Wouldn't that be reason to doubt, to consider whether your loyalty and dedication was misplaced? Take Gaby - that was ridiculous they had no reason. Ah, but when have the Gestapo needed reasons or excuses? Face a few facts, Heinz, allow yourself to use your brains.

The insistent voice would not be stilled; ask yourself, whom can you really trust? How many neighbours, friends? Even your own children? Get wise to yourself, you cannot keep your head down forever. Germany today is a nation of stool pigeons all waiting to shop each other. Webber's words rang in his ears. So did another familiar pedantic set of phrases, phrases that stemmed from Littner that he had heard second or third hand. 'You are all tools, pawns in a ghastly game of fatal chess. The pieces moved at the slightest whim of one who is a power-mad maniac. The Führer will destroy the German race, drag us all down to oblivion and degradation through his manic depressive super ego.'

Usually, Heinz thought, one could not remember what Littner had said. Possibly it was because once he started, the phrases would roll off his tongue in high German, studded with words that sounded a metre in length. In the cold and complete silence Heinz struggled with his thoughts. A week ago, no, he corrected himself, it was much longer than that. Three months ago he would have considered Littner as a traitor. Now, he asked himself, was he? Time had flown.

He did his job as well as he knew how. Took the same risks. Heinz could never recall him complaining. Was he a traitor just because he dared to criticise, questioned the decisions of the Führer and, and what? Heinz prided himself on being fair, just. Maybe it was because Littner irritated him or perhaps he was jealous of an intellect, not superior exactly but different?

Different, but then all of them were different. He was aware of the change in himself over the past six months. Otherwise he would have been content to soldier on out here. The change had not been quick but gradual. The long months in this empty limitless wasteland had in the beginning been a challenge. At times he had enjoyed it, real soldiering, hectic, exciting. Sidi Rezegh had, for him and many others, been a shock. The sheer fury of the actions, day after day, the sapping grind of the long month and the utter confusion had done more than hint at the future.

It had sounded a warning that the Brits would never give in. A year later the crest of the wave had ebbed in the tide of defeat. Morale and superiority, certainty of victory had come down to survival and disillusion. Overweening confidence to near despair. There must be more now who questioned even if it was only silently. His own perspective had widened and suddenly he realised he was empathising. His rough-hewn soldier's character revolted for a moment. Next thing, he thought, I'll be going round to kiss the bastard. Makes you think though where we shall be next year or in three years' time.

Could it last that long? Christ, I hope not, but the news of the Americans, the sheer amount of kit they could produce, the stalemate in Russia and that sentence in Gaby's last letter. It had worried him. They didn't get much sleep, she had said, then hastily she had added they did not really need it; they were too busy. He had read it several times and he could only draw one conclusion. It must mean the Brits and their night bombing. Back in May they had launched a thousand bomber raid and flattened Köln.

In his reply he had suggested the garden be dug deeper to get good results. It was all he could do. At that time they had been digging and blasting every day and part of the night. That basic discipline had been all that they had to counter the enormous barrage that commenced on 23rd October. The hellish racket had taken him back in time to the first months of his service on the Western Front.

The armoured steel of this old stager wasn't much good against sixty or ninety pound high trajectory shells. A direct hit would have spattered this hunk of steel all over the desert. When you think about it, it takes a lot of shells and a lot of bullets, bombs and mines to kill one soldier. He looked at the darker patch beneath his feet that was Stollenburg.

Quite a character that one. Not unfeeling but stoical, difficult to get to. Getting words out of my friend there was like pulling teeth. In battle he was quick and competent but almost uninterested. Heinz wondered mildly for a moment whether that attitude was due to a semi-permanent half cut state. If there was any alcohol within a hundred miles, Stollenburg would find it. Pissy-arsed bastard but dependable. Gold right through. April '41, that had been the first time, he and I, the only originals of that crew left. Suddenly his eyes closed. His last conscious thought was the dial of his watch on the screen of his mind, set for two hours later.

Heinz awoke five minutes before his mind set time. His skeletal structure locked into a rigid inverted j. Carefully he tested feet, knees, arms and neck. His spinal column felt like a bent saw blade. It was only seconds before he attempted to move; they stretched into hours as creaking like a rusty gate hinge he finally stood upright. Every joint in his body protested violently. He saw the condensation of the night trickling down the steel walls of the cupola. Gritting his teeth he waited as the agony of returning circulation sent armies of pins and needles carried by unravelling red and white corpuscles. The picture of himself, old, white-haired, bent double on frail shaking legs with toothless mouth over shrinking gums, flashed through his mind. Savagely he blotted the picture out and grinned inwardly at the caricature. Poor old bugger - I remember saying that about Sergeant-Major Schulz in - 1924 and he was only twenty-nine. He rubbed his thigh, have to change the bandage tomorrow, starting to lose feeling. He stood up on the commander's seat, the cold morning air damp and unfriendly on his cheeks.

As he looked around, the almost imperceptible false glimmer of dawn came from the east. Clouds were higher, not as thick, a low mist covered the ground, could get some sun later on. Not much wind though. Blowing through the commander's voice pipe he shouted:

'Wakey, wakey. *'Raus! 'Raus*! 'He heard Stollenburg moving. Satisfied he clambered out of the cupola and stiffly bent to jump. The shock of landing reverberated from his ankles to his skull.

Scholz loomed up, Schmeisser under his arm.

'Wake the rest up,' Heinz said. 'Start up in fifteen minutes.'

He started walking the length of the three vehicles. His circulation was steadily increasing as he shook one leg after the other and stamped his feet. By the time he had circled the small leaguer he could see that Stollenburg was out of the Mark III and Braun with Webber were lighting their first cigarettes of the day. Littner was rolling his bedding.

Fifteen minutes later Webber and Braun had inserted the handle for the inertia starter. Scholz mounted the tank, dropped through the cupola. He reappeared and shouted,

'Right.' The two commenced turning the handle. Scholz disappeared. It was stiff, the engine cold, they both sweated as they overcame the arm-weakening resistance. Faster and faster, breath jetting in the cold air, chests heaving until a wheeze, a cough and an intermittent chug, as first one then another piston caught and fired. They withdrew the handle as gradually the remaining cylinders burst into life. The engine settled into a smooth, pulsing beat. Scholz slid down and stood listening critically. He turned to find Braun at his side. They walked to the rear of the Mark III. Here they repeated the starting ritual. The horizon was lightening steadily, the mist looked like cotton wool. Heinz gave instructions to Stollenburg to tow the Lancia. When it got lighter they could stop, have a hot drink and Scholz with Stollenburg could take a look at the diesel engine.

Heinz tested the radio link, no problems.

'Right, let's go. 185 degrees. Advance.'

Both panzers lurched forward and slowly picked up speed. It was going to be restricted by the towed Lancia. It was jerking and swaying as the tow rope whipped taut, then slackened with disconcerting rapidity. It was going to take time for Littner to get used to it. He could see nothing in front but the bulk of the Mark III. The tow rope was virtually invisible from this high vantage point in the cab, the huge expanse of the bonnet was not improving matters either. Even though there was more light the benefit was not much travelling south. It was still dark to the drivers and to Heinz.

He peered into the gloom ahead. It told him nothing. They were travelling blind. His only fear was the chance of going over the side of a wadi and finishing up with one of the panzers on its back. That was always the danger, on moves at night, if you were not following a marked track. Still, it was worth the risk; it would get lighter and if they only covered eight miles before first light, it was eight miles nearer their goal.

Littner, almost standing at times to wrestle with the huge steering wheel, was vainly attempting to pick out the tow chain through the dust and gloom. At the same time he was trying to avoid losing his spectacles and stop the big truck crashing into the panzer. He was sweating freely, this in spite of the near freezing cold. Desperately he took one hand off the wheel, pushed his spectacles back into place and blinked his eyes rapidly as he strained to pierce the dense gloom now aggravated by swirling dust from the Mark III.

The cab rocked and lurched under the spine-shuddering leaps that set his teeth on edge. The minutes passed slowly. He prayed for the dawn.

Webber perched on the edge of the cupola, watched from time to time the faint promise from the east of a new day. He was the only one who could see the pale unearthly glow that spread in fingers and shafts of luminous light. Reluctantly, it seemed, the ground began to reveal features that moments before had been shrouded in darkness. The horizon on all sides greeted the dawn slyly and provocatively, like a dancer shedding veils that revealed beauty.

To the west the huge rugged outline of the escarpment lit by fire appeared, gentle pink turning to fiery red under Webber's gaze. The ground mist flowed like a cottonwool blanket, fragmented in places and varying in depth from two to six metres. To the east and flowing back to the north was another escarpment, visible but only just against the background of the breaking dawn. The country in front undulated, with wadis as yet unlit by the rising sun. The mist hid the camel thorn, rocks and the frequent gullies.

Webber felt like the commander of a submarine high above the sea waves of the mist. Scholz was finding it difficult. Vision was bad. Constantly he referred to the gyroscopic direction indicator, his whole being concentrated on keeping the bearing steady.

Littner was doing better although his eyes felt raw behind the spectacles. His shoulders ached and he hoped that soon, Heinz would call a halt.

Heinz asked for mileage from Stollenburg and Scholz. The replies came back swiftly. Fourteen kilometres. He contacted Webber and told him the first wadi on the right. Two minutes later they entered it. Littner got out and waited for Braun before unhooking the tow chain. They dragged it to the Mark III. It was heavy and it took all their strength to get it stowed away. Webber was lighting a petrol fire and putting the water on. Both panzer engines burbled softly. Scholz and Stollenburg arrived at the Lancia with a box of tools.

Between them they unclipped and lifted the bonnet off. Scholz took a look and turned to Stollenburg.

'We'll have to strip the injector. I think that's favourite. Soon tell if there's water there or air.'

Stollenburg nodded agreement, Heinz arrived and they quickly explained what they intended to do. Heinz walked away slowly. Automatically he was chafing at the thought of more delay but accepting there was nothing he could do. It was vitally important to their chances that they kept the truck and contents. And it had to be a runner. Without that precious fuel any hope of getting back disappeared.

Webber called softly that the tea was ready. They were all getting used to tea. The cylindrical respirator containers were ideal for holding tea and sugar. They stood sipping the hot brew, dirty, unshaven and no two dressed alike, scuffed boots, sand-heavy shirts and jackets, forage caps jammed over sand-rope hair. Expressions relaxed as they smoked and drank but conversation was limited. It was too early in the day.

Stollenburg and Scholz drifted back to the truck. Littner followed. They had the injector stripped and were cleaning it with petrol. Littner sat on the running board. Out of the six of them he was the solitary non-smoker. There were times when he was tempted to have just one cigar. He gazed at the scene around him. No man is an island? John Donne was not referring to him. He had always been an island. A chip on someone else's shoulder. A burr under the saddle. He didn't seek for reasons. It was a fact of life, or death. He thought of yesterday, before their ambush of the Tommies.

They had passed a graveyard of derelict tanks and vehicles. An open charnel house with blackened skeletons. Ignored by the Hauptmann it had affected Littner. It had seemed a sacrilege to ignore the final resting place of so many, like being billeted in a fire torn crumbling and devastated church. He had said a short prayer for their souls, a Lutheran prayer.

He was aware suddenly, that they had fitted the injector back. He climbed into the cab. They were turning the starting handle slowly with Scholz leaning back, eyes on the injector pipes.

'Air bubbles,' he confirmed to Stollenburg.

They carried on turning until the frothy bubbles disappeared. Littner watched the deft fingers of Scholz connecting and tightening the pipe nuts. A round peg in a round hole, doing what he knew best. Littner felt, for a brief moment, envious. In the short time he had known Scholz he was aware of the command driver's obsession for his family. Had listened, been bored and dismissed Scholz as very ordinary.

As he watched he hastily revised his opinion. Scholz was an artist, his material, engines. Far more use than he was, square peg in a round hole. Over-educated, under-muscled and probably a pain in the neck to all of them. Scholz stood back nodded to Stollenburg; they picked up the heavy bonnet and replaced it. The clips fastened perfectly in alignment.

'Okay,' breathed Scholz. 'I think that should do it. The air's gone. Time to see if the old cow will do her duty. Switch it on.'

Littner switched on. They commenced turning the starting handle. The exertion darkening faces under their tan. The diesel sucked, sweat trickled, ran down their cheeks until the pressure suddenly detonated. The roar of the big engine split the air, accompanied by the dense black smoke from the exhaust. It drowned the burbling throb of the panzer's engines.

Heinz came over, he grinned.

'So, the magicians win again. Good.' Scholz returned the grin. Heinz's words were better than a medal. That was the good news. Now for some that's not quite so good. His face now serious, he said:

'Sergeant-Major.' His voice was barely heard over the thud of the diesel. Heinz gave a questioning look.

Scholz moved away from the engine's beat. 'We've got a problem though. I think the cylinder head gasket is just about *kaput.* ' He waited.

Heinz, his face impassive was thinking. Cylinder head gasket?

That meant, sooner or later, water in the sump. It was not often a sudden catastrophe, more a slow deterioration. The end result was the same, it could ruin the engine.

'How bad?' he asked.

Scholz looked at Stollenburg before replying. Stollenburg said flatly, 'It'll last maybe a hundred but not more than two hundred and fifty kilometres. No more. You can tell by the rust stains on the block.'

'That'll be far enough,' said Heinz. He was once more in command.

'Webber and Braun are topping up the tanks now and filling all the jerricans. When this packs up, we'll fill up again and take a couple of drums on each panzer. No problem.' He turned and stomped off. Stollenburg looked at Scholz, he said sarcastically.

'No problems, eh? That's what *he* thinks. Off he goes putting his feet down like ready money. Jesus Bloody Christ! We've only half the Eighth Army to get through. Fuck my luck!' He spat moodily, searched and found a cigarette, lit up and dragged hungrily. Smoke trickling from nostrils he looked at Scholz, saw the surprised expression. He bared stained teeth in a rueful semi-apologetic grin.

'Finished the rum last night, bit jarred off with this lot, things get worse, even Old Fifty-Seven's not too happy, I know - sorry.'

Scholz acknowledged with a deprecating gesture. So that totalled four, four who, including him, were riddled with doubt. That wild scheme of Braun's didn't seem so wild anymore. He walked back to the Mark IV and stowed his toolbox away. Webber and Braun came back from the Lancia carrying two jerricans each. He helped them strap the cans firmly in the holders. They got mounted. Heinz was ready and Webber moved out on his command.

Down the wadi, into further wadis avoiding crests like a plague, the mist swirling over the height of the panzer's tracks. Jinking as they travelled in a rough V formation but always steadily creeping along the 185 degree bearing. The sun was weak above clouds that were thin and high. Warmth would not come in less than two hours and it was likely the mist would remain for another thirty or forty miles.

Littner followed fifty yards behind. The land was still rising but the ground was firm with sand and shale predominating.

He took the opportunity to wipe his bifocals. He felt much more relaxed now he was not attached to the Mark III. He was beginning to enjoy the freedom and solitude of the big cab. His thin ascetic features bore a trace of worry, his domed forehead wrinkled as he wondered what the day would bring. The analytical brain had long since assessed the situation. He was not unduly nervous but neither was he optimistic.

The loss of the Hauptmann had been sudden but to Littner it had been a relief. Not that it improved the outlook particularly. That remained but now there was a new dealer, the sergeant-major. He wondered idly if he could find more than fifty-two cards in the pack. Today they all needed aces. Old Fifty-Seven was competent. He was also cautious and crafty. A product of the old Germany, the Fatherland and had obviously spent more time in the Wehrmacht than in civilian life. Rough and ready, quick to chastise, biting in criticism but for all that, he had humanity and he inspired confidence.

Littner looked up at the sky, that part of it he could see and hoped the RAF were still grounded. They were making good time now. Scholz had stepped up the pace and they were holding a speed of between twenty and twenty-five kilometres an hour. If their luck held, who knows, they could reach Agheila, If, that little word. If he had only been born different, kept a watch on his tongue. If common sense would only seep through, just a little, into the minds of the German people. If there had been only loyal Germans listening to that last lecture at Göttingen. If he had only volunteered for the Corps of Interpreters.

The swift arrest by the Sicherung, cancellation of his 'unfit for military service pass' the *Untauglich für Wehrdienst* had been followed by immediate induction at the *Ergänzungsstelle*. He wondered for the hundredth time how he had survived, but he had. The threat hanging over him like the sword of Damocles had terrified him; *Sonderaktion Wehrmacht* - the concentration camp of the Wehrmacht.

He, who had only the sketchiest knowledge of panzers and detested the stink and noise had finished up in a panzer division. It was survival in a different world. Only the tough kindness of the common *Soldaten* had brought him this far. Rough and crude, ignorant and unfeeling, nevertheless they were the core, the heart of Germany. If they survived, so would Germany.

They had even listened to him as they helped, maybe they did not understand half of what he had said. Possibly they humoured him and eventually he had been accepted. Heinz had cursed him up hill and down dale. Threatened to put him on charges for undermining the morale but had never pursued any. Heinz was more of a humanitarian in some things than most people. Deep down, Littner thought, he and Old Fifty-Seven might have more in common than either realised.

The time would come when Heinz and then a few more would grasp the significance of his words, words that he had dropped into the ponds of their minds. The ripples would spread to the banks of common sense and, ultimately, revolt and overthrow of the vile Nazi hierarchy. Littner hoped, God willing, that he could be usefully employed in the re-education of the German people. It could be done although in the doing, history would have to be rewritten. The task was gigantic, tear out the Nazi creed root and branch and utterly destroy it. On the ashes, build for a new Germany. Time and dedication was needed, he knew he had a part to play. God give me strength for the mission.

The sun made a brief flashing appearance for a few minutes before retiring behind the thin shelter of the cumulus. The cold air numbed the lips of Heinz as it swept past his head. Once more, for the umpteenth time he swept the horizons with his binoculars. If there was life and movement, it was underground. They came out of a long wadi and faced ground that sloped up to a long crest. There seemed no apparent way to circumvent the obstacle. Heinz frowned, as a veteran of armoured warfare, any crest was anathema to him. He recalled the numerous times he had been the lure, asking to be chased and the Tommy tanks swallowing the bait. They paid for the experience, heavily, before learning the lesson.

He halted both panzers halfway up the slope and slid down off the Mark III to walk to the top of the crest. He wriggled flat on his belly for the last ten feet. Through the binoculars he studied the country ahead. The ground sloped away for another - he guessed - eight kilometres. Beyond was the blue-hazed gap. His gap, the one he had aimed at on the map. The bottom of the slope he was surveying was still mist-laden. He felt like Columbus sighting the shore of the new land, fulfilled, satisfied, the marksman hitting the bull. Carefully he traversed with the powerful lens seeking anything foreign, unusual in the expanse before him. A small sigh of relief escaped him. The way was clear. The two horns of the escarpment reached out from the gap stretching in a lazy purplish crescent, to the north-west and the north-east.

He got to his feet and waved the two panzers forward waiting whilst Stollenburg drew level and stopped. The squat, dirty yellow-green brown outlines of the panzers, followd by the sandy grey of the Lancia eased slowly down the slope. Chameleon-like their presence blended into the landscape.

Webber, perched on the cupola rim, thought of a pubic bush and gigantic tits; he liked the role of commander.

Littner thought of a friend of long ago, a Jewish colleague forcibly removed with his family to a concentration camp.

Stollenburg licked his lips, stoically accepting the prospect of a dry future, his mind empty of guilt.

Braun was tense with purpose, a spanner and white, or nearly white towel ready. Would it be today?

Scholz wondered if he had missed anything by getting married. Tooling the Mark IV skilfully down the slope, he had already placidly accepted the future in a British Stalag.

Heinz thought of the country beyond the gap his mind leaping ahead. Mechili, Msus, Agedabia, Agheila - home. He crossed his fingers.

IX

Bell had decided to do Cockney's stag. He sat on the polished wood of the layer's seat. In the last hour he had asked himself a lot of questions. He was calm now and relaxed, even the shame had died. Only the soreness of his lips remained. He had tried to answer the questions objectively. It had not worked out too well. He was still making excuses, he seemed to have an endless supply.

The adjustment that he was trying to make should have been a simple matter. From the bullet in the brain to end it all he had been painfully yanked back in to the world of the living. He was grateful, Cockney had saved his life but had he been watching, expecting, or was it just blind chance? And was he right? After all, he wasn't a doctor.

He got up and began to walk, the thoughts tumbling willy nilly in his mind. Doctors to Bell were creatures on another planet, skilled in matters the laymen never questioned, omnipotent with an authority and knowledge that only the universities provided. Seven years of dedicated study before they were allowed to treat patients. Households were hushed when they entered, whispered consultations cloaked in secrecy. Prescriptions in Latin, symbols and dots, hieroglyphics deciphered only by the pharmacist. Bell stood in awe of their pronouncements in childhood sickness. The feeling of respect had never left him. Solicitors, accountants, teachers were not on the same level but they too, commanded his respect and homage. So, how could he be sure Cockney knew? He was only - say it - working class.

The penny dropped and his mind pulled the lever. A sudden clarity came over his thoughts, that he didn't much like. Grammar school, then a secure job, Father an Alderman, had given him pride of class. His friends before the war, the girls, the parties on tended lawns had been his real life; not this - this interruption in the scheme of things. He yearned to be back, back in those idyllic surroundings with its private jokes, easy familiarity, the maids, cook and the gardener. The insulated superior luxury and comfort. Abruptly he stifled the yearning. Objectivity crept into his thinking.

In the first place he could see nothing wrong in pride of class. It was an integral part of him. Other people, particularly in the army, were different. Comradeship made a nonsense of it. Nevertheless it did not mean he had to sacrifice his own standards and accept lower ones. He realised slowly that the hurt lay deeper than he had imagined. Unconsciously he was feeling resentment as well as gratitude. It was difficult to accept that a comparatively uneducated working class comrade could be right. But he had to accept it, hard as it seemed. It was a matter of trust. Class did not enter into it.

They each trusted one another on the gun completely, he admitted wryly. He had been a fool, a complete idiot in his attitude. Now the boot was on the other foot, now he had to change. He still needed support, his fears, the thought of being ridiculed had quickly assumed a role of unimportance. He was wrong to ask Cockney to keep his physical distress a secret. The rifle, well that was secret. How does one change from an introvert to an extrovert? Slowly, he thought, and it all has to come from me. I can and I will.

He wondered for a moment whether his previous inadequacy, his temerity to share fully with the others his thoughts and feelings, would improve. Half the time it was because he had little to relate in comparison to the hundreds of tales dwelling on working class life. The rest of the crew drew from an unlimited source of poverty, hardship and hard work experience. He always felt outside the cosy circle, bereft of any similar or different personal and interesting episodes in his own life. A partial solution occurred to him. You can't match the tales, so discuss what you know. The war, current affairs, reminisce, don't keep it to yourself, think up a few tall stories, jokes if you know any; at some time you've got to laugh at yourself. While you're at it think about your cushy existence before the war, that should raise a laugh. Absently he stroked the rough paint of the piece. Guns have a smell to gunners, a mixed evocation of oil, grease, cordite, explosives, steel and leather. That slim looking barrel with slightly flared muzzle shouted an arrogance to the skies. Sky which now was definitely less dark. The mist dropped in skeins of cobwebby tentacles. He looked at the watch. Today was here, so far it didn't look any different from the night, or feel so. He went from bundle to bundle giving a firm squeeze to shoulders or ankles.

They came awake with varying degrees of alertness and left the snug warmth of blankets venting their displeasure on boots that were stiff and cold and coats that perversely seemed to have lost armholes. The initial waking up curses died down naturally as they accepted the new day and what it might hold in store. The clutch of sleep slid quickly away. Bedding rolls were chucked up and tied on the roof; the mist laden atmosphere struck bitingly cold. Visibility was ten yards. Chalky was topping up the radiator. Dodger, Muscles and Bell stood at the trail of the gun.

'Unload the cartridge,' James called. 'Put the muzzle cover on. Run off and hook up. OK, Chalky, start 'er up.'

Cockney was loading the mines and grenades back into the truck, as they hooked up and replaced the shells made ready a few hours ago. He finished loading as James approached.

'Keep close. It's gunna be slow. Should 'ave a man in front with a white stick. It'll get better after first light.'

'Right, Sarge.' Bell arrived. '*Saieeda* Dinga. Got the mines in the back, ready 'an primed. You never know, 'an as our chief scout ses' be prepared. That way you die, but not as quick.'

James had travelled on odd occasions with a round up the spout and the charge. But funny things could happen and sometimes unpredictable accidents occurred. Removing the charge was just a normal precaution. He stuck his head through the hatch astonished to find he was clear of the mist. The faint lightening of the sky promised the new dawn.

'Right, Chalky, turn right out of the wadi. We should find that track. I'll stop you when I pick it up. OK, let's go.'

Hesitantly the quad moved off, James bobbing down to guide Chalky with hand movements. Thirty seconds was long enough.

'Hold it!' James said. They had a problem.

Even with just four in the quad and the door missing, the warmth from their bodies was steaming up the windscreen. James cursed as he negotiated his passage around the tank on the floor, the pipe and Dodger's outstretched boots. He swung down through the vacant door space.

Outside it was cotton wool, dense impenetrable, the top of his head was level with the radiator cap. He looked up at the split windscreen. Wiper blades and arms had been discarded months previously when this had replaced the old worn out quad. Useless then, never used at any time or needed. Now he could do with some. The two cleared strips on the glass looked like blind cartoon eyes. Still, it would be the same for the panzers. The reminder of what was behind, the menace, activated the hairs on the back of his neck.

An urgency rose within him, powerful and insistent. Savagely he fought it down. Think! Desperately he tried, forcing himself to be calm. Despite himself the questions began, pessimistic of course. He grimaced. What if back there, it's clear, no mist? They could be on top of you before you know it. This cotton wool deadens sound, not like last night. How long have you got before those two clanking bastards reach here? How much time to live? Bollocks, he answered. If they get here, they're no better off than we are. They've not got X-ray eyes. Got to get moving though. The indecision vanished.

'Get the windscreen open, Chalky. Do mine as well. I'm gunna look for the track. Keep the engine runnin'.'

He walked from the radiator into the mist pausing to listen for the quad engine and searching the ground. Fifty yards on he stumbled, the edge of the track, the rut stretched to his right. He stood listening, picked up the engine sound and walked confidently back. He reached the quad noting that there was an opaque diffusion of light, so faint that he at first wondered if it was imagination.

'Follow me,' he called up to Chalky. He noticed that Dodger was in his seat, head almost touching the windscreen frame. Good, another pair of eyes, maybe stop Chalky running me over. He started walking, the quad ground away behind him in low gear. Reaching the rut of the track he stopped. The quad halted. He stepped back and waved Chalky to the right. He waited whilst the full length of the quad and gun then the 15 cwt passed him before shouting, 'Halt!'

Reaching the front of the quad he stopped, then walked forward, he could see the ground and the ruts fairly well. He estimated his distance as six yards from the quad, the limit of his vision.

'Chalky, Dodger, can you see the ground - the ruts?'

'Yeah,' came the chorused answer.

Satisfied, James climbed back through the doorspace and picked up his compass. It would only be a rough guide, he knew, but all he wanted at this time was an indication that the track was heading somewhere along his bearing. It was. His compass showed 175 degrees.

They moved off, the minutes passed, the track, like all tracks, meandered, the ruts deep with hidden rocks. They lurched along, Dodger, and Muscles huddled together, both asleep. James sat on his seat. He could see what he wanted better than from the hatch which he had closed. It was cold, damp icy cold that drove deep into bones. Progress was desperately slow but, he thought, it was progress in the right direction.

Babes in the wood, he thought as he looked at the sleeping couple behind him. That's one thing about this war. Sleep on a clothes line. Never stand if you can sit, never sit if you can lie and grab all the sleep you can. At the moment he felt curiously wide awake. He looked at his watch, they had been going for a little over an hour. That's about six miles. He lit a cigarette, remembered Chalky and lit another from the glowing end.

'Ta,' Chalky said. He gestured to the radiator from which a tiny trickle of steam was escaping.

'*Tora Garrum,** Sarge.'

'It's got to last us. Got to. When we stop we'll give it a drink. Dawn should be soon. Maybe we'll be able to see a bit more then, but we must make all the ground we can, get out the way of those fuckin' panzers, if the worst comes with this - we've still got the fifteen hundredweight.'

Chalky nodded; like all of them he was a bit of a fatalist. They were doing their best. Luck! That's what they needed, the run of the ball. The indefinable something that meant the difference between winning and losing. Only in their case it wasn't a game. Well, it was in a way, a deadly game where they might finish up being the ball.

Forty-five minutes later James had the hatch up; he was above

* *A little hot*

the mist and even though he had seen what was happening a thousand times, it still surprised him. In the last ten minutes the breaking dawn had rolled back the curtain of the night, the blue and copper red bulwark of the escarpment to the west glowed under the gentle shafts of virgin light. The first of the day.

He raised binoculars and looked ahead. There was the gap. After that, home and dry. The blue and purple Vee was still some miles away but already it seemed to beckon a welcome. The mist was clearing too, not very fast but enough for them to increase their speed. Chalky slipped the gear lever into third then to fourth. The quad had been in first and second gear now for the past two hours. Fifteen then twenty miles an hour the mist receding to seventy yards on all sides. The quad and gun started to bounce as wheels hit unavoidable bumps and rocks. Their progress now was a weaving dance that awoke the other two occupants.

'Kerrist!' complained Dodger, as a particularly vicious lurch and pitch of the quad battered his spinal column. He nudged Muscles.

'Hey, mucker, where the bleedin' 'ell are we?'

Rayburn opened his eyes and glanced through the open doorspace. He turned his untroubled gaze on Dodger.

'Bombay. All change, Sahib.'

'An' up yours too,' retorted Dodger. 'Cor - could do with a brew, mouth's like the bottom of a swill tub. Arsk the shuvver' my man. Tell 'im to see to it, pull in some place. Ah, the Savoy will do nicely.'

Rayburn grinned and pointed to the number one. Dodger grunted in disgust and lit a cigarette.

'Might as well smoke mesen' to death then.'

The gap was much closer now and their approach more of a straight line. James could see the rocky fissures of the escarpment on both sides. He had the advantage of height and could see the gap narrow roughly two miles ahead. He thought he saw a track leading off to the right and felt for his binoculars. Suddenly he saw it.

'Turn *right - jildi*!' His voice cracked like a whip. Chalky, hand over hand, spun the wheel expertly to the right. The quad turned abruptly in a circle with the nearside front wheel just shaving a vertical length of angle iron and halted. James had his arm raised, palm vertical in the halt sign. The truck drew up behind.

'What's up, Sarge?' asked Chalky. The others were out of the quad yawning and stretching rubbing eyelids free of dried mucus.

'Minefield,' James said shortly.

His binoculars focussed to the west, the direction they were now facing. One by one he picked them out through the lens. Some upright, others leaned drunkenly and some were flat. The remains of minefield markers, the barbed wire long absent. They were virtually invisible in the camouflage the desert winds and sand had provided. He swivelled round and looked to the east, the mist still limiting his vision to a hundred yards. It was the same. The minefield blocked the gap. Looking to the north the ground rose to a crest about seven miles away. From the quad, mist stretched solidly for two miles until the beginning of the slope. From that crest and down that slope would come the danger if he was any judge unless the panzers had followed the track. Whichever way, this new obstacle had put the cat amongst the pigeons. Well, I can't stand here admiring the scenery. He ducked down and swung out of the quad. Bell had come up and was standing by Rayburn and Dodger. James said.

'Right, pay attention. This minefield might be one of ours, an old one, or a dummy. There has to be a gap - somewhere. Stay 'ere. I'm takin' the truck. One of you keep a lookout from the hatch - and there's no time for a brew. Any minute a couple of panzers are gunna 'it us up the arse. We'll just 'ave to 'ope, trust in the Lord, Buddha or Mohammed. It's time they did some work too.'

He walked swiftly over to the truck.

'OK, Cockney, straight along the outside of the angle irons. Move it. I don't think we've too much time.'

Cockney let in the clutch and they roared off. The markers seemed about seventy yards' interval, the ones that remained. In five minutes they reached the last one, driven in on a steep slope. Cockney turned the truck in a circle and they roared back to the quad and past to the east.

'That's it,' James had found what he was looking for. He tapped Cockney's shoulder to stop the truck and jumped out. He leaned across and shouted.

'Straight back. Bring the quad. I'll have a look round, it's about in the middle, I think it's Hobson's Choice.'

The truck roared off, James lit a cigarette and walked slowly to the gap studying the ground, looking for tyremarks. The entrance, if that was what it was, seemed to be at least twenty yards in width. He walked in. Even this closer look told him nothing. The winds and the recent rains had efficiently obliterated any evidence of wheels or tracks.

He moved further in striving to pick up any trace. A minefield was the last thing he had expected. His growing irritation was now sheer bad temper. In regimental parlance, he had a hell of a liver on. The prospect before them he viewed without enthusiasm. It could be British, the markers indicated that but there were no signs. No skull and crossbones with *'Minen'* painted in stark warning.

It could be a dummy, yeah, and you could be the Queen of Sheba. What if the Jerries had been here and booby-trapped? A minefield was different to just the odd Teller or 'S' mine. Even the Eyetie ones, the long oblong mines painted grey he could disarm; thermos bombs, the toy child's pillar box grenades painted red were dicy. Blow those up with a rifle bullet, that was safest. But a whole bloody minefield, it's like Russian roulette. He walked further, scanned the ground through the binoculars, saw the ruts - not fresh but at least it proved that traffic had moved over the ground. He could pick out the track now, like all tracks it curled and bent.

To the east and west of them rose the escarpments, a solid wall that would mean sixty miles of travel to get round. He turned and started to walk back. He knew he was prevaricating, reluctant to take a decision. Minute by minute the sun was gaining strength. Already he was feeling the warmth on his face. That was another factor added to the rest. The mist was an ally at the moment and the strengthening sun an enemy.

He heard the quad and the 15 cwt approaching. Five lives and his own rested on doing the right thing. You and nobody else, mate. Your clapped-out quad just hanging together with a radiator liable to pack up at any time. No spare wheel. The truck, two wheel drive, it wasn't exactly new either. Running either east or west was a gamble, if they weren't spotted first. There was a chance if they crossed the minefield to find a defensive gun position. That's if they didn't get blown to smithereens.

As he got closer to the two vehicles the sound of Dodger's voice came to him clearly.

'What a bleedin' turnup for the book, as though we ain't gorrenuff' to put up with. We 'ave to drop on the one spot in the blue an' find a fuckin' minefield. To crown it all, I'll bet it's one of ours. Now what? Bleedin' tanks behind, millions of mines, all booby-trapped in front. An' the best of British luck to you, sir. I know what I'm gunna do when we get back. I'm seein' the Colonel, ask 'im for me bleedin' cards - I resign.'

He reached the quad in time to hear Cockney's reply.

''Ang on a minnit while I get me towel out an' a bucket to catch the bleedin' tears. Resign, I should say so.' His voice changed to that of their Colonel. 'Of course, Green, if you feel you must go, it might be in the best interests of the regiment.' His voice reverted to his own. 'Kick the cunt out - 'e never was any fuckin' good.'

The two of them were pretending to square up as James arrived. Chalky got out of the quad and joined the little group around the Sergeant. James thought: Bell. Then he remembered; he was still in the quad leaning on the rim of the hatch facing north. He moved closer to the quad, the group staying with him. He looked around at them, faces cleaner than yesterday, he thought, looked up and saw Bell. Umm - cut lips; wonder what he's done? Must have a word.

'I'm not much wiser. Looks smooth at first, then there's tracks, can't really tell whether it's OK. I think it's British, but I'm no expert. We either go through 'ere or we take a detour. With those panzers in mind, that's limited to the east. Could get caught in the open, get shot up, or break down, I just don't know. You pays your money and you takes your pick. It's a gamble, whichever way.'

He looked again at them. No one offered any comment or suggestion. This is still all mine, James thought, another baby to carry. Bell's voice came from above his head.

'You'd better make your minds up quick.' The words tumbled out urgently, although Bell seemed cool enough. 'There's a couple of panzers behind us, coming down that big slope, too far to tell what they are - and there's a big truck just behind them.'

James walked clear of the group and scanned the slope through his binoculars. He knew they were panzers, even without the drop in his stomach. The truck looked like an Eyetie ten ton diesel. He couldn't make out whether they were Mark III's or IV's. They both had long barrelled guns.

'Right, get mounted. We've no choice now. I'll lead. Cockney, fifty yards interval, in my tracks. Don't stray for Chrissake or you'll go sky 'igh. We've a chance that they 'aven't seen us. Let's go.' His voice crisp, decisive and commanding.

Chalky let in the clutch and they started rolling. Bell settled in the passenger seat of the 15 cwt. He held the machine gun upright, between his knees. Cockney spat out the butt of his cigarette and tried to relax.

At ten miles an hour the quad nosed through the minefield gap. In the land of the cowboys this would be termed a draw or small canyon. James watched the faint track with concentration. The cleft in the landscape no longer seemed a thing of beauty. Even the increasing light did nothing to reduce the atmosphere of menace, the innocuous featureless ground in their path sown with hidden danger.

Leaning foward on the edge of the hatch he was wishing for all sorts of aids, X-ray eyes or radar and praying to a God whose existence, when not in personal danger, he had often doubted. He tried to clear his mind, put everything out of his head but the here and now. His eyes concentrated keenly, afraid to blink, sweeping the ground twenty, thirty and fifty yards ahead. The skin on the back of his neck crawled with a thousand pin prick eyes, all of them blind.

Questions came uninvited. How far away were they? If just one of the panzers was a Mark IV it was probably armed with the long barrelled 75 mm gun. Fired a mixture of ammunition and had a muzzle velocity of 3800 feet per second. If they were both Mark III's it would be the 50 mm and that didn't hang around when the shell left the muzzle. Quickly he glanced to the rear and beyond and blessed the mist. No dust, the truck following easily in their tracks. The panzers were halfway down the slope their camouflage blending into the backdrop. They did not appear to be in a hurry. He guessed the distance to be about three miles, between five and six thousand yards. Let's hope the bastards are still asleep. Just keep your fucking eyes closed until we can get out of here. He ducked down and said:

'Speed it up a bit, Chalky. Don't want 'em to catch us in the middle.'

'That's right, Chalky,' came Dodger's voice. 'Get the fucking whip out, *bot jildi*.'

'Who's drivin' this bloody vehicle eh? Shit innit.' Chalky also had flocks or swarms of butterflies bouncing around in his guts.

James was back up through the hatch. The track from the entrance had swung in a curve to the left. He reckoned the minefield to be just over a mile deep. They were a third of the way through. The track clearly starting to bend to the right. There was a bluff on the right just about where the minefield, if they got through, would end. There must be a track up to that bluff but he couldn't see one. They were nearly halfway.

It was then that he saw the scattering of mines, the grey and red of British and the black Tellers. By the time he saw them it was too late. His throat constricted and the shout he had intended died to a gurgle. His stomach knotted then writhed and seemed to disappear. He waited hopelessly for the explosion. He felt the front then the rear wheels of the quad bounce on the steel cases. In his mind's eye he already saw the shuddering deep-seated explosion and the vertical sheet of flame. Then, in a split second, he knew the mines had been disarmed.

The sign of relief came from the soles of his boots and his intestines uncoiled but only to tighten again as they hit a cluster of four.

If I get out of this bastard alive, he thought, I'll have snow-white hair at twenty-seven. He tried to relax as they ran straight over six mines in a row, — bump, — bump bump bump bump, — bump. He cringed inwardly expecting the deafening crash that would signify it was all over. Each time - nothing, Russian Roulette. His nerves were strung like piano wires that were being strummed by a diabolical infant, intent on driving him mad. The torture went on, the awful screwed-up expectancy that the next would be the last. Sweat trickled into his eyes, the back of his neck felt electric, his eardrums expanded and contracted and his heart pounded like a sledgehammer, wielded by a monstrous giant of a blacksmith. Each time it came, he wanted to close his eyes, each time the lids locked open to force him to look for the next one. The one that would blow them all to kingdom come.

Bell and Cockney in the 15 cwt were experiencing similar emotions. Even though they saw the quad wheels hitting the mines, when it came to their turn Cockney would try to avoid them. It was impossible. Involuntary reflexes curled their guts, caused Bell to grip the steel of the windscreen frame. Cockney's knuckles white under his frantic grip of the steering wheel. They huddled and cringed as they waited for the inevitable to happen. Neither spoke. That was impossible too. Each had their jaws locked, teeth clenched, lips at times curled in a rictus death's head grin. Bell thought it was hell. Cockney thought: Christ, when will it end?

Two days earlier, on that same track and in eight different places, the engineers of General Karl Buelowis had been busy. In holes sometimes four feet deep lay sandwiches of mines. Some booby-trapped, others normal. Some held three, others four or five Teller mines, earth, mine, earth, mine, earth, mine, sandwiches of death. The quad, gun and truck added their weight and compressed the earth just a little more. No one, even the men who had created the silent waiting menace, would ever know when they would erupt. Only one thing was certain. When they did, it would be totally unexpected.

James realised they were nearly through. Fifty yards to go, the track free of loose mines. He looked at the bluff to his right. The binoculars picked up the area. It looked right, a natural gunpit that would command the minefield. A faint track led up the slope. They came out between the angle irons. James pointed to the right. Chalky changed down to second then first; the quad speed dropped as it hauled the gun and trailer up the fairly steep slope.

James looked back and saw that the truck had stopped. He was about to yell at Chalky to stop but swallowed the yell as he grasped what was happening. Bell was at the rear of the truck and Cockney was handing him objects down. They were using the captured mines, both now scraping rough holes with fingers and covering the mines with sand.

Unbidden the words escaped his lips.

'Good lads. If they get as far as that, they'll get a taste of their own medicine.'

The satisfaction that he felt at them using their own initiative outweighed the prick of pique he felt. I should have thought of that but I missed it. He bent down to warn the other two to get ready. They saw his figure stoop before he saw them. When they came into his line of sight they were sat normally but with hands over eyes, brass monkey fashion. Dodger said.

'Can we look now, Sarge?'

James grinned, managed a look of surprise, then said,

'Oh you two still 'ere? Thought you'd got out at the last stop. Get your fingers out. *Action rear!*'

He was past the petrol tank and already halfway through the doorway. Rayburn and Dodger followed him like greased eels, one from each doorway. They loped alongside the gun trailer until the quad cleared the false crest. James's cry to halt had them unhooking the trailer. Two rapid bangs on the body of the quad and Chalky accelerated forward. Dropping the trail of the limber they moved round and unhooked the gun. The fifteen hundredweight flashed past with a roar, Bell and Cockney were out, the truck still rolling, in gear and its ignition off.

Chalky arrived at the same time and in seconds the gun was on the gun platform. The massif of the escarpment loomed behind them and the rock in front might well be the stone battlement of a castle. In effect they were in a huge cave, without a roof, the quad tucked into the right corner, the truck coming to rest against the solid back wall. Bell had the breech open.

'Check the shell,' James ordered. Bell inserted the rammer and pushed. It was solid.

'Charge three.' Dodger slid the cartridge case in the breech. The breech closed with the familiar clang of heavy steel. James, on the handspike, moved the trail to the left by twenty degrees. Cockney, outstretched hand with palm facing to James's left, gave the silent message that he needed a few more degrees. James moved the handspike slowly to the left. The hand closed into a fist. Cockney was ready.

James was now flat, observing the approach of the panzers. They were entering the minefield. Range, fifteen hundred yards. He realised as he watched the small convoy negotiate the first two hundred yards, that the track was shaped like a ? with the left hand curl broken off. The panzers were now halfway down the right hand side of the ?. Range twelve hundred. It occurred to James that they might have been seen. Otherwise the sight of a minefield directly in their path would have, at least, made them pause. Instead one might think they were on the Autobahn. Range one thousand.

This was a rare experience for James. He had time. Felt confident and in control. Let them come on. The closer the better. The twenty-five pounder rested on the gun platform that tilted slightly. The tilt would give another ten degrees' depression. The closer the panzers came the less their guns could elevate. And here they were three hundred feet above them, and sheltered. The only thing that could hit them the panzers hadn't got, a mortar or a howitzer. Range eight hundred. He heard Rayburn humming. He waited, a trickle of sweat ran down his cheek. The tune Rayburn was humming became words as well. It was 'Abide with me,' the verse was slightly different from the original.

'Abide with me,' then the verse, 'French Greek and Spanish bints, all around I see. Come oh Horse Artillerymen, Abide with me.'

Bell giggled. Cockney gritted, 'Come on - come on - '

James could see the white edged black cross on the leading panzer's turret through the lens. The two panzers and the truck were coming out of the curve, beginning the nearly straight length of track. Range six hundred.

'Lay on the truck - five hundred, as it levels out on the track. Hallo, what's this?' James could not contain the surprise in his voice. Through the binoculars he saw a grey clad figure leave the cab of the ten tonner, hit the ground and roll away. Now what the hell was that all about? he thought. He couldn't see any other signs of movement, and pushed it out of his mind. The leading panzer was three hundred yards away.

The truck ambled gently into the crosswires of the telescopic sight. Cockney's deft fingers softly finished the movement of depression that took up any slack in the elevating gear. His grip on the firing lever tightened.

'Fire!' His voice was a whiplash. AP - *Load - super-charge!'* With HE in the bore he really hadn't got a target choice.

Cockney's arm shot back. The firing mechanism released the firing pin to hit the primer. The wicked crack of Kelly shattered the silence. It reverberated off the rock behind, magnified and ear cracking in its fury. A part of James, the liverish part, seemed to disappear with the shell. He watched with satisfaction and a kind of unholy glee. Be my guest.

X

Webber's voice came through the headphones.

'There's a minefield ahead, I can just see the markers, sir. I think it's British. There's a truck - a British 15 cwt - it's belting up the slope. It came out the minefield. I thought I saw something else, couldn't tell what it was though.'

Heinz acknowledged. 'Reference?' he snapped.

'Right-hand edge of right cleft, five o'clock, two thousand metres - Sir.' Webber's voice carried apologetic undertones; he was mentally kicking himself for forgetting the primary target rule.

Heinz said, 'We go in. Follow the track, that truck went through. I think the minefield's a dummy. Keep your eyes skinned and be ready!'

His binoculars picked up the cleft, came down to five o'clock. Rock - nothing moved. If there was a track up that slope, they could forget about a single truck. A Sherman would be a vastly different story. The minefield was an added complication. He reassured himself it had to be a dummy. And another thing, it was still part of the ground captured in June. Engineers would have cleared it. No problem. He slid into the gunner's seat, the gun was loaded with HE. Grasping the traversing handwheel he traversed right, picked up the rock face in the telescope. they were travelling east on the track, another hundred metres and the track curved south.

With the rubber pad against his forehead, he looked again. He was sure there was something. Blast. His eyes were watering. Have to get up top, get a steadier view through the binoculars. He slid out of the seat and began to haul himself up the cupola.

Littner, nearly a hundred yards behind the Mark III, guided the Lancia in the track ruts. The big truck nearly steered itself. Had anyone asked him to explain his actions of the next few seconds they wouldn't have got an answer. It was someone else doing these things. He watched his fingers set the hand throttle, the door opened and suddenly he was hitting the sand and rolling away. Flat on his belly he lifted his head and watched the truck follow the panzer. He was suddenly horrified at his action. His head dropped, he contempleted the grains of sand on the back of his hand.

Heinz came up from the turret steadied himself and jammed his back under the rim and raised binoculars, forearms locked.

There was a brilliant flash from the spot on the bluff, no question what that was. He let the binoculars drop onto his chest. The whoosh of the shell nearly parted his hair and from behind he heard and felt the tremendous explosion and blast of heat. He was aware that the Mark IV's 75 mm had fired. Saw the explosion high up above the enemy gun. Took a quick glance to confirm his fears about the Lancia.

A huge mass of flames and dirty black smoke. The truck had disappeared. His heart fell through his boots. Jee-suss! All that fuel - *kaput* - *shit*! Now we're right up shit creek, never mind the paddle, we haven't even got a fucking boat. His movements were quick and automatic to get into the gunner's seat. But first, he lifted the binoculars, saw the enemy gun, twenty-five pounder and it was having trouble. The muzzle was close to the shield, still on full recoil.

Savagely he thought, time, the commodity he needed. Tommy - you've had it. He slid into the seat. Something niggled. Ah yes, Webber - bloody poor shooting. Then he remembered: it would have been Braun who fired.

In the Mark IV Webber watched the burst of the 75 mm. Too high, too far - fucking amateur. Anger took control.

'Get out of the fucking way. *Dummkopf* - idiot.' He screamed as he launched himself down to take over the gun. He overestimated his ability and the cramped space he was aiming at. His bootsole hit the only patch of oil on the perforated steel floor. His head hit the gunner's seat. Braun looked, mouth open, head full of confused thoughts and emotions. Anger at Webber's insulting yell. Shame at the thought of deliberately aiming high, then relief. Enormous relief slightly tinged with worry at the sight of Webber's crumpled figure. Keeping a grip on the breech guard rail he braced himself against the motion of the tank. Looked at the swelling that was growing, even as he looked, on Webber's forehead. It was on the left side. He felt for the pulse in the neck, found it and sighed with relief. Definitely unconscious and, if we get out of this lot, he'll have a headache for a week. He spoke throught the intercomm, closing down the inter panzer communications.

'Scholz, our friend had a little accident - speed up!'

*

The yell of delight that went up as the HE blew the truck to smithereens, died as quickly in the millisecond that followed the explosion. The sight of the breech still in the recoil position shattered their exuberance and brought them all back to earth. James recovered first.

'Depress!' he yelled to Cockney. 'Right, everybody! Start pushing - or we've 'ad our chips.'

Slowly, agonisingly the reluctant piece, inch by inch began to move up the guide rails of the recuperator carriage. Thirty inches they had to move it. To them it felt like thirty miles. The sweat of hard physical effort mingled with the sweat of fear. Rayburn, two huge hands planted on the breech surround was using all his terrible strength. The veins stood out on his dripping forehead. The tendons and sinews of his neck rippled like rope snakes. Epithets spat from his lips. It had moved twelve inches - fifteen - sixteen - . How long, how many hours had they been pushing? Twenty - twenty-one - hearts pounding, pulses racing, muscles screaming for relief. Twenty-three - twenty-four, sweat was now streaming off their foreheads, trickling in rivulets down taut faces, down their backs, into their socks - twenty-seven - It was like pushing a giant hydraulic jack back into its sheath.

'Twenty-nine! That's it! Load!' Relief in James's shout. Dodger held the black, spherical, sharp-nosed armour-piercing shell ready to ram, Bell's rammer propelled it into the bore with a clunk. The supercharge cartridge followed, the breech clanged shut. Supercharge would give the shell a muzzle velocity of two thousand three hundred and fifty feet per second.

'Take the second tank, Cockney. That's the danger.' He had noticed the leading tank, a Mark IV he now recognised, had speeded up. There was something strange about it too. The turret had traversed left, barrel depressed and a hundred and eighty degrees away from them.

A shell from the other tank exploded on the rock face thirty feet above them. Everyone ducked instinctively. Slivers of rock, splinters of steel hummed and ricocheted like angry bees. The body of the quad clanged as a splinter came to rest.

'Let it get to three 'undred. The other one's wavin' a white towel or somethin' - out of the turret.' Jame's voice was calm but with a rising tremor of excitement.

'Christ! They want to surrender. Watch that Mark Three - shout when you're ready.'

They waited, all eyes on the panzer as it maintained its steady pace. As James watched, the panzer was obviously slowing.

*

Heinz was busy. He was also furious. His shot had missed and for him, even though the shot had been difficult, that was unforgivable. He was loading the 50 mm. Two men on a Mark III, on any panzer that crewed five, was no joke. It was hard enough work with a full complement. He slid the round into the bore and closed the breech. The twenty-five pounder was still silent. He said.

'Slow it down a bit, Ernst. I want this one to finish the bastards off.'

Stollenburg nearly fell off his seat in surprise. Ernst! Wonders will never cease, I never knew the old bastard knew my name.

Obediently he slowed the speed of the panzer. Heinz settled his forehead comfortably, finger on the tit of the electrical firing control. Gently, gently, he crooned to himself as the sight lined up on the enemy shield. Should be two hundred and eighty metres. A fraction of a second later the track rolled over a Teller mine sandwich. Not the biggest but Heinz was not to know that.

The nearside track took the full force of the explosion that flipped the panzer through the air on to its side. The four mine sandwich with forty-four pounds of explosive detonated under the track pressure of nearly twenty tons.

Unbelievably, Heinz was still conscious, his fingers locked around the breech guard rail. Dazedly he realised that his body was hanging from that grip and legs trailed on the floor. But now, the floor was the side, the other side the roof. He released his grip and crawled his way forward. Stollenburg was unconscious. He found his pulse. It beat strongly. Shaking his head doggedly he used all his strength and dragged him from the wireless operator's position where he had finished up. Heaving and straining he dragged the driver past the projections of the new floor which, seconds ago, had been the side.

The hull was full of dust and smoke that was gushing out of the cupola, that was now the roof, light came faintly through the gloom. He dragged Stollenburg one-handed below it, braced his feet on the guard rail and pulled the limp body up and through, into the fresh air. He collapsed on the sand for a moment breathing heavily. Getting too old for this lark. He reached for Stollenburg again and started dragging the unconscious Stollenburg away. Blearily his unfocussed gaze followed a grey-clad dimly perceived figure. He made a tremendous effort, staggered to his feet and followed. He was fifty yards from the panzer when it blew up. The blast knocked him off his feet. 'Oh, shit!' He was the only one to hear the words. A black dung beetle, six inches from his head doggedly rolled a ball of excrement ten times as large, to a destination that only it knew.

*

Cockney eased his grip on the firing lever. His eye clamped to the rubber eyepiece told his brain what was happening. His brain refused, for a moment to accept the evidence. The Mark III, solidly in his sights, had suddenly erupted. Flung casually on its side, a snake-like steel track whirling slowly through the air, the black fountain of smoke already drifting and spreading. The dull deep thud of the explosion reached him. A mine, and a big one at that. For a fleeting second his flesh crawled as his mind flashed back to their passage over that same ground. The crisp voice of James concentrated his attention.

'Fresh target!' His mind cleared. There was still the Mark IV. The gun wheels were already moving around the platform rim. His hand made a fist and slapped against his rump as the Mark IV moved steadily across his front.

'Four 'undred!' The voice was calm. James was elated; the ball was running for them.

'Ready!' He had extreme left traverse on deliberately; it gave him a full ten degrees to follow the panzer whose profile looked as big as a house. A hand holding a machine pistol from which drooped what looked to be a towel, waved frantically. Left to right the panzer tracked across his front dead in the centre of the telescope crosswires. Just like the ranges on a tank shoot.

Abruptly there was a flash of flame and black smoke coupled with the deep thud of a mine explosion. The offside track, the nearest one to them had been severed, laid neatly on the ground. The panzer half turned then stopped as the undamaged track was controlled. The throb of the engine ceased.

'Hey, Sarge,' remarked Bell. 'That's one of ours, the one our gallant layer and I put down - '

James nodded. He was still keeping the tank framed in his binoculars. They all turned as a massive explosion ripped across the minefield. The remnants of the Mark III whirled at the pinnacle of the mushroom. One that contained flame smoke, oil and old iron. James resumed his observation of the Mark IV.

There was movement as a figure climbed out of the turret, stood up then reached down to pull another figure from the turret. The one being pulled out flopped like a grey rag doll. A third man came into view. Together they laid the unconscious man down on the flat cover over the missing track.

'Make safe.' Cockney flipped the safety catch over. 'Dodger, get a brew on. I think we're overdue. Put two cans on. I'm expecting company.'

'Not before bloody time, Sarge. You could use me tongue for sandpaper.' He trotted off to the quad.

They watched as the panzer crew, or what remained of them, commenced their stumbling progress out of the minefield and up the slope towards them. They supported the injured man whose feet dragged uselessly on the end of rubber legs. All three were encumbered with water bottles and holdalls.

The drag of the hill, the sand and the dead weight of their comrade forced them to take frequent rests. Finally they reached the twenty-five pounder and the waiting crew. Scholz and Braun laid the unconscious body of Webber on the ground, then both came to attention. The word came out in unison. '*Kamerad*'

The tension of the little party eased.

'*Sprechen Sie Englisch?*' James asked.

'*Nein*,' replied Braun.

'Look in their bags.'

Rayburn and Bell rummaged through the three holdalls.

'Clear, Sarge. Just personal possessions, razors, comb, letters, towel, usual stuff.'

James nodded. 'Thanks,' as Dodger handed him a mug of tea. He took the first swallow with relish and felt for a cigarette. 'Get the three prisoners over to the quad, Muscles. Stand guard. Give 'em a drop of tea, Cockney. After we've 'ad a drink we'll get off down. See how many survivors - five minutes.'

James concentrated on the warm tea and the welcome cigarette, the panacea of the desert. The sun warmed his skin, he realised the mist had fled. It was going to be a nice day. He took off his overcoat and tied his bootlaces, rubbed an errant speck of mucus from an eye corner. Nothing like chah, maybe they should bottle it, after the war, make a fortune. His eyes roved over the crew, prisoners and the gun. Lucky, dead lucky. It was time to see what lay down there. Hope there's not too many of them, have a job to fit them all in.

He saw that Bell had the MG 34. Rayburn held the Bren with no more effort than holding a toothbrush. The others held their Lee Enfields. He walked over to the quad, reached in and retrieved his webbing belt that held the holstered .38 Smith and Wesson revolver. He buckled it on. Passing the gun he picked up the Thompson and tossed it to Cockney. Wells caught it smoothly. They walked down the slope. They paused to lift the Teller mines, disarmed them and flung them well off the track. Cockney climbed to the turret of the Mark IV and leaned inside. He came up with a Schmeisser and a cloth bag of magazines.

He grinned at James. 'Might as well, Sarge. Which one d'y prefer?'

'I'll 'ave the Schmeisser. Toss it down. Always wanted one of these.' Catching the machine pistol in one hand he examined it, took the safety off, cocked it and fired a short burst into the sand. He looked at Cockney who had landed like a cat next to him and said.

'It works. Trust the wily Hun.' They grinned at each other. It was at once a joke and a reminder of other days.

*

Heinz came back to the world slowly. A voice was shouting in his ear. It was insistent, annoying.

'*Oberwachmeister*, wake up please, *Oberwachmeister*.'

He opened one eye. His head felt like the belfry of a church tower. Come to think of it, he could still hear the bells, huge clanging massive bells. He swallowed to try and relieve the pressure in his ears. Now, there was just a rushing noise. He raised his head painfully. Gradually the rushing sound changed into the deep thud of a regular pulse. Christ! Am I deaf? The prospect horrified and depressed him. It was replaced instantly by a more optimistic thought. That meant the *Krankenhaus*, honourable discharge and a cushy number at some rear base.

The voice penetrated his mind again, it sounded forlorn.

'*Oberwachmeister.*'

He opened the other eye and after two attempts managed to focus on the grey-clad figure kneeling bside him. The face swam into view and the steel rimmed spectacles. Littner! No, not that. Now I know I'm fucking dead! For the rest of eternity I shall be marching alongside this bloody egghead.

Obstinately the face remained in focus. But it couldn't be. There was nothing left of that truck, just flame and smoke. No, it cannot be. Wearily he closed his eyes again. Fingers shook him. The pounding in his head settled behind his eyes. Resigned, he opened his eyes and made a supreme effort to struggle to a sitting position.

'How the fucking hell?' The words came out in a jumble of sound, slurred and distorted by lips that were numb. He swallowed, bit his lips, felt the return of some control and tried again.

'How the fucking hell did you get here, Littner? The truck! It went sky high. There was no chance, none. How for Christsake?' Heinz shook his head in bewilderment. It was a big mistake as steam hammers throbbed massively in his skull. He kept very still and gradually the painful vibrations diminished. Littner grinned sheepishly. It changed his whole expression; he almost looked, Heinz thought, handsome in a way and - happy?

'Let's just say, sir, that I had a premonition. For once I took notice. It saved my life.' He stood up.

Heinz looked around slowly. Stollenburg was struggling to his feet. His eyes took in the scene, the remains of the panzer and a hundred yards behind, the smoking remnants of the Lancia. And, he wasn't dead. They were going to finish up in the bag, bloody *Kriegsgefangener*. Still, he consoled himself, I'm still alive. He didn't know whether to be pleased or sorry.

He got up, paused whilst the world stopped spinning and went slowly over to help Stollenburg remain upright. Stollenburg blew his nose through his fingers and shook his head, like a punch drunk boxer trying to find an opponent, who had hit him harder than anything he had ever experienced before.

'What happened?' he asked haltingly. 'Whooo - eeeee - my head!'

Heinz was now almost in full control of himself, his *Feldmütze* jammed firmly on his head remarked sardonically:

'Pissed again, Stollenburg?'

His driver's head shot up at the unjust accusation, he winced at the pain the sudden movement caused, then grinned slowly. Old Fifty-Seven was back to his old form. He looked at Littner questioningly. Littner said cryptically:

'Nine lives - like the feline species.'

Stollenburg tried but failed to grasp the reference. He gave it up in disgust. Heinz said:

'We've got company.'

They watched the two figures, one in a sheepskin coat and suede desert boots, the other in khaki battle dress the upper sleeves bearing the three chevrons and brass gun. They walked casually towards them, both carried automatic weapons.

James and Cockney reached the three men. Heinz and the others sprang to attention. Heinz saluted.

'Oberwachmeister Karl Heinz.' He looked vainly for any sign of insignia on Cockney's attire. Cockney was enjoying himself. Airily he gave a casual wave of his hand that resembled accurately, the aristocratic acknowledgement of a duke.

James said quickly, 'Knock it off, Wells. *Sprechen Sie Englisch?*' he enquired neutrally.

Littner said 'I speak your language. Do you have an officer that we would wish to surrender to?'

'No,' James replied. 'No officer. I'm a sergeant - Sergeant James, Royal Horse Artillery.' He caught Littner's look of surprise. 'No, no horses. My detachment is up there. We 'ave three more prisoners —from the Mark IV. I'm in charge. Who are you?'

Littner thought quickly. There's nothing fancy about this one. He looked at the craggy features, the cold green eyes and the stocky muscular body. The other too, moved like a cat, the automatic an extension of his arm. Surely they knew the rules of war? The Geneva Convention? They could decide to shoot them. He suddenly developed a respect. Here, in this isolated wilderness the three of them had no rights. Maybe, they even knew about the three trucks and the armoured car of last evening. Quickly he stood to attention and said:

'This is Squadron Sergeant-Major Heinz. This is Panzer Driver Stollenburg and I am Soldat Littner. I drove the Lancia truck.'

James grinned. 'Ah! So you were the one who bailed out before we brewed you up?'

Littner gave a small smile of embarrassment and nodded. The one in the sheepskin coat was grinning too. James said.

'Tell the Sergeant-Major to pass over his Luger.' Littner spoke to Heinz who immediately passed over his pistol. Heinz was reaching back in his memory. At one time, a long time ago, he used to have a fair command of English garnered from the British Army of Occupation in the Saar. The words, some of the phrases were coming back.

'We are your prisoners, *ja?*'

James hid his surprise; it showed only slightly in his eyes.

'That's right.'

He had been sizing up Heinz. Must be over forty, grey showing in the blond hair, good teeth, an old soldier, looked as if he knew what it was all about. He searched for a word. Efficient? No, not quite. Competent? Not quite that either. It was something more. Expert, that was it and vastly experienced with it. He'd bet money on the Sergeant-Major to handle anything, from tanks and guns to bar room brawls. The question had not really been a question. More an opportunity to try out his English. He would know, better than any of them that for them, the war was over.

The bespectacled, thin, intelligent-looking one looked like a teacher. The driver just stood there looking dazed but his expression told James nothing.

This, James thought, was the enemy. On the guns they saw them clad in armour, squat deadly shapes advancing remorselessly. Otherwise they were the far-off dim figures in tropical drill or grey green. Some would wear the coal scuttle helmets or forage caps with the small roundel on the front. These were the *Herrenvolk*, the master race, the conquerers and enslavers of Europe.

Shouldn't he be feeling something? They, or some like them had killed his best friend. Shouldn't he feel hate, want revenge, some kind of retribution? His eyes flicked over the epaulettes of the Sergeant Major. They bore two pips, more like a lieutenant's rank in our army. His knowledge of German Wehrmacht badges of rank was hazy, to say the least.

He answered his last question. No, it was difficult even to feel animosity. After the last thirty-six hours he was satisfied just to be alive. The dead were the dead, let them rest. It was over. Finished, gone. He had a sudden thought.'

'Your papers - identification!' he demanded.

Littner interpreted for Stollenburg. Heinz understood and passed James his wallet. Too late he realised he had handed over the late Hauptmann's wallet too. They waited. James said.

'Are you lot Nazis?'

Stollenburg and Littner shook their head. Littner said.

'We are not Nazis.' His tone was defiant, even proud. 'We are Germans.'

'But you are?' James looked at Heinz. He had his party card in his hand.

Heinz hesitated as he searched for words.

'*Ja* - yes - that is card. That is all, it is a card. It - it, was required. I was in Reichswehr - nineteen eighteen - like you, *ja*? - regular?' His look said it all, you and I, we are soldiers.

Christ, James thought, nearly a quarter of a century. He believed him. He opened the second wallet and took out the party card of Hauptmann Schmidt. Now, that's more like it, that's what I expected a bloody Nazi to look like. Arrogant sod. He turned over the photograph of the girl and let out a low whistle. Cockney looked over his shoulder and gave a gasp of admiration. James beckoned Littner and asked him to read out the written message. Littner read it verbatim, even he had to smile. James and Cockney let out a roar of laughter. James said.

'Well, she's certainly direct. Christ! She's got enough there for two women, I reckon she'd put life in a dead body.' He paused, asked Heinz:

'Who's this Hauptmann Schmidt. Where does he fit in?'

'He was our commander. A British soldier shot him in the head yesterday evening.' Heinz glanced at Stollenburg who saw the look. So - he knew.

James was holding up the photograph of Karl Schwarze. Cockney looked and nodded. Heinz said.

'You know him?' The meeting was producing some surprises. James nodded. 'Yes, he was our prisoner until yesterday. We knocked out one of your halftracks, infantry carrier. He was wounded, in the head, just a kid. We didn't know 'im long, nice kid. He died. We buried him.'

Cockney said, 'The Sergeant's mate - best friend - he got killed too. Just before.'

Heinz murmured, 'Sorry, *c'est la guerre,* - It is the war.'

He retrieved the wallets from James and walked over to Stollenburg. The driver looked at his face. There was a relaxation in the features of Heinz that was new.

Stollenburg said, 'Thanks, Sergeant-Major - I know you saved my life, I could have - 'He broke off, could not restrain a shudder.

'Littner too. He did most after I got you out.' Heinz paused, uncertain, then decided. 'It makes up - just a little bit - for Rheinhart.' He saw the unspoken question in Stollenburg's eyes. '*Ja*, I knew. It is over, forget it.'

He turned and walked after James. Questions were swimming up in his mind and he was puzzled.

'Sergeant,' James paused and looked. '*Bitte*, why you knock out truck first before you knock out me?' James grinned.

'Well, I'd got a round of HE up the spout — in the bore. It had to be the truck. I wanted armour-piercing shot for the panzers and, - I didn't knock out your tank - '

Heinz stopped, incredulous. 'If you did not - who?'

James said, 'Blame your own mates - you hit a sandwich - four Tellers. Your own mines. That's what knocked you out.' Heinz knew all about mine sandwiches, his training had been thorough.

James, magnanimous in victory said sympathetically.

'You couldn't know, neither did we. We were lucky - you weren't, *c'est la guerre, eh*!'

They continued walking with Cockney bringing up the rear. James shouted to Littner.

'Any spare water - petrol, on that Mark IV?'

'Yes, Sergeant. Water marked with a white cross on the jerricans, petrol in unmarked cans.'

By the time they reached the damaged panzer the English of Heinz was more fluent and James had the story of the panzers' journey. So had Heinz as James related the better part of what had happened to them. Stollenburg and Littner carried two jerricans each. Heinz and James one.

Heinz said, as they struggled up the slope to the black circle of the twenty-five pounder's muzzle.

'Are you leaving the panzer there?'

'Yeah,' replied James, 'Why, were you thinking of repairing the track and taking off?'

The thought had crossed the mind of the German Sergeant Major briefly, but it was only a thought.

'*Nein*, no, that is what I mean. What we hoped, is impossible now. The war for us, soon for all of us, two, maybe three years, even less, will be *kaput*. Russians, Americans, too much. The war, it is lost.'

They reached the gun. Braun and Scholz greeted Heinz and the others. Webber was in a sitting position against the quad wheel. His eyes looked vacant. The desert brew was circulating. James took his mug, swallowed half of the sweet brown liquid and passed the mug to Heinz. He took it gratefully and took his first swallow.

'*Ist gut* - very good.' He pulled out a small cigar as James lit a cigarette. Both shared the light. They smoked in silent companionship. James thought, fraternising with the enemy, - what the bloody hell next? Heinz spoke.

'Would you - how so - grant me a - ' he groped for the word ' - a wish?' The keen blue eyes searched James's face.

'You mean - a favour? Depends, you know, what it is.'

'Let me blow up the panzer.' The request was a plea.

James understood immediately. Why not, it was only junk. He wondered cynically had the positions been reversed would Heinz have agreed to let him blow up his own gun? He rather doubted it, anyway he was a gunner, Heinz a tankie. Not the same. Well, it was no skin off his nose. He called Cockney over.

'We're goin' to blow the panzer up before we leave. It's your tank. If you want to blow it up, that's fine. If you're not bothered about it? Well, it's the Sergeant-Major 'ere. He'd consider it a favour if he could do it. Sort of last farewell.'

James stopped. He felt he'd made a hash of the halting explanation. Cockney, on the other hand relished the irony of the situation.

'Yeah, why not? 'Sall right by me.' He stood back. James pointed to the gun. He knew Heinz needed no instruction. On the way back to Alamein the Afrika Korps had more twenty-five pounders than the Eighth Army. Heinz slid into the layer's seat, took off the safety catch, traversed a millimetre, slight touch of depression and said, 'Ready! *FIRE*!'

The result was impressive. The Panzerkampfwagen IV received the twenty-five pounder armour piercing shot in the fuel tanks slightly in front of the massive engine. It disintegrated with a huge whoosh, the turret sailed majestically high in the air preceded by what was left of the cylinder block and twenty-three or more tons of Ruhr steel, armour plating, bogie wheels, Very lights 75mm ammunition and assorted extras. The black oily smoke ballooned vertically smudging the clearing skies. Then there was just the roar of the flames and the crackle of exploding small arms ammunition.

Heinz said, '*Auf Wiedersehn.*' He murmured, '*Dankeschön*' to James and then to Cockney. They pushed the piece back. Rayburn thought how easy it was - now.

Cockney was conscious of a feeling, difficult to describe as he watched the rest of the crew and the prisoners, former enemies, talking, helped not a little by Littner. Then he recognised it, simple kinship. Under the skin and if they could understand each other, they were the same. Fighting men doing a job they believed in. He looked at this German sergeant-major. That was what he was. Not particularly a German, but another sergeant-major of any army in the world.

He had a thought, a wicked shaft of humour.

'There's one thing, Sergeant-Major - ' Heinz looked questioningly. 'You'll be the only sergeant-major who finished off his war by knocking a Mark IV out that belonged to his own side, with a British gun.'

Heinz smiled. Whomever they met in the Stalag or whatever, he would remember these impossible yet likable Brits.

The battery sergeant major was known as Tiger. Disbelief at what he was seeing fought with the evidence of his own eyes. The battered quad towing that scarred A sub gun was coming on to his gun position. The battery was trails down but not in action.

Another truck, a 15 cwt followed. Men in German uniforms stood and some sat in the back. The open doors of the quad revealed more strange uniforms. Standing by the side of Sergeant James another German uniform. The quad pulled up in front of him. He looked up at James and bristled.

'Which are the fucking prisoners then? You or them?' As James opened his mouth to reply he continued sarcastically:

'I suppose you're going to tell us - I know, I know - There's Hell on at Fuka too. Jump down, you Geordie bastard. Introduce me to the Afrika Korps. Don't suppose you've got Rommel in the back?'

The crew of Kelly's Eye had arrived home.